Springs and Autumns

Springs and Autumns

Baltasar Porcel

Translated from the Catalan
and with an Introduction by
JOHN L. GETMAN

The University of Arkansas Press
Fayetteville 2000

04   03   02   01   00   5   4   3   2   1

Designer: John Coghlan

⊚ The paper used in this publication meets the minimum requirements of the American National Standard for Permanence of Paper for Printed Library Materials Z39.48-1984.

The English translation was made with the help of a grant from the Institució de les Lletres Catalanes.

Publication of this work has been supported by the Program for Cultural Cooperation between Spain's Ministry of Education and Culture and United States Universities.

Title of original edition: *Les primaveras i les tardors,* © 1986 by Baltasar Porcel. Published by Enciclopèdia Catalana, S.A., Diputació 250, 08007, Barcelona, Spain.

Library of Congress Cataloging-in-Publication Data

Porcel, Baltasar.
    [Primaveres i les tardors. English]
  Springs and autumns / Baltasar Porcel ; translated and with an introduction by
    John L. Getman.
    p.   cm.
    ISBN 1-55728-609-4 (pbk. : alk. paper)
    I. Getman, John L. II. Title.

PC3941.P63 P7513 2000
849'.9354—dc21

                00-028627

This work has been published with the support of the Ministry of Education and Culture of the Government of the Balearic Islands.

Tx'uen Ts'iu,
or Springs and Autumns,
is the title of the annals
of the small and mystical
Chinese principality of Lu,
the homeland of Confucius,
from a time much earlier than ours.
And even though this novel
has nothing to do with all that,
I think everything I am going to narrate here
could be symbolized in that evocative name,
Springs and Autumns,
because of its singular perfume,
its marginal lives
in their flight through time,
the remote setting,
borne witness to by
those ancient annals. . . .

Acknowledgments

I would like to acknowledge the cooperation and support I have received during this project from the Institució de les Lletres Catalanes, Barcelona, its director, Francesc Parcerisas, and Ms. Iolanda Pelegrí. The guidance given by Dr. John Du Val, director of the translation program at the University of Arkansas, Fayetteville, has been invaluable. Critical reading of the manuscript by Dr. Kay Pritchett of the Spanish department was helpful in setting the work in perspective. Prof. Joanne Meschery of the English department creative writing program graciously critiqued the completed English version. Special thanks are due my editor, Brian King, for his perceptive suggestions that have helped bridge those often murky waters between two different languages, their cultures, and usages. Finally, this book would not have been born without the enduring patience and support of my wife, Pilar Eraso Aquilué.

My deepest gratitude to all of you.

Introduction

Catalan is an ancient Romance language, akin to Provençal, dating from the time of the Marca Hispanica around the year 800. The Catalan-speaking peoples originated in the Eastern Pyrenees and spread to the southeastern part of France (the Roselló); the northeastern Spanish coast, including Barcelona, Tarragona, and Valencia; inland to the west of Lleida; then north to the principality of Andorra; as well as the Balearic Islands of Majorca, Menorca, Ibiza, and Formentera, which lie just to the east of Valencia.

Majorca became part of Catalonia by conquest in 1229. An island people, located on the crossroads between Southern Europe and North Africa and ruled from afar, the Majorcans have been left alone to do pretty much as they pleased, engaging in piracy, smuggling, and other seafaring enterprises. Andratx, located on the western tip of Majorca, was home to all of these activities until relatively recent times.

Baltasar Porcel was born in Andratx in 1937, heir to the rich traditions of its people. However, the persistent poverty and insular mentality of Andratx did not match Porcel's aspirations for a literary life, so in 1960 he began his first adventure by moving to Barcelona. He survived the first six months by working in a furniture store, while at the same time writing articles and stories about his native Majorca, which were published in *Destino* and *Serra d'Or,* two Barcelona literary magazines.

His first novel, *Black Sun,* was published to critical acclaim in 1962, receiving the City of Palma Prize. Both ambitious and prodigious, Porcel produced more than ten books and many short stories and essays during the next decade, through which he attempted to free himself from the weight of the past and deal with an agonizing present, that of the declining Franco regime.

The more critical his outlook became, the more demanding he became of himself and his writing. He progressed from polemic essays in the sixties to a leftist-oriented existentialism based on the realism of the man in the street. He sought the historical roots of his own and Catalonia's reality through exploration of the collective memory of his people. A thorough reading of Proust was invaluable to him at that stage. The Paris student revolt of 1968 deeply affected his course of action in that it forced him to define himself more clearly in the dichotomy of individual versus tradition, to reexamine the value of individual freedom as opposed to the collective good. Porcel joined the growing crescendo of voices favoring Catalan independence, while at the same time doing research and traveling widely in Europe, the Middle East, and Asia, absorbing new insights.

As the translator of both *Springs and Autumns* and *Horses into the Night*, I have had access to and worked with Porcel's Catalan and Spanish texts, plus the editorial notes of Rosa Cabré, editor of Porcel's twelve-volume *Obras Completes* and the introductory notes to the *Obras Completes* contributed by Professors Joaquim Molas and Carme Arnau of Barcelona. These resources have proven invaluable in understanding Porcel's creative process. In the Andratx of Porcel's youth, they spoke a dialect of Catalan, Mallorquín, which neither he nor his family nor peers could write because the Franco Regime prohibited the public use of Catalan. He was faced with a crippling realization:

> I lived submerged in an illiterate bastardy: all that was important and grandiloquent, from politics to science, including literature, came to me in Spanish. All that was basic, daily, and domestic, my life and that of my people, was carried out in my local Catalan dialect.
>
> When I was fifteen, I decided to learn a language, the only one I had access to: Spanish. First I learned it in books, and later, thanks to an Andalusian friend, I was able to practice it orally. . . .
>
> But speaking was not enough for me, as I also felt the need to write. And Spanish, that language so useful to converse with the marine commander or to read novels by Baroja or Valle-Inclán, was showing itself harsh to me whenever I tried to compose an article or a story: words got stuck, descriptions became long and unfocused. It was then that, quite casually, two books in Catalan with nineteenth-century realistic topics fell into my hands . . . I devoured them page after page, and with each new line I read, it became more and more evident that this was the world I wanted to describe, and also the way I wanted to write. In the twinkling of an eye I found myself condemned in my literary endeavors to a fossilized wilderness, to a marginality without an iota of importance. It was a disagreeable discovery. It seemed to me I was being forced to return to the caves. But I wanted to write, and with the same voracity with which I had learned Spanish, I undertook the learning of Catalan and the reading of books in Catalan. What followed was

grotesque: between the ages of fifteen and twenty, I, a high-school student and the citizen of a civilized state, had to learn two languages in order to speak with my fellow beings and write to them, since from childhood I had been deprived of a normal language.

And I wrote. I wrote a lot in Catalan from that moment on and would only use Spanish for bare-bones newspaper copy. Until one day I experienced a strange phenomenon: I discovered how to write in Spanish. Precise wordings, sensual and correct adjectives and adverbs, phrases with the musical naturalness of the language came to my pen. The explanation, once I found it, had a radical simplicity and logic: since a language is at once a creation of the world and a means for communicating within it, I was able, for the first time to describe a world—my world—as soon as I could put together my experiences and my Catalan speech within their proper cultural context. But underneath, unconsciously, my brain was carrying out another job—muted, deep down, like a computer. My brain was looking for the Spanish equivalent to all that I was creating in Catalan and thus brought about in Spanish a second creation, based on the world created in Catalan. Then I managed to write in Spanish with a certain expressive decency, and without rhetorical dryness.[1]

In an article which appeared in *Destino* on May 6, 1975, written in Spanish and entitled "Caballos hacia la noche," Porcel goes into specific detail as to how he constructs his novels:

> More and more, pre-planning means very little to me at the conscious level. In fact, what I do is drive myself, sometimes aggressively, to try to force into narrative form the images, the atmosphere, the feelings that are boiling around in my subconscious mind, and which form the porous, existential substratum that remains beyond time and desire. That is the definitive magma which comes to have the weight and the measure of who we really are. The novel, then, is already there within that magma, from the moment in which I sense its first stirrings.[2]

The question of which came first, the Spanish or the Catalan version, is really not germane if we are to understand the creative process in Porcel's subconscious as he has described it, within the context of his linguistic origins and how and under what socio-political circumstances his linguistic

---

1. Baltazar Porcel, "Succincta explicació de Catalunya per a castellans," in *Debat Català* (Barcelona: Ed. Selecta, 1973).

2. Baltazar Porcel, *Obras Completes,* vol. 5 (Barcelona: Ed. Proa, 1993), 609.

personality was formed and sought written expression. Thus, the "translation" process for Porcel is unique, in that it involves the free transfer between two sets of language codes of the seminal, subconscious energies which lie at the root of his creative being.

Porcel quotes Pío Baroja to demonstrate the formation of his concept of the world and human relations within that world:

> "As for me, I have noticed that my emotional base was formed in a relatively short period of time in my youth and young adulthood, a period that covered about a decade, from age ten or twelve to about age twenty-two or three. That period was for me transcendental: people, ideas, things, even the boredom, were all graven deeply into my being, indelibly so. I believe that this emotional base, which is tied to one's infancy or youth, to one's country, to one's loves, one's studies and one's dangers, is what gives the novelist his character and makes him who he is."[3]

Porcel enjoyed the distinct advantage of having his emotional base and his character formed in two languages.

In a 1962 article he wrote in Spanish for *Diario de Mallorca,* entitled "Recuerdo de Pavese," Porcel used that writer's existential approach to justify the need of the individual to rediscover his past in order to place himself within his own historical context and discover meaning in his life: "We are the sum of all that we ever have been. We discover who we have been through the memories we can recall."[4]

From this search and its written expression in his novels, Porcel has created the "myth of Andratx" bilingually, as he has lived it. *Horses into the Night,* and a decade later *Springs and Autumns,* became for Porcel the culmination of that search, the beginning and end of the "myth" series. Porcel brought the results of his deep searching to focus in the novel, *Horses into the Night (Cavalls cap a la fosca)*, which was received by public and critics alike as perhaps the most trenchant Catalan novel since the Spanish Civil War. The novel was honored with four prestigious literary awards: the Prudenci Bertrana Award in 1975, the Spanish Literary Critics' Award and the Serra d'Or Critics' Award in 1976, and the Internazionale Mediterraneo d'Italia in 1977.

Springs and Autumns delves fearlessly into the atavistic: "We are fire," Dioclecià of Pula affirms in a Heraclitean spirit after Beautiful Egèria's funeral

---

3. Baltazar Porcel, *Obras Completas,* vol. 5 (Barcelona: Ed.Proa, 1993), 612.
4. Baltazar Porcel, *Obras Completas,* vol. 5 (Barcelona: Ed.Proa, 1993), 614.

oration, in one of the most impressive—and most emotional—moments in the novel. The Taltavulls—or at least the majority of them—*are* fire, people who seek happiness, who live their lives passionately, and who find meaning in each of their personal stories through their sense of belonging within the family. It is only through the rediscovery of their past, of their family traditions, that they can begin to reconstruct their own mythical history and identity. In *Springs and Autumns* Porcel has given his readers an authentic work of his maturity as a novelist.

Porcel shows us the transient nature of the reality we know: the brain's attempt to give order, structure, and meaning to universal chaos. Once the human condition is recognized for what it is—at the same time weak, fragile, violent, fearful, tender, perverse, and loving—then we can fathom its existential nature.

Porcel's prose style is often lyrical. His ability to describe what he sees and feels in his reality is astonishing in its evocative power and richness of metaphor. His landscapes often become prose poems through which he mirrors his characters. The moon, the sea, and the green and the bloom of the almond trees become recurrent mood themes. Through these and other stylistic resources Porcel has instilled in his home town of Andratx/Orlandis mythical qualities which endure. His imagery runs the gamut from musical to violent to pastoral, surviving in the reader's imagination long after the book is put down.

Springs and Autumns is perhaps Baltasar Porcel's best novel. It received three awards in Spain upon its publication in 1986: the Premi Sant Jordi, the Premi Joan Crexells, and the Premi de Literatura from the Catalan Ministry of Culture. This English translation follows the earlier success of *Horses into the Night*, published in 1995 by the University of Arkansas Press. *Horses into the Night* was chosen as one of the twenty-five best fiction books of the year by *Publishers Weekly* and as one of the eight best translations of 1995 by the *San Francisco Review of Books'* Critics Choice. I second the Spanish and Catalan critics who awarded *Springs and Autumns* three prestigious literary prizes at first publication; I believe it to be comparable in quality to its predecessor.

It is my hope that this translation of *Springs and Autumns* faithfully conveys the author's poetic vitality and imagery to the English reader because Porcel's work deserves a broader audience.

Note: All character and place names in the novel have been retained in their original Catalan form. In Catalan, as in Spanish, a person's name consists of three parts: the first or Christian name (Ignasi), then the first of two surnames (Taltavull), taken from the first surname of the father, and the second surname (Oliva), taken from the first surname of the mother. Sometimes double first names are used, such as Joan Pere. The only possible confusion for the English reader is the name Joan, which is the Catalan form of John.

1

The southwester shook the night with its insistent howling, driving the trees to invisible spasms. Clouds of smoke swirled back down the chimney and snorted out the hearth, spreading in tumultuous gusts, converting the vast hall into a mass of nebulous uncertainty. Irritating clouds of smoke turned the people into shadows. Coughing and cursing broke out. Someone ran to open the door and windows and managed to clear the air. And then the Taltavulls slowly emerged from amid the smoke, young and old, close and distant relatives.

• • •

"Silent night, holy night...." The children sang excitedly, off-key, having already lost interest in the saintly little clay figures in the manger scene laid out beside the cistern: damp moss, the little cave harboring the angels, the three kings astride their camels, the squatting urchin defecating beside the make-believe river of crumpled aluminum foil. The tumult of children appeared and disappeared in the gray pall of smoke in the hall. In a tone wavering between melancholy and naive, a voice that could only be Beautiful Egèria's asked, "And the children? Where are the children?"

She was right to ask because nobody had seen them for quite a while. Parents and uncles and aunts and other relatives began searching all the corners of the hall, the dimly lit staircase, and the feverishly busy kitchen. Aunt Pollònia, looking like a pharaoh with a huge comb stuck in the knot of hair atop her head in preparation for matins, whined that the children—unfortunate wretches beyond salvation—had probably gotten lost in the dark valley, that somber world beyond the house.

Tomàs Moro, her nephew, raised himself lugubriously from the wicker rocker where he had been breathing heavily, rocking up a sweat. His bloated body appeared to be undergoing a spectacular chemical transformation. He was an apprehensive and imaginative man. He lurched to his feet in horror when he heard Aunt Pollònia's wailings, a lurid vision flashing through his mind of his twin daughters carried off by the lashing wind, scratched to bits by the sharp, naked branches of the almond trees, carried off into the insanely infinite sky.

Led by Tomàs Moro's gelatinous bulk, the gaggle of people, including his fierce mother Paula, Beautiful Egèria, Joan Pere Tudurí (who was narrating another adventure to the crowd), the robust Marianna Mas, and Albert the Younger, all swept out through the door and stood facing the valley and the night. They listened, holding their breath. They cried out for the children, their voices rising and fading, echoing the sadness of all humanity.

"Childriiin!"

But the deep blackness plagued by the howling wind consumed their cries, leaving nothing but a murmur in the night.

"Childriiin!"

They returned to the house. The smoke was swirling through it again, completely invading the long hall.

"They'll probably appear out of the smoke," someone commented.

But the truth was the children had slipped off to their secret attic world, so near and yet so far away from their searching parents. They were discovered by Grandmother Brígida who frequently wandered through the solitude of the ancient house, mumbling erratic exclamations. With her ashen hair and faded smock, the aged grandmother seemed a pale shadow floating at the edge of another world.

Damp tangles of thick cobwebs hung from the dusty and broken heirlooms in the attic, cracked mirrors reflected silent horrors from the past: the eternal decapitated toys, rusty piles of arms that misguided generations of Taltavulls had brandished in all the uprisings and revolutions of the past, a remote past filled with peasant famines and religious revolts, with the burning of the Jews, the war of the Bourbon king, and every onslaught of the Moors. And nearer at hand there were the joys of September, 1868, the vendettas of the Carlists with their incomprehensible rages, the pigheaded militia, the pronunciamiento by Colonel Horacio Perelló to save the honor of the weak, the Civil War of 1936 and its lust to kill and kill again.

A funnel-mouthed blunderbuss, a couple of pikes crowned with crosses, the little drum from the Spanish flag, a saber sheath, an enormous Reffye machine gun, seven .38-caliber Colts, two stone cannon balls as round and fat as melons—the whole of it a useless clutter of martial glory at the sight of which somebody from the family would always recall the heroic deeds of Great Grandfather Bartomeu, the one with the red beard who, armed with a

14-gauge shotgun, had confronted the enemy on the hillside by the beehives right there at Taltavull Hall and had killed a man from Cordoba.

Grandmother Brígida—at the time an ingenuous young lady who had just married Benigne, the founder of the alarm clock factory and the son of Great Grandfather Taltavull—had sat beneath a jujube tree with a kitten in her arms and watched the drama. Even after so many years, they would still ask her the same question they always asked her, over and over again, "So why did Great-Grandpa shoot him, Grandma?" Her sober answer would be, "Because he was on the other side."

"And who were the ones on the other side?"

The old woman would think for a moment, caught off-guard by the question. "Well, I don't know.... Maybe I never did know.... But they say the one from Cordoba was a good dancer, and I noticed he had a little tooth-brush mustache...."

"And why were you carrying that kitten, Grandma?"

"His name was Marcellí. Or maybe Marcellí was the tiger cat, and the one I had was that one-eyed cat, Cariñito? He wore a pink collar."

"But Grandma, don't tell us it wasn't strange, you sitting out there on that hillside among the beehives with shots flying by!"

"Oh, the bees. Yes, I like honey.... Some cats do too. Our honey was very light-colored and sweet because in the spring the mountains are covered with wildflowers. Maybe it was May when my father-in-law shot the Cordovan. Now that I think of it, when he fired the shot, the kitten took off through the poppy fields, their funny red petals fluttering in the breeze."

On that Christmas Eve, the children had become captivated by a box of candle stubs left over from the funeral last spring of their grandmother's eldest son, Francesc de Borja Taltavull. The children were marching around the attic each with a lighted candle raised high in each hand—the lively, scatter-brained scarecrow Gori; Carloteta, the relentless inquisitor; the obtuse Nofringo; the Moro twins, looking like music-box figurines; and Bielet the cripple—all of them crowned with brilliantly glowing orange halos of candlelight as they marched in orderly ranks around the jumbled dark of the attic, looking like specters, disembodied floating faces.

Enchanted, Grandmother Brígida followed them with her eyes, imagining them to be a blessed apparition from the Golden Legend. That's what made her happy when she visited Taltavull Hall: there she found everything that brought back years and years of memories, as well as everything her heart still yearned for.

2

Suddenly three ceremonious blows sounded at the front door and echoed through the hall. Everyone turned to look at the solid pine door, its carrot-colored grain, its hinge straps a rustic wrought iron. If the newcomer had been another Taltavull come for the Christmas Eve supper, he would simply have walked in without knocking. Who could it be then, at this unseasonable hour in that distant valley? No one moved. Aunt Pollònia stifled a groan.

Finally Commander Ignasi Taltavull Oliva, whose modest appearance hid a stubborn, frigid interior, rose to open the door. The thundering wind burst through the doorway on the heels of Ramon Consolat with his hat in hand.

"I've come to talk with Bernat," he croaked hoarsely. He blinked his eye-lids several times, surprised by the bright light and the large gathering standing motionless, staring at him through the pall of smoke. . . .

That hall and those fairy-tale people reminded Consolat of that sorrowful Day of the Dead in the year of the great rains, the unreality of the cemetery lingering in the mist, its marble statues appearing suspended in midair. Dressed in mourning, all five young ladies from La Paret, locked arm-in-arm, advanced toward the family tomb—its dove of peace shattered by a lightning bolt—their long black skirts swishing, sweeping the desolate pathways between the niches. And Ramon, his bull neck and square head perched atop a squat, robust body, walked behind them, saddled with the tin wreathes, the box of glass vials and wicks for the feeble little votive oil lamps. . . .

Bernat Taltavull the Wise came over and said, "Oh, Ramon, I didn't expect to see you here."

True enough, for Bernat's ears still rang with Elisa's proud, dry words when he last visited her: "We aren't selling anything!"

And as she spoke she had pointed with her bony forefinger at the impressive German grandfather clock that dominated their cramped little living room. Its works had stopped ticking five or maybe fifteen years ago—nobody could remember exactly when.

Bernat, bewildered by the bitter rebuke of the old lady and driven by his convictions on universal harmony, still wanted to maintain a friendly atmosphere and so invited the ladies to join the family supper. After all, La Paret and Taltavull Hall were houses related by blood.

But the imperious Elisa, sitting stiffly on the worm-eaten Isabeline sofa, lashed out at him, "We aren't going anywhere!"

Bernat forced a disheartened smile. Of the other four sisters, Miss Felícia, Miss Margarida, and Miss Caterina supported their elder sister by nodding their heads in unison, their arms folded rigidly over long, starched bodices, their faces contorted by expressions of anxiety that seemed to consume them. Only the youngest sister, Antonieta, red-faced and stuttering, added, "We . . . we . . . don't go out very much. . . ."

Outside the sun was shining timidly, the December calm suffused with a subtle sweetness that seemed to come from far away. But inside La Paret's sparsely furnished living room with its frigid atmosphere, the blinds were half-drawn and only a weak light illuminated the sisters' blurred silhouettes.

"Have something to drink," invited Miss Caterina.

"No, no thank you. I don't need anything," Bernat said, courteously declining her invitation.

"Oh, yes, you must have something," insisted Miss Felícia.

The visitor yielded, "Well, if you insist . . . do you have a . . . ?"

But he was interrupted by Miss Elisa, who interjected, "What I really love is water!"

"Oh, yes, cool water, what a blessing!" added Miss Margarida.

Bernat tried to speak again, but in vain. Antonieta insisted, "Cousin Bernat, would you like a glass of water?"

Bernat accepted with an exaggerated gesture, feeling a flush of pity for them and for himself a blush of shame for having tried to snatch one of their few remaining possessions from them, taking advantage of their poverty.

But that wasn't it, exactly, either. What had brought him to visit the sisters was the focus of their existence: the splendor of La Paret. By that he meant the richness the manor house had possessed in the past, the grandfather clock perhaps its only surviving symbol.

The clock had been transported by ship from Hamburg, Germany, and stood as a representative of and a tribute to the alarm clock factory founded by Bernat's father, Benigne Taltavull—Brígida's husband—together with the participation of their godson, Diumenge de La Paret, father of the five spinster sisters. Bernat the Wise had retold the venerable, epic tale a thousand times, just as he had heard it told by others a thousand times before.

The graceful *Twelve Apostles* was a sailing ship belonging to Diumenge, the lord of La Paret. It had glided into the small semicircular port of Orlandis at full sail, its bow cutting a straight and frothy trail through the water as if it were a proud and marvelous harbinger of good news. And it was, for it bore the grandfather clock from Hamburg. The gigantic crate it arrived in was unloaded onto the dock with nervous care, witnessed by a gape-jawed throng of the curious. Mysteriously and incomprehensibly, the machinery hidden inside began sounding out the hours.

"Now it says it's five o'clock," grumbled the sailor Canuda.

"But it's only twelve noon!" replied Bett the fishmonger.

"Well, in Germany they're in a different time zone. The clocks in each country chime in their own way, you know," explained the blind lottery vendor, Pere Capó Esteve.

And so the great clock, nestled in blankets atop a wagon, rumbled through town, pursued by a gaggle of curious children. Bernat, who was also a child at the time, rode on the wagon. And if his chums got too close to it, he threatened them with a lash of his whip.

For a long time now Bernat had imagined that having the grandfather clock from La Paret in his office at the factory would be tantamount to possessing another of the bolts that held together a perfectly rotating world, especially his own and his family's. That very morning, stimulated by the vague but unmistakable optimism of the Christmas season when he passed by the peeling façade of La Paret, he had suddenly remembered the grandfather clock and so had knocked on the door.

Cloistered as they were in that ruin of a house, the sisters only ventured out at the crack of dawn for early mass. The five of them sat through the service huddled together in the dark as one shapeless bundle on the pew. Very few people in town were still sensitive to the waxen respectability that had emanated from La Paret in the past. The sisters had already become anachronistic, aloof silhouettes. Bundled up in their mended mantillas and their haughty, outdated dresses, walking through town tightly arm-in-arm with their eyes to the ground, barely responding to the greetings of some of the neighbors who still spoke to them, the old maids of La Paret represented the unremitting will to reign over all that was long dead and gone.

But they were unaware of the void through which they walked, for they formed no part of anything hinting at community, neither in the town of Orlandis nor in the church. If they deigned to visit that temple, they were drawn to it neither by faith nor tradition, but by the implicit conviction that the category of the stone edifice and the richness of the priestly vestments—

their emblematic embellishment, the most singular milestone in the life of the town—constituted the most unique and elevated relationship La Paret could maintain without losing its dignity.

Father Arcadi Frau Taltavull, the rash and long-suffering rector of Orlandis, was just starting his car under the linden trees in the church square at the very moment Ramon Consolat knocked on the door of the ancient ancestral home in the valley. The priest had on more than one occasion thought of denying communion to the five old maids.

"They don't share any of the dogmas of the Faith," argued the Bishop of Majorca. But the priest's only answer to that comment was to raise his eyes to heaven and change the subject.

La Paret meant The Wall. The mere mention of the name guided and absorbed the sisters like the paper star in the manger scene at Taltavull Hall with the twenty-five-watt bulb behind it that had hypnotized the children earlier in the evening. The sisters proudly continued to pronounce those words, La Paret, even though they now lacked any hint of meaning even remotely related to power or property, for the manor house itself—their only remaining possession—was mortgaged. Their stock in the alarm clock business brought them only a miserable income. After the Spanish Civil War, Bernat the Wise had bought the factory from the sisters out of pure compassion because it had neither raw materials nor any possibility of an export market and consequently was forced to close down for a time.

But the sisters, either unaware of conditions in the real world or unconsciously desperate, as no doubt befitted their stubbornness, continued to hold forth as the vestal defenders of a cult that had already become a metaphysical mirage.

Lord Diumenge de La Paret as a ship owner—though of only one ship—had always dressed in a blue blazer of imported English cloth with anchors engraved on its golden buttons. He wore a captain's cap decorated with gold braid. His wife, in a constant state of discrete exhaustion, died after her eighth pregnancy. Three were miscarriages and five were live births. The sweeping presence of Diumenge in the town square and at the port of Orlandis became the incarnation of respectability. His daughters, flaunting their expensive finery, accompanied Diumenge de La Paret wherever he went and looked down their noses at the rest of the people in town.

It was inconceivable to the girls that the young lads of Orlandis should dare tag after them with pretensions of marriage. They wouldn't even listen to such oafish peasants. The delicate, milk-white hands of the girls were to be promised only to parties from other social and territorial galaxies. Diumenge cleared his throat, caressed one of the girls' cheeks, gave eight pesetas to another to buy some violet ribbons newly arrived at the dry-goods store, and made a suggestion to the third. He was surrounded by skirts, curls, and giggles, the picture of utter contentment.

The lord of La Paret usually embarked on the *Twelve Apostles* when it was about to undertake a long voyage. Thus he had sailed through some of the most extraordinary seas and tied up in some of the most unusual destinations: the South Atlantic and its icebergs; the wharves of Bombay with the scorching odor of starving people; the South Pacific and its gracious, comic isles; the leaden estuary of the Thames, riven by the shrieking of its sirens. In Bangkok he had been honored by the King of Siam, and in the Black Sea he had emerged victorious against the mutiny of some Cypriot sailors. The wake of the ship, the sparkle of the waves and the long trail of seagulls behind, the toy-like, make-believe horizon through the circle of his binoculars: he had experienced the tension of the tiller tightly gripped in his hands and the terror of many storms, like the one off Madagascar that split the masts of the ship and filled its deck with thrashing swordfish.

With his charter fees, his estates, and his other businesses, he created feverish activity among the scanty investment resources of Orlandis, and although he only managed to produce two sacks of hard coal from his eccentric mining ventures, he put quite a bit of money into his own pockets. He wasn't originally from La Paret, because La Paret didn't even exist at the time—it belonged to a branch of the Taltavull family who lived at the Hermitage.

The largest of the estates consisted of flatlands in the very middle of the valley of Orlandis, which centuries ago had been a bog inhabited by an enormous dragon with a fiery, sulfurous breath, a swallower of chaste maidens. The dragon was defeated by the Knight of Orlandis, who arrived by sea on his frothy steed, armed with his lance and the blessing of God. He thrust the lance into the dragon's only eye, causing the beast to disappear, the bogs along with him. That miraculous and heroic deed was commemorated by the construction of an oratory called the Hermitage. But the torrent that rushed through the valley in winter used to burst its banks and flood the freshly sown fields. People whispered among themselves that it was the dragon who still lay buried beneath the mud and stirred it up, causing the floods. After one of them had turned a noble expanse of wheat fields into an immense quagmire, the ship owner declared, "Let a wall be built!"

And the wall, La Paret, was built. Months passed of wagons and peasant labor, of hauling and cutting stone non-stop until the torrent, held captive between two long and sturdy walls, never again burst its banks. And every June thereafter, the crops on the plain ripened and were harvested. And thus the dogma of The Wall was born, the kind of work respected by the Romans and—logically—by the Lord of the Wall, Diumenge Taltavull.

And according to the law of life both would die, Diumenge before the name of La Paret. But he died before any of the ideal suitors for his daughters could find their way to La Paret, bearing a bouquet of roses in one hand and a gold wedding band in the other. And so his dream collapsed. In spite of the fact that the daughters felt the disaster coming, they procrastinated and gave roundabout excuses for what was happening, then signed over their control of the estate, giving power of attorney to Ramon Consolat. He then became the one who sold off the estate piecemeal and brought ruin to La Paret.

The girls never really wanted to know what was going on, cloistered as they were in hostility and confusion after they were suddenly orphaned by a father they both loved and enjoyed. They had lived according to the firm belief that their world—in reality the bell jar built around them by their father—would last forever.

Elisa, the eldest of the five, was a tall, square-shouldered explosion of bitterness in every thought and word she uttered. She gave orders day and night, driven by a rigorous standard: to be, but not to do. Margarida, on the other hand, outdid herself with sweetly flowing gestures, rolling her eyes, her skin pale and transparent. She obeyed without being aware of what she did. And Caterina, heavy-bodied and weak-minded, finally married Ramon Consolat.

Consolat owned a van and worked as a delivery man. He was always dirty from rolling barrels, hefting sacks and baskets of produce. His father had been the last farm manager at La Paret. Caterina married out of desperation and for a chance to flee the despair of her family. The sisters needed money, however little it might be, in order to survive after years of eating fowl from their chicken house—whose occupants had become progressively scrawnier from lack of grain—and the few vegetables they were able to grow in a corner of the courtyard.

But well before the wedding and with his father already retired as farm manager, Ramon in his own churlish way had begun to do more and more jobs for La Paret without having agreed with the evasive sisters on any payment. At least on the surface, these labors were inscribed in a mythical, brutish book of reckoning, a continuation of the ancient hierarchical scheme of things that had bound his father to the estate. But in reality, other appetites were at play: Ramon, as he worked around the house, would often run into Caterina, ogling her with gluttonous eyes, drinking in her prominent hips and heavy breasts. The sisters observed his stares but held their tongues.

Until one day, what everyone had expected to happen happened. Elisa told Ramon in a tone as dry as that she used when ordering him to bring firewood or fix the roof, "You can marry Caterina whenever you want."

His only reaction was to grunt in agreement.

His behavior had been based on simple-minded intuition: by lowering himself and becoming the young ladies' most humble servant, their dependence on him would soon become absolute. Like a crude and powerful god, Ramon granted them his devotion, but demanded sacrifices from them in return. The five young misses offered up one of their own because in truth survival in slavery was their only option.

Early one morning at six the wedding was held in the dark and empty church. The ceremony, however, did not alter the relationship between the sisters and Ramon. Whenever they spoke to him, they never looked him straight in the eye, and he in turn manipulated them with feline cunning. But at night in the dark warmth of her bed, Caterina embraced Ramon's well-muscled body with preemptory grunts, groping for his feisty penis, trembling and moaning as her crotch swallowed it up.

On Saturdays Consolat would show up with a few baskets of provisions for the coming week which he had bought in the market at Palma, the capital of the island, on one of his many trips with his van. Soon the sisters fell into the habit of waiting and watching for his arrival from behind the window curtain. The van would pull up, and Ramon would unload it. The sisters never ventured out to greet him, pretending they had chores to do. But when he left, they threw themselves upon the market baskets, pulling out the goods and marveling at them between exclamations of surprise: a pound of Swiss chocolate, a package of macaroni, a bunch of fresh green onions, a bottle of strong, sweet wine.

But some Saturdays Ramon Consolat brought nothing home with him, not even an excuse for the empty baskets. Nor did the young misses dare to ask him why. Sunday would come and go . . . and Monday, and Tuesday, and the sisters of La Paret—their pantry drained, their table more and more bare of food—seemed to change in physical appearance. They began to prowl like animals when they came near food. Their bodies became aberrant highly sensitive olfactory, tactile, and visual organs, their sole mission to ferret out food.

But all that happened after the crazy episode of Felícia's love affair, the only affair there ever was at La Paret. She never understood what had happened to her or what it all meant. Nor did her sisters, because the story had taken shape outside the strict confines of La Paret, their only point of reference.

The sisters had not even noticed the presence of Maurice in Orlandis, and when he burst into their lives, they were more surprised than indignant that such a person had been able to gain such influence over La Paret. A swarthy Algerian with curly hair, tightly tailored shirts and trousers, Maurice Borrassà had appeared in town toward the end of the fifties to spend his vacation at his parents' house.

They were fishmongers who operated a little shack down by the docks. The great flat expanse of the wharf was like a peaceful breath of fresh air compared to the narrow, winding streets of the barrio, which stank of fish. Those streets smelled like a closed cellar, so humid and narrow that the sun never reached lower than the eaves of the buildings. The houses were a rabbit warren, a slum. Old man Borrassà was an experienced water witcher. He had been to Taltavull Hall, searching with his pendulum for its hidden underground veins of water. All the cats in the valley used to follow him wherever he went, yowling at the fishy stench he gave off. Maurice always doused himself generously with cologne to disguise the smell.

The jolly and mysterious people from Pula, who knew everything in spite of the fact that they lived in the inhospitable and isolated place called Les Exèquies, had already figured out the Algerian.

"Any day now that guy is going to strike gold," some of them had commented at Taltavull Hall, where they also had relatives.

Then unexpectedly, one afternoon as the sea breeze barely rocked the boats and murmured softly through the halyards, Maurice and Felícia were seen strolling along the wharf hand-in-hand. How had they met? She was rarely seen on the street and had no friends. When her sisters questioned her about it, she was unable to give them a straight answer. She would either stammer from shame or rebuke them defiantly. For some days now, with her heart in her throat, she had been meeting Maurice in the tranquil pine forest atop the terrifying rocky cliffs at the mouth of the harbor.

For the rest of her life the memory of Maurice would remain unaltered, a singular and indecipherable vision linked to her initial intimacy with the Algerian: three crazy barking dogs, she all sweaty and weepy, her hair mussed up; the stunning, blinding whiteness of his shirt, his swarthy face, his drifting arms; a ship on the sleepy evening sea swaddled in the mellifluous cadences of a distant flute, the delirium of his vigorous penis in her hands and then in her mouth. Maurice.

At the time, Felícia was thirty years old. And she had not even had a whiff of a male until then. Her slim face with its morbid, sunken eyes, her shapely, angular body. . . . The first thing the sisters noticed about her contact with Maurice was the exquisite perfume she started drenching herself in. It affected them emotionally, for since that paradisiacal time of their father—now gone forever—they hadn't smelled anything like it.

They reacted in alarm, and in unison. And as they were demanding explanations from her, the stench of fish drifted to their sensitive nostrils. The intruder had insidiously burrowed to the epicenter of La Paret, on the one hand formed by their firm habit of waiting, which had made their maidenly fates second nature to them. On the other hand, the denigrating appearance at La Paret of the Borrassà clan, represented exactly what the haughty sisters thought ought to be groveling at their feet.

However, Felícia did not give him up. Maurice's orgasmic embraces drove her crazy with fear, after first driving her crazy with pleasure. She realized that insufferable deprivation would await her should she lose her man. Thus she was also the only one of the sisters who grasped the direct relationship between La Paret and nothingness. But, incapable of analyzing the situation because she had been brought up only to believe and feel, her only response to her sisters' accusations was to rave at them in scorn.

And when the Algerian returned to Africa, Felícia wept a flood of tears and pursued the mailman every day because she was getting letters, ardent love letters. And so, prisoner of her own foggy thoughts on commitment, Felícia married by proxy, with Ramon Consolat representing the groom. He was the only male La Paret had at hand, since they no longer dealt with the people in Taltavull Hall. To have done so the sisters would have had to explain a little, or a lot. And that they could not do, nor did they want to, sequestered as they were from reality. They preferred to lose rather than share.

"Was that grievous wedding scene real?" they asked themselves. The priest and the justice of the peace had ratified it, but the sisters didn't feel any echo of conviction, of inner emotion. The bride left immediately for the unknown land of Algeria. Her sisters in Orlandis heard nothing from her for months and months because the OAS, the *pieds noirs,* the FLN, the French Army, the Christians, and the Moors were locked in an exasperating confrontation saturated with bombings, uprisings and torture—revolution and war, the torrid accomplices of the sinister scythe of death.

And then late one evening, as the sky over Orlandis became tinged with purple clouds, an emaciated Felícia appeared at the door of the family manor with no luggage, nothing but a shabby dress hanging loosely over her scarecrow frame. Her face showed fright and astonishment, she opened and closed her arms like a robot, as if expecting somebody, a body, any body, a body that never came.

In Algiers, Felícia hadn't been able to see very much of Maurice—hasty meetings amid the chaotic throngs in the port, crazy encounters in the squalid, motley, terrifying bedrooms of the Casbah. She soon learned that Maurice was a supporter of one side against the other. People she didn't know and whose language she didn't understand were constantly moving her around. She found herself as often in miserable rooms among sheet-draped Muslims as in shabby apartments full of irate Frenchmen.

Before that, she had contemplated the Arab peoples and their faces only in the pastoral images of a collection of books her father had brought from Marseilles, entitled *Le Tourisme du Salon.* The innocent young ladies at La Paret used to leaf through them in the glassed-in balcony on quiet afternoons or in the sewing room beside the jar of chocolates, with the iridescent macaw clumsily clutching its perch, the screeching of the bird the only reality the sisters were able to link to those picturesque book plates.

But *Le Tourisme du Salon* hadn't the slightest to do with the reality of the Algiers Felícia slipped and slid through, galvanized by terror. That seething crowd of Moors with ambiguous rancor in their eyes constituted a beastly, incomprehensible rejection, the maximum vision of her own private hell, the overwhelming misfortune described by the nuns and priests at Corema School, something she had evidently never imagined could touch her life. Felícia had never noticed people in Orlandis, but in Algiers she discovered that her own inner tranquillity depended on others, that she was also—and perhaps above all—the others.

Felícia lay curled up on a dirty straw mattress, half-awake, half-asleep, suffocating amid the heat and flies, staring at the squashed remains of bedbugs and mosquitoes on the whitewashed wall. The police suddenly burst in and dragged her away screaming. She faced a glaring bulb in a suffocating room and was interrogated between beatings.

Felícia stood on the deck of a steamer as it left port, huddled against a lifeboat, beaten and swollen, observing the porticoed city square as it grew smaller in the distance, the palm trees becoming tiny sticks on the horizon. She knew everything was finished, that another, stranger and more specific hell was beginning: herself alone with her self.

"Well, what about him?" her sisters asked in Orlandis. Felícia's only answer was to open her arms in a gesture of desolation.

Antonieta was already nearly forty, but still enjoyed using the wheedling gestures of her adolescence on that Saturday Christmas morning, dressed in the style of a quarter of a century ago in the only rags she had. Antonieta was a delicate, fussy blonde. And her nervous movements, the constant frightened look in her eyes, hinted at the dark fears that haunted her.

As a sprightly young woman, the beautiful and fragile Antonieta had been the last hope of redemption for La Paret. Every Sunday her sisters would send her out on the streets alone at the time people strolled in the square, hoping against hope that there might be some young lads who would perhaps show an interest in her. If the sisters had only dared years ago, they too might have been courted.

Antonieta walked like a duck in her high-heeled shoes, embarrassed among the Sunday strollers, her fan dangling in her limp hand. Young men either didn't notice her or hid their smirks and kept their distance. She didn't allow herself to get too close to them, either. A few minutes after arriving at the square, she would slip away down a side street and walk contritely through a deserted neighborhood, feeling sorry for herself as she sucked on a tender stem of grass, waiting for the time when she could go home.

Bernat Taltavull supposed he had really been in love with Antonieta. "Falling in love doesn't cost a thing when you're young," he used to think. And she was like a breath of sweet and gentle air. . . . He greeted her on the street. She blushed. Sometimes he was able to walk with her down the lanes leading out of town, lined with verdant almond trees. The young man talked on and on, masking his inner timidity with a free and easy manner. Antonieta answered in monosyllables, her large beseeching eyes defenseless. Bernat took her hand, and in her indecision she didn't resist. And then one afternoon he kissed her clumsily. Antonieta fled from him, dropping her fan in the roadway. . . .

"Come on in, Ramon, and warm up a bit and have a glass of champagne and a piece of Christmas candy. At least you'll enjoy the party with us, because those ladies over there. . . . Are we relatives or not, by God!" exclaimed Bernat, clapping Consolat heartily on the back that Christmas Eve.

"Afterward," replied Ramon. "Now come outside and help me."

They went out into the windy night. Despite the dark, the white balustrade of the wide terrace stuck out as if it divided the world in two. Ramon Consolat's van was parked beside the tall, round, thickly-branched cypress tree that swayed lazily in the wind. He opened the rear door and pulled back a blanket, revealing the potbellied German grandfather clock from La Paret.

Ramon mumbled in Bernat's surprised face, "It's yours. The girls don't want to sell anything here in town, out of pride. And even less to someone they know. Bah, and if they try to speak to anyone on the street, they have to identify themselves first because everybody has forgotten who they are. So I truck their things into Palma and sell them to the antique dealers and junk men. They think I've gone there now with the clock. I suppose you'll give me a good price for it, won't you?"

3

Beautiful Egèria was standing beside the wide fireplace, talking in her seductive, sleepy voice with her uncles, Albert the Younger, bewitched by the popping, flickering flames, and Honorat Moro, hunch-backed and hairy, the misanthrope from the high plains on the outskirts of Orlandis.

"And of course Uncle Bernat wants the clock because it symbolizes an infantile fixation of his, but also because it's German—the best piece of clock-work we've ever had in Orlandis. What does that tell us? That foreigners do things differently. They live life differently. Oh, how I'd love to travel to other countries and get to know their people! It makes me sad when I think about it. Isn't happiness sort of a dream about new and different things?"

Albert the Younger's face—so noble, covered with such fine wrinkles—grew devilishly flushed from the fire. He gazed at his niece, stunned by her question and failed to understand why she had asked it. He didn't know what to say to her. In reality, he never did know what to say, unless it had to do with some whim of his own.

His brother-in-law, Honorat, who was gobbling roasted almonds, answered with a skeptical shrug.

"The human animal never changes. And if it does, it's always for the worse."

"My dear uncles, how old-fashioned you sound!" laughed Egèria heartily, not allowing her eagerness to get in the way of her enjoyment. "You, for example, Uncle Albert, are asleep in a sort of vacuum. And you, Honorat, have retreated to prehistoric times. You'll see, I'll prove it to you, and very simply: let's take the differences between us and foreigners. They have the advantage. Look, what's your opinion of hedgehogs? What is a hedgehog?"

Uncle Albert appeared even more perplexed. Hedgehogs? Of course he knew they existed, and he had even seen some, but he didn't understand why anyone should have to notice them, least of all talk about them.

"A hedgehog . . . ," he mumbled, his mind a blank.

"Hedgehogs?" Honorat raised his head in interest. "Well, yes . . . I find them quite often in the thickets and along the edges of the fields . . . they carry a lot of lice among their quills. And they are meat-eaters. If they get into a henhouse they'll gobble up the brood of baby chicks and even attack the hens. They come at night when the birds are asleep and can't defend themselves. They nibble away nonstop with their little snouts. . . . I used to have a little black dog who was an ace at hunting hedgehogs. And oh, is the meat of those little critters tasty! During the Civil War with all the famine they were a prize. We used to cook them up with rice. Sucking on those little legs was a delight. And if you baked them until the skin was crunchy, they made a great main dish."

Albert the Younger grimaced, with theatrical delicacy.

Aunt Pollònia was busily setting the vast table. She seemed like a glider emerging from the cumulus clouds of smoke, landing in the middle of the hall and serving all the Taltavulls their Christmas Eve dinner. Discreetly she listened to her brother-in-law Honorat, nodding her head in agreement.

"Ah, Uncle Honorat, I knew you could tell us!" applauded Egèria. "Listen to me now. I've just received a letter from that Swedish lady who rents the chalet on West Beach, the one that used to belong to La Paret. She and I are friends. Let me read you a couple of lines from it: 'I remember all of you very well, and I especially remember the Taltavull Hall countryside. And the little animals from the woods surrounding our house there. Imagine! Every day a family of hedgehogs would appear on the lawn, the mother and five little ones. They waddled across it in an orderly little row. We kept a bowl of milk ready for them. They are incredibly graceful as they drink it up in little slurps. They lick it up to the last drop. Then they turn around and leave in a procession, until the next day.' What do you say to that, Uncle?"

Before Honorat Moro could answer, Pollònia, who was gliding by with a plate of radishes, suddenly stopped, goggle-eyed, and asked Egèria incredulously, "Where'd you say they were from, Albania or Switzerland?"

"Who's that, Aunt?"

"Who? Who else? The hedgehogs, of course!" answered Aunt Pollònia impatiently.

"From Sweden."

"Well, then, from Sweden or wherever, because out there beyond the sea there's a hodgepodge that beats all . . . Swedish hedgehogs, come on! Are they really hedgehogs?"

"Of course!"

"But hedgehog-hedgehogs, just like ours?"

"Exactly," smiled Egèria.

Aunt Pollònia thought about that for a moment, "And . . . hedgehogs like the ones here just waltz up to that foreign lady's house with the whole brood following her?"

"Are you thick, or what, Pollònia?" Honorat was annoyed. "Didn't you hear what she said?"

"Yes, of course I heard! My God!" she answered in a fluster. "I haven't gone deaf! But do they give them real milk?"

"Yes, Auntie."

"And they actually come up and drink it?"

"Yesss . . . ," smiled Beautiful Egèria.

"There's nobody as thick-headed as my sister-in-law," snapped Honorat.

Pollònia thought that over for a moment, then burst out indignantly, "And does that foreign lady sweep up the droppings from those hedgehogs? They're shameless, drinking milk like that, as if they were little kids! Not only people, even the animals are topsy-turvy today!"

Tomàs Moro, comfortably ensconced in his glistening fat, took very little part in the general conversation; he listened furtively and disdainfully to the conversation between his father, Honorat, Aunt Pollònia, and Cousin Egèria. "Bah, things are so superficial . . . ," he commented, seated meditatively in his rocker, rocking slowly back and forth.

The only time he got up was to edge his bulk over to the bar, where they had laid out an abundance of hors d'oeuvres. He nibbled at the stuffed olives, attracted by the oily bitterness of the anchovies inside. Then he went for the cod balls, which he really liked, then the salty chunks of cheese from Mahon. He didn't drink very much, just a few swallows of vermouth.

What he really missed, especially when eating at Taltavull Hall, was the homemade wine they used to make in Orlandis, the kind they themselves pressed on the farm. But those were the good old days. The wine was always a bit muddy, a color that ripened to a pale green, just a bit tart. As a little boy, Tomàs had stomped the grapes inside an enormous cask while Grandmother Brígida sang along, excitedly watching the intoxicating juices flow from the fruit.

Now the cavernous wine cellar had been converted into a kitchen outfitted with a freezer, a water heater, and an electric oven. The monumental cask where they used to store the wine, its oaken staves clamped together with iron hoops, now served as a decorative piece at the entrance to Taltavull Hall. And the long narrow terraces on the hillside where they used to grow the grapes had been invaded by the ever-hungry, ever-expanding pine forest, casting its compact, velvety shadows over the vines, ultimately devouring them.

Moro smiled. The engineer Fèlix Albornoz, married to his cousin Marieta Verònica, the daughter of Bernat the Wise, got into an argument with Marianna Mas every time he heard the story of the shade killing the vines and insisted that it wasn't the shade that demolished the vegetation; it was the pine roots themselves that abused the soil and sucked all the nutrients out of it and caused the other plants to degenerate.

"And that could well be true," Tomàs hurriedly granted, believing prudence essential to guarantee his quiet independence.

"It *is* true!" added the engineer Albornoz, glaring at the rest of the people, while he expounded on a generally accepted truth: the roots of the almond tree reach out three feet beyond the circumference of its crown; the pine tree and the carob tree both send out roots thirty feet beyond the spread of their foliage; a fig tree and a grapevine have no limits.

But when the Spaniard Fèlix Albornoz wasn't present, then Tomàs Moro, his huge eyes bulging and his arms spread wide, would venture to make some innocent comment: "It could also be true that the unfortunate death of vegetation was due to the shade created by the pine. It isn't that I want to argue with the theories of Marieta Verònica's husband, whom I dearly love and who builds roads and bridges for the Public Works Department, but let's look at this more closely: Can one know everything about everything? Absolutely not. Why can't shade kill, then? Every plant has roots that spread out underground. Is it possible that some are thieves, shall we say, and others are stranglers? Nobody from around here has ever heard of that. And it's been demonstrated that any plant you give enough water to—even though it's a delicate, recently-grafted fruit tree—will thrive tremendously. On the other hand, the rapid development of the pine is accompanied by another, even more important factor: the shade it creates. It grows and grows, wider and thicker until the sun's life-giving rays can no longer reach the ground under it. The shade of the pine is the shade of death."

Tomàs Moro paused to observe his audience's reaction. If it looked as if they understood, if there was nobody among them the likes of the engineer or the priest Arcadi Frau Taltavull—"Another inveterate and rancorous resister of the spontaneous; he who, on the contrary, believes himself to be God's representative of Eternity, which surely is unusual," grumbled Moro to himself. Then he lowered his voice, half-closed his eyes, and whispered ecstatically, "Who has not heard it from the old sailors, from our parents and our grandparents, through whom we have come to know everything about all things created and yet to be created? Who has not listened to the carefully detailed stories of poisonous shade on remote islands and coasts? A ship with its billowing sails on a sea as flat as a plowed field that suddenly enters the shadow of a solitary black cloud and sinks straight down like a rock as if someone had pushed it to the bottom. An inhospitable shoreline, rugged cliffs dominated by a very high pinnacle like the tooth of a fairy-tale giant casting its own long, triangular shadow. Well then, under the protection of that shadow, there is a cove with a beach full of coconut palms, a fresh-water fountain, and multicolored songbirds. This shadow moves, of course, to the march of the sun. And the cove moves too, appallingly following the solar movement, like the hands on a clock. Long ago, some mariners disembarked in an unknown land and saw a man sitting quietly under the shade of a tree. They drew near to ask him news of the place, but the figure turned out to be a skeleton, sitting in the shadow of death. And what about the most beautiful woman on the island, whom they embraced and felt her dissolve in their arms because she was only a shadow?"

Tomàs Moro took a deep breath and opened his eyes a bit to check the reaction of his audience: the people were listening, serious and concerned. Moro opened his mouth, but did not speak. The idea that had just come to him produced a visible shiver throughout his massive frame. However, he finally spoke in a thin, reedy voice, "Even the shadow of the pine has an aroma, as if an invisible being were living inside it." If he had dared, he would have added, " . . . a Being from the Other Side that has uncorked the flask of an extremely rare essence, both very bitter and very balsamic."

Tomàs Moro, nestled in the rocker among the swirls of smoke in the hall, smiled again, his mouth awash with the bitter aftertaste of the stuffed olives. There was an infinity of mysteries, of powers, out there. In order to capture them—in spite of the fact that to get to know them would require even more enigmatic operations—it would be enough to investigate and listen without prejudice to the opposite of what things appeared to be because appearance was just one of the multiple dimensions of any organism or idea.

What he was conceptualizing was the voices and shapes of silence and the unknown, sudden sensations of well-being or horror; a sigh in the middle of a room where no human voice existed; indescribable and constantly changing colors; an animal with an expression of abominable intelligence; the nothingness of water and sky; a mark on a stone; the unintelligible voices of the heirs of the Grand Design.

Tomàs Moro was able to divine all that with much more intensity at Taltavull Hall than anywhere else. His ancestors had inhabited the old manor house since the century of the Conquest of America, the century of glorious arms that made things happen. It was the center of the world. And once installed in the valley—even though his ancestors had no written documents—wouldn't their Catalan and Provençal blood have mixed with that of the earlier inhabitants of the isle? An Arab slave girl with a delicate beauty, the close-knit and unctuous Jews, the crude captives from Slavonia: men and women of such mixed races that by Tomàs Moro's time they had been absorbed by a long line of generations, by the endless seaways that always opened their maws then snapped shut again: the sinewy Berber race, the ferocious Maltese, the Carthaginians with their tremendous talent for commerce, the pompous Byzantines, the midgets and the giants. Yes, all vanished, but they left their mark ingrained in the inherent wisdom of the people who survived. Didn't Grandmother Brígida herself come from the family in Pula, those redheads who arrived from unknown parts of the Adriatic? At the manor house Tomàs Moro felt bathed in a balmy atmosphere more amiable and tender than at any other place.

Moro had often lived at Taltavull Hall, especially as a child, when his father abandoned him and his mother, and went off to live in that little mountain cabin. His father claimed he couldn't stand it in Orlandis, that he felt surrounded by threats, while up there on the mountain he could commune with everything: "All I have is just this one life, and if I don't live it for myself, I shall have lived it for others . . . what a swindle!" he repeated stubbornly as Tomàs and his mother cried and implored him not to leave.

So Tomàs and his mother went to live at Taltavull Hall. Grandfather Benigne reigned over everything there, constantly giving orders and more orders, watching over the corrals and the newly sown fields. They were short of everything. It was wartime, and there wasn't much to eat. But in their labyrinthine larder were stored sacks of wheat and fava beans; parts of the butchered hog made up into sausages, the rest salted away in barrels and boxes; strings of dried tomatoes and garlic hung from the rafters; a bread made from figs, wrapped and stored in grape leaves. Grandmother Brígida spun the yarn for her own clothes, humming ancient tunes she didn't understand, vague old hymns from another time.

The people who lived at Taltavull Hall were self-centered and withdrawn, insulated both materially and psychologically. Though the hall limited them in some respects, it also created the mettle and intensity out of which grew their belief that everything was a repetition of something that had happened before. As a result, just as native species survive but atrophy in closed-in spaces (one of the characteristics of Majorca, of islands), old habits, customs, and wisdom from distant antiquity persisted at Taltavull Hall, contributing to the myth of the creation of the race. It was but the visible tip of a vast iceberg of clan and tribal traditions, which if viewed by outsiders would have appeared irrational.

Because, no doubt, they were just that. Or would have been, if they could have been separated from the family genes. In that atmosphere laden with echoes, the daily rituals, the unspoken understandings, the spirits risen from the distant past had all fused with daily life. They were life itself, for they fed off the driving forces of life. And within the confines of that life, nothing was out of harmony, for the repetitive mix became transformed by secular influences into a stylized subtlety of gesture and perception.

Deep in his solitary meditations, Moro stood by the bar where he absent-mindedly continued stuffing himself with hors d'oeuvres. Father Arcadi went by with a platter of roast chicken stuffed with fragrant apples and prunes. He feigned dumping the platter on his cousin Tomàs, as he warned him, "You're as fat as a sow, and yet you stay at the trough. You should go on a diet!"

Tomàs Moro didn't even bother to answer. The priest opened his mouth only to vituperate others, always finding or inventing something negative to say about them. Moro disliked him, especially his appearance. Arcadi was a tall man, thin and stoop-shouldered, with an enormous knot of hair, sunken eyes, a mouth twisted to one side, large and yellowed teeth. If he tried to show someone his good nature by affably clapping them on the back, what they received was the full ham-fisted force of his hand.

"If he believes what he preaches about the brotherhood of man and heavenly redemption, then why does he only tell rotten lies? Like everybody else, he's hanging over the abyss by his fingernails, but at the same time, invoking the name of his God and refusing to admit he is barely hanging on. And that's why he's a phony. His bitterness is the vomit of his own contradictions."

The abyss, or the truth—truth, the result of the incalculable essence of the ages. Tomàs Moro owned a home appliance shop, the best-stocked in Orlandis. He had graduated from high school, and he read. He was aware of and appreciated what was up-to-date and modern; the electric refrigerator was to him a wonderful appliance, and color TV was a prodigious tribute to man's ingenuity.

"But those things only represent the outer shell of man. Progress has to do with how you live, but it's not life itself. Bleatings of desperation and songs of love, on the other hand, have always been the same. In the old days, since people had fewer material goods to weigh them down, they were more aware of who they were. If we separate man from passing fashions, all we are left with is a lowly disciple of banality. And under those circumstances man learns very little or is often wrong."

That's what was wrong with the engineer and the priest, as well as the immense majority of people who crow about the absolute truth of contemporary values based on the lone truth of a single faith. "They measure everything by immediate empirical evidence." Just the opposite of the Taltavulls, who had been brought up amid the turbulent and sharp-edged attitudes of their ancestors and thus were able to detect the ambiguous and twisted presence of that which is silent by nature.

"Bah, Albornoz and that priest are idiots," Tomàs Moro declared, blissfully curled up again in his rocker in spite of the fact that his brain, stirred up by the obviousness of his ruminations, was still alert and receptive, like a greyhound in hot pursuit. If Arcadi had become a priest, there were others in the family who had never darkened the doorway of a church, such as Tomàs's own great-grandmother, Anna de Gràcia—the mother of Grandmother Brígida—kin to the people from Pula.

And why didn't she go to church? Tomàs didn't think she had ever gone to confession. She had been born in the marshlands beyond the port of Orlandis on that rugged shore, scene of shipwrecks and home to pirates. And when she heard anyone mention going to church, the fairy-tale pink of her cheeks would turn a deep purple. She would begin to grumble, her eyes wandering as if she had suddenly lost her balance.

Did Tomàs think that Arcadi and the church were lying, that they were wrong? No, not exactly. A lot of people in Orlandis respected religion, even though they seldom went to church. But there were many more who considered it a superficial system imposed on the genuine forces of life, those which every man was directly involved with: the basic, visible forces on earth.

"Just because something alive has been buried doesn't mean it's dead," Grandmother Brígida used to say with mystical and vengeful fervor, even though it had nothing to do with the conversation.

An image flashed through Tomàs Moro's mind that gave him goose pimples: the old lady's unbridled excitement every time she saw the White Mule.

"It's her! It's her!" she would murmur in awe, pulling Tomàs by the hand as she nervously paced back and forth on the terrace of her daughter Paula's house, her eyes gleaming as she watched the grotesque and enigmatic White Mule advance down the street. Some of the bystanders cheered the beast while others looked on suspiciously.

The Last Days of Mardi Gras, the famous Last Days . . . pure joy, burdened with the sweet uncertainty of the masked figures. The most extravagant prelude to the Lenten season occurred when the children ran through town shouting, "The White Mule! The White Mule has just come out!"

The older folks would join the melee, asking where that prodigious, dread figure was going as they followed her with their eyes. They hadn't seen her since last year's Mardi Gras, and depending on the year, sometimes she wouldn't appear at all . . . until they would unexpectedly run into her at a street corner: a tall, rigid figure, so precariously balanced that she looked about to tumble over. She moved ponderously, covered with a vast white sheet crowned with a mule's skull.

That totemic sacrilege never spoke a single word. She would only buck back violently, rearing up like a jackass at anyone who dared come near her. She would run her course through the town, and then return to the place she had come from with ghostly secrecy.

Tomàs Moro asked himself what furious, secret mockery did her barbarous costume represent? Who kept her cadaverous rags and icy-white bones during the year? And what was she trying to prove with that stupid, primitive ceremony? Better yet, who was she trying to honor with her charade, as obscure and intangible as the name might be? Moro's suspicions grew. Grandmother Brígida exuded such a degree of satisfaction that it seemed to ooze from her whole body. The White Mule would withdraw at dusk, as the little lamps on the street corners came to life. It was as if a breath of menace were slipping down the placid lanes of almond trees. Her mournful bulk made pathetic, repugnant twists and turns as she advanced. And in the year of the big snowfall, the White Mule left immaculate tracks for all to see. A gang of children, Tomàs Moro among them, bucked up their courage and decided to follow her.

Then out of the ecstatic glow from the almonds in flower along the lane a spell arose. What was it? Impossible to say, but all the children felt as if something were blocking their way, and they could go no further. They turned and fled, while the ghostly figure of the beast, outlined against a hill of carob trees, brayed barely audibly to the rising moon, full and blood-red.

4

When the wind stopped, it felt as if the valley had suddenly acquired a new, sensitive dimension. The zephyr that followed made the dark feel overwhelmingly heavy, more impenetrable. If one ventured into the dark, it felt like one might bump into some obdurate rock or something even harder. But what appeared diminished had in fact become an unexpected vastness in which the gentle rustling of the leaves, the cautious grazing of the rabbit, the velvety smoke rising from the chimney all wrapped the night in a cordial warmth. And out of the pitch-black the faint sound of church bells from a distant town echoed as counterpoint to the deafening crash of the waves on the beach just over the hill from Taltavull Hall.

"Whip them egg whites hard, Joan Pere, and we'll make us some good fritters!" exclaimed Marianna Mas, the wife of Bernat the Wise, as she downed a slug of brandy from the bottle she was basting the roast with.

"That's right!" Joan Pere Tudurí responded jovially. He had been whipping the egg whites in the bowl so vigorously his arm felt as if it were coming unhinged, so he switched the whisk to the other hand. His jolly demeanor was not a pose; he breathed in the mood of the crowd just as deeply as he breathed the air around him. He lived generously, spontaneously. What he most enjoyed was to submerge himself in something as trivial as making fritters in the kitchen at Taltavull Hall on Christmas Eve amid that atmosphere of jolly bustle. That's what he had been looking forward to since his return from six months of wandering from one country to another over the globe.

Joan Pere Tudurí had arrived the night before. The plane had glided softly out of that dark blue sky, its solitary, lively stars just beginning to disappear. The cool earth, the sovereign, still-reigning night was about to become morning. Joan Pere was filled with the sensation that who he was, who he had been, and who he would become floated in the quiet, fragrant air.

He rented a car at the airport and drove toward town. He wanted the snug solitude of the deserted roads that seemed to trace a border between him and a foreign land: thick woodlands, one after the other, redolent of the aroma of pine resin and the acrid smell of a recent forest fire. The sea, glimmering from the depths of the coves, appeared to offer sparkling, enticing advice through its majestic murmurings. The horizon was filled with huge white stars that seemed to rise out of the arid hillocks of Orlandis, crowning the town with an imperial diadem.

Twenty years ago, Joan Pere had taken that same road but in the opposite direction. He had left the island out of necessity then, his breast crushed by panic as he prepared to face the hungry maw of the world awaiting him. From behind the frost-covered window of the bus taking him from Orlandis to Palma on that frigid early winter morning, he had observed a tall, gaunt, sad-faced man standing at Pous de l'Om.

When he had returned the night before, he remembered the thought that had crossed his mind when he first left the place: "What is life all about, after so much discouragement?" At the time he had surely projected his fears into the future, of which he had caught only a glimpse.

The alarm clock factory had been closed during the Civil War, and for some time afterward, for lack of raw materials and markets. Eventually, they were able to re-open it and begin to make clocks again, but almost nobody wanted to buy them. The competition of the precision-engineered clocks from the Swiss factories made the European market clearly out-of-bounds. There was only one way to go, and that was to exploit the emerging third-world markets, which were demanding more and more technical innovation but had little money and couldn't be too choosy about quality. The Taltavulls could work cheaply. So a family council decided that Joan Pere—the son of that dreadful Pollònia and the deceased watchmaker Tudurí who had done so much to make the factory survive—should therefore travel the world as its sales representative. The young man had no choice but to obey. His father, a modest man and a hard worker, had left his family in abject misery. The passing of the last twenty years found Joan Pere still doing the same sales work, and he was content with it. Thanks to it he felt free, had gotten to know women of every race around the world, to the point where he felt quite at home anywhere on the planet. He often returned from a trip with very lucrative contracts.

He drove the rental carefully, humming some tune he couldn't remember the name of. He circled the steep sides of Saints' Hill, where as a child he had always imagined a couple of saints strolling in perpetual meditation. He observed how the broad valley of Orlandis appeared from the shadows and began to take form under the slowly rising moon. The car's headlights startled a series of little animals from the dark roadside bushes: an owl with severe and angry eyes; a lumbering hedgehog; a pair of rabbits zigzagging and springing crazily into the stony roadside thickets of furze and wild olive. Clumps of trees flashed by in confusion, followed by the musty marshlands with their clusters of reeds, cattails, and bulrushes overlooking the muddy flats, suggesting the floating tips of a submerged landscape.

The ragged walls of the castle stood silhouetted against the Penyal de Ca ridge. Joan Pere could barely make it out in the murk. Its walls were broken and tumbled down, its tower a pile of rubble, the chains in the dungeon thick with rust. The devilish ghosts of the dukes stood patriarchal guard over the sea, on the lookout for a strange sail that might be the Turk. The ancient, cruel, and dictatorial duchess, quaintly elegant in her outlandish garb, never visited the castle anymore. During a storm the doors would bang and crash desperately in the wing of the building that was still intact. At dusk, throngs of bats would flap and chitter from a thousand holes. The coat of arms of the duchy, carved in obsidian—a stone not native to the island—shone in all its black splendor, glinting as if alive. It contained a heart and a thistle, representing all that man was, from lover to penitent.

"I'd like to live in a castle and hear my footsteps echoing under its arches; I'd watch the sunsets from the battlements . . . ," Tudurí thought to himself with tender irony.

The bay of Orlandis was artfully laid out, silver-surfaced, below the magical, deserted castle. It faced west and was framed by the powerful breakwater, an eruption of leaden rocks, and the wildness of the Camp de les Exèquies, a wasteland thinly covered with scrub brush. Shaggy silhouettes of palm trees stood out against the docks, their stiff pole-like trunks nodding at the quiet sea. There were few lights along the coast; the warm colors of their reflections shimmered on the water, resembling the faded flags of a sleeping army. The streets of Orlandis lay naked in the silent early morning, the murky vigilance of their empty portals tracing dark voids.

Marianna Mas, Joan Pere's aunt, scooped up a gob of the fritter dough on a tablespoon and plopped it into a kettle of boiling oil. The oil crackled and spattered, a drop of it hitting Joan Pere's cheek. He rubbed the burn with some spit on his fingertip while he stared in fascination at the fritters as they puffed up and grew golden brown in the boiling oil.

5

A tan cat dashed across the hall with a fat rat clamped in its teeth.
"Ai! It's a rat!"
"What is that?"
"What rat?"
"It's horrible!"
"The cat! The cat!"
"Ow!"
"Where'd it go?"
"Hit it! Hit the rat!"
"Where'd it come from?"
"The cat! On the stairs!"
"It's a rat! It's a rat!"
"What'd you say about a cat?"
"Everybody shut up! Sounds like you've gone nuts!"
"Ugh! It's ugly!"
"The cat's likely to hide the filthy thing in somebody's bed!"
"Aiii!"
"Hit it with the broom!"
"It's still alive!"

Three or four of the Taltavulls headed up the stairs after the cat. Damià, Egèria's brother and a professor of sociology, forced a wry smile and sarcastically addressed Joan Pere Tudurí, who had appeared at the kitchen door to see what the uproar was all about.

"You must have learned how to eat rats in China. If you want, we'll fry it up for you."

"Oh, yes, in South China they eat rats, monkeys, snakes, and everything else that feeds off the vegetables in their soggy gardens. But I haven't had the pleasure. It's a shame, considering how well I like Chinese food. All those little chopped-up pieces of things served on little plates. You get a variety of things to eat without stuffing yourself. That's what I don't like about the big servings here at home: they're boring, and they bloat you."

The retired commander, Ignasi Taltavull Oliva, couldn't agree more with Joan Pere Tudurí, "Ah! Chinese vegetables—all they do is bring them to the boil and they come out crunchy and sweet."

Beautiful Egèria laughed, deliciously envious, "And have you tasted the Chinese girls, cousin Joan Pere? My, my, the countries you have seen, the experiences you must have had . . . oh!"

"Once a Chinese lady singer came to the Lyric Theater in Palma and danced very mysteriously. I had a chance to greet her," added Albert the Younger, as he adjusted the frivolous silk cravat around his neck.

"You did what with her?" asked Damià acidly.

Albert, suspicious of what he had just heard and with a malicious glint in his eye, raised his hand cautiously to comment, "There are certain things a gentleman does not mention. And I mean just what I said: I greeted her and kissed her hand."

"Hand could be a Chinese word for . . . what were you implying that you kissed?" insisted Damià obliquely, as he leaned his scrawny body forward in his chair with the disagreeable insistence of a bird of prey.

His sister nudged him and said, "Come on, Damià, don't keep rubbing it in! Joan Pere, you still haven't answered my question . . ."

Tudurí a man of many worlds and at least as many women, poured himself a glass of champagne, took a sip and murmured, "Ah, this is the best aperitif there is, when it's well-chilled and dry."

He handed a glass to Egèria and filled it slowly.

"Oh, thank you. Joan Pere is as gallant a gentleman as you, Uncle Albert."

Joan Pere leaned against the cistern and, assuming an evocative posture, began to tell his cousin the story of Hai-yun, on an afternoon in Shanghai under the gentle but incessant rain of the Southern Empire.

Beneath the protection of a waxed-paper umbrella which the listless water from heaven drummed upon, Joan Pere walked in silence beside the young Chinese girl, Hai-yun, in the Imperial Gardens of the Mandarin Yu. The glistening rain seemed to anoint her skin and hair as if with oil. The elusive fog appeared and vanished, giving everything a lightness, a weightlessness, disquietingly close to the abyss.

A frog splashed around on its grotesque hindquarters in an oval pond. If the weather had been better, the pavilions with their curvilinear tile roofs would have been reflected in the surfaces of the small ponds where stately lilies bloomed. But that day the rain sliced at the mossy surfaces of the ponds and left them tremulous and turbid, blurring the solitary goldfish below. The acid scent of the lemon trees, the bushy green of each little tree seemed suspended among the enormously eroded rocks, converting the garden into a labyrinth of worm-eaten masks, mute witnesses to the ancestral horrors of long ago.

Delicate trefoil windows opened from the whitewashed wall where scaly, frisky lizards flashed. And further on beyond that space guarded by the sorcery of the centuries, the entrails of old Shanghai lay piled and twisted upon themselves: narrow lanes with sooty, decrepit wooden houses and the stolid, tireless hustle of the lively eyed Chinese. But in the lonely garden nothing of the Mandarin Yu remained except perhaps the last wisp of his spirit, which could be found suffused in the breath of nostalgia nestled in the indecisive hearts of Hai-yun and Joan Pere Tudurí, the Asian Taltavull.

Suddenly a rather pretentious question from Joan Pere surprised the commander and young Damià, but left Egèria and Uncle Albert unaffected, "Are we the bearers of eternal and hidden truths similar to majestic constellations, or are we only a lethargic, elusive struggle resembling that of a frog hopping about in an oval pond?"

"Well . . ." commented the retired commander.

"Hey! What's going on here?" Damià the professor cuttingly demanded.

Albert the Younger said nothing; Egèria awaited ecstatically, more beautiful than ever. She was amazed by everything she didn't know. Her daily routine was only a wait in an antechamber, a way-station to the truth.

"And what am I waiting for?" she would often ask herself, standing before the mirror. She would shrug her shoulders and think, "I guess I'm waiting for the whole universe to appear in the color and form of a tiny wildflower, waiting for something to happen that would shake me splendorously." Indeed, Egèria was very beautiful: her hair was the color of golden wheat, with splashes of frosty light; her eyes were a deep green, every movement of her body an inflection of gracile curves. But perhaps her most seductive attraction lay in that dreamy air about her, in her capacity for wonderment.

But Joan Pere, the inveterate traveler, had not been addressing himself to his audience at Taltavull Hall. Instead, deeply stirred by his own rhetoric, he was attempting to recall the moment and the question to Hai-yun on that late rainy afternoon in Shanghai. He continued, as if he were again speaking to her, "Three hundred years ago, the dignified mandarin in his stiffly embroidered robes was perhaps taking his tea in the company of his ladies, all of them seated with their legs crossed before a low table in the Western Gallery, the one done in red lacquer with the elegant and bristling phoenix silhouetted against a bamboo screen. The ladies were dressed in their heavily embroidered soft silk kimonos, their faces in white makeup, resembling faces of the moon. Would the ladies and the aristocratic Yu have observed the slight bow made by the frog? Would they have noticed amid the persistent drizzle Hai-yun's certainty that happiness was unstable and ephemeral?"

Joan Pere Tudurí Taltavull was the exact opposite of his cousin, Egèria. In spite of all his travels, there was nothing unknown that didn't attract him. Wherever he was he immediately connected with his surroundings, however exotic. His mother, the god-fearing Pollònia Taltavull, considered humanity and nature only in terms of the frights they gave her. Her son, Joan Pere, also had a personal relationship with the thousands of variations of the universe, but with another purpose: they only stirred his interest if he could set up a sort of theatrical production with them, as passionate in appearance as it was superficial in content.

As a youth Joan Pere had become fond of acting on the stages of Orlandis. And he still felt that excitement of his youth: nothing had ever stimulated him so much as that game of masks where he would play a different role in each show, each of which was very familiar to him, and none of which offered any of the surprises or anguish inherent in life itself. He had lived through the slow, painful death of his father, an exhausted desperation. Joan Pere avoided all that through his performances on stage: today as a lawyer who had fallen in love, tomorrow as a swank military officer, and the next day as a flabby butler. From then on the degree of enthusiasm or sincerity in whatever life circumstance befell him paralleled the intensity he achieved in his acting. Furthermore, that way he could never get hurt again, even though his father died all over again. It was his crazy but simple way of dealing with the fact that everything always came to nothing. It would not be he himself who expressed the emotional anguish, but his mask, which would also be the only thing that suffered. If it hadn't been for the theater, his youth would have finished one stormy day at the end of the breakwater. He would have thrown himself into the waves, which at least would have turned his death into a great tumult.

That rainy afternoon in Shanghai after the evocative digression he had indulged in, Joan Pere smiled with affected sadness at his friend Hai-yun, who avoided looking directly at him or answering his questions: "Hai-yun, is there anything that might be reborn, as the phoenix constantly was in the Golden Age?"

The girl's cheeks blushed red. She knew that the European was really referring to that time many years ago—too many—when they were both young, and she had resisted the love that drove them both. It was an anguished love, vehemently repressed by her, capricious and superficial for him. It was the time of the Great Proletarian Cultural Revolution, and Hai-yun suffered its consequences every day and every night, suffocating in grating fear at a time when she should have been living out her greatest hopes and dreams.

Joan Pere, in spite of not having sold a single alarm clock, felt the contagion of the red banners, the epic turmoil in the streets, the chairman of the country—who was both poet and guerrilla warrior—greeting the assembled masses in that vast Tiananmen Square.

The girl shared the astonishing morality dictated by the revolution and the visceral Chinese caution when faced with a foreigner. She had just married, and her husband had been transferred immediately to the far-distant city of Sian to labor in the wheat fields under a blinding sun. Theirs was only one of the millions and millions of separations imposed on young married couples in order to slow the birthrate, to keep the population down and insure that people did not establish bonds with others stronger than those with the state. Hai-yun suffered for her husband, for the uncertainties that might drag them both down. And she suffered from the growing temptation of infidelity that was encroaching on her spirit.

If her relationship with Tudurí had been discovered, it would have meant years of "re-education" on a prison farm. Or it could have had her thrown into the insane and slimy chaos of being stoned by the Red Guard. As a result, she and Joan Pere never even kissed. The Chinese girl accompanied the Majorcan as his official guide and interpreter during his travels. The long, disturbing conversations they had about themselves both drew them closer and forced them further from each other, and in that way they managed to sublimate their enforced chastity.

Joan Pere Tudurí returned to China again in an attempt to establish a network of regular commercial markets. And from Spain he had requested, along with his travel itinerary and visa, that Hai-yun serve again as his guide and interpreter. When he landed at the Shanghai Airport, there she was courteously awaiting his arrival. Tudurí had lightly grazed her cheek with his forefinger, barely touching her, moved and grateful to be with her again here in this far corner of the planet after the indescribable events that had recently occurred in the old Empire of Heaven.

And she, in a neutral voice, had wished him a happy sojourn in the People's Republic, indicating that she not only spoke for herself, but also for her honorable husband—who had returned from Sian and had obtained his degree in optometry—and in the name of their young son, Ying the Fat.

On that afternoon in Shanghai Hai-yun had answered Joan Pere and his emotional siege with her eyes lowered, taking evasive refuge in the historical parable, the impeccable model of oriental good manners.

"No, nothing can be brought back to life. Not even the Mandarin Yu— important state functionary that he was—whose gifted life and eventual disgrace have all disappeared. Now it is as if the man had never existed.

"Yu was the designated scholar and personal consultant to Chong Zhen, he who would become the last emperor of the Ming dynasty....Yu was seated on the floor near the throne with his legs crossed, atop a very soft cushion on that early morning in 1644. He had the tablets and brushes over his knees, ready to draw the pictographs that would form the edicts and letters of the Son of Heaven. Chong Zhen was wearing an exquisitely embroidered purple tunic. He commanded his private eunuch, Wang Chen-en, who sat at his side, to ring the bells announcing the usual audiences.

"But no one came to humble themselves at the feet of the Son of Heaven, because the enemy armies led by the invading Manchu had already encircled the Forbidden City and were beginning the final assault on its great walls decked with bunting the color of dried bull's blood. Crushed, the Mandarin Yu wept for his lord.

"Chong Zhen removed his traditional robes and dressed himself in a white cape—the color of the dynasty—sewn with silver threads. From that time, white has been the color of bereavement in China. He then appeared at the pavilion of his first wife, whose eyes already reflected the enormity of her terror. He obliged her to commit suicide: her hypnotic reflection at the bottom of the well was to be the last thing she saw. According to ancient belief, the true inhabitant of the well should have been the green dragon of good fortune.

"The Emperor then ordered his children to flee as best they could, at the same time praying to the Mandarin Yu that he provide them with all the aid he could. But no horse, however swift, could penetrate the compact lines of Manchu archers. Yu then pointed out the imperial stable to the frightened little children and followed the Emperor.

"Chong Zhen left the Royal Palace through the Door of the Divine Military Deed, accompanied only by the eunuch Wang. Meditatively, he ascended the steep hill called Coal Peak, between the murmuring pines and the majolica-tiled roofs sparkling in the sun. When he reached the top, he let his eye roam for the last time over his beloved and revered city of Peking." As Hai-yun told the story she was overcome by both the historical sorrow and her own, model of patience that she was.

"And with a very fine brush, Chong Zhen drew the characters on his sleeve which said, 'Weak and short of troops, I have offended Heaven. The rebels have laid siege to my capital because my ministers have betrayed me. Ashamed to face my ancestors, I choose to die. I remove my imperial robes, and with my hair in disarray, I allow the rebels to destroy my body. All I beg of them is that they not harm my people.'"

And then he hanged himself from a juniper tree. At his side, the eunuch Wang joined him on the tree. The Mandarin Yu later recovered the imperial tunic with its poem of farewell. He ended his life in a secluded garden of Shanghai, right where the two young people met on that late afternoon when the rain finally let up and left only a trace on the tiles and the lemon trees, dripping as if they were predicting better times.

"Please, Hai-yun, I'm tired of death, of history, and of your coldness toward me. Why don't we talk a bit about ourselves," protested Joan Pere as he caressed her straight black hair.

But she acted as if she hadn't noticed his touch, distraught as she was after telling her tale, absorbed in the contemplation of a magnificent cherry tree in bloom as it caught a reflection of the sunlight just beginning to peek through the clouds. Then suddenly she turned to him, looked Joan Pere straight in the eye and stated dryly, "What about us? At least the Mandarin Yu and the Emperor Chong have left us a record of everything they accomplished. But for me, you are the pitiless memory of what has never been and what can never be, as if I had to play the adolescent forever, the projection of your dream as if my own destiny had escaped my grasp before it was really mine. So I have become the sum of my sorrows."

"Well, I . . . I think . . ." stuttered Joan Pere, aware she had caught him off-guard. His act was beginning to waver.

The girl cut him off, "'Lament for a Capital' is the title of a poem, written by K'iu Yuan in the Period of the Fighting Kingdoms. If you don't want history, maybe you can accept the truth of these verses:

> Over the immense waters of the God of Waves,
> like an arrow I flash toward the unknown.
> I could break the chains about my heart,
> but my spirit wanders, eternally wounded,
> ship without direction, at the mercy of the winds."

The wind and the smoke.... In the old Majorcan manor house, Joan Pere stood in the middle of the hall amazed, his face bearing the deep lines of tragedy, his imagination overflowing with those emotional memories and the poignancy of recalling them. He concluded, "And I had to leave China, having successfully completed my task. With Deng Xiao Ping's policy of economic liberalism, which was just beginning to bear fruit, the sale of alarm clocks, bicycles, sunglasses, bedsprings, and television sets had increased tremendously. It was a splendid spring morning the day I left. Hai-yun, with whom I had not talked again about our feelings, bade me a silent good-bye at the airport with a delicate bow. Ah, woman of love and misfortune, dressed in her rough gray uniform, her face so small, consumed by silence."

Tudurí returned to China twice again, increasing his export market for alarm clocks each time. On both trips he had requested Hai-yun as his interpreter, but in vain. However, he was able to see her once again in spite of that.

A train was roaring down one track while another rushed by in the opposite direction. They crossed at a very high speed, the man and the woman startled as they recognized each other in that split-second through the train windows . . . a moment, a skipped heart beat; then all was gone. The train whistles faded, their tremulous echoes rending the air. Joan Pere Tudurí Taltavull, on that Christmas Eve in Majorca, dropped his jaw to his chest and fell silent.

"What is it about the Chinese girl that you especially remember, nephew?" Albert the Younger asked circumspectly.

Beautiful Egèria had her eyes closed. Joan Pere responded without hesitation, "The tone of her voice, so varied and well-modulated, as if she were singing . . . it sounded as if the birds were speaking."

6

The cat with the rat in its teeth stood still for a moment on the stair landing. There was a barred glassless window which looked out over a hidden part of the roof in the direction of the scrub oaks.

Only light gusts of wind found their way in through the window at the height of the ceiling beams and were immediately dissipated. But outside a mastic tree was being whipped about by the wind from the southwest. The light from the kitchen shone on it dramatically, making it look like a frenzied fetal mass. The cat bristled, poised itself, and jumped through the window with the rat still clenched in its teeth, disappearing over the roof and into the night.

There were three more windows in the stairwell. One looked out over a small vale, and during the day there was a peaceful view of the almond trees and the fruit orchard and the old broken waterwheel. Another window faced the thick woods, the mountain that embraced the vale, the huge pines, the furze, the palm trees, and the blackberry bushes, all of which seemed to announce the beginning of a world of evil. The third window opened onto the spacious hall filled with smoke and the Taltavulls chattering away as they set the table.

The stair landing was a strange place suspended right in the middle of the house. It was difficult to describe with any precision, since it had first been a terrace. When the original house was enlarged, the old terrace was absorbed and became a sort of nexus around which the complex interior of the house evolved. Together with the windows, five different stairways converged on the landing: one led to the great hall; one led to a stable that wasn't used anymore, where a grotesque knot of worms writhed in a heap of fetid, curdled manure; another stairway led to Grandmother Brígida's dank bedroom; another led to the upstairs rooms, some with high ceilings and others low enough to bump heads on; the last was a spiral staircase that rose without seeming to lead anywhere.

The stairway landing possessed a disconcerting quality: its drafts and its light coming from unsuspected directions. It was the funnel for all the noises in the house: everybody's voice could be heard from there, some with an eerie clarity and others distant and reedy, laden with agony. Sometimes when two Taltavulls happened to meet in that narrow jig-sawn spot they would stop to chat a bit and smoke a cigarette, just as if they were meeting on the street. Often an owl or a lost hoopoe would fly in, unable to find its way out.

Only the lay of the land and the needs of its inhabitants had dictated the growth of the house. In one room there was a rock that had been impossible to blast out, and so it stood there still. A little passageway led to a well full of stagnant water nobody ever drank; it must have been built as a secret water reserve back in the times of the Barbary pirate raids. An oaken door bound with iron straps had not been opened in recent memory. Some of the rooms were very warm and others frigid.

There was something of a link between the structure itself and the echoes of life it housed, as if old laws from the time of its first dwellers were still in control of certain parts of the house and still held vague prerogatives there. One of the family would suddenly get the impression that a wall or a room had been modified, but couldn't say how. Another relative would get lost and instead of coming out in the larder would emerge in the tiny interior patio completely overtaken by an enormous decayed old fig tree.

From the outside, the building looked long and low with an excessive number of doors and windows and with sections that rose like little towers toward the sky. The extensive grape arbor produced dark purple grapes that hung in abundant clusters in summertime, seeming to symbolize an endless joy.

7

The wind suddenly grew fierce, bellowing with Vandalic fury against the house. It roared between moss-laden tiles, through cracks in the doors caused by sun and rain; it drove against loose-fitting windows and swirled around the many unequal corners of the old house. Inside the hall, the wind drove waves of smoke that swirled and billowed. They had fed the fire with carob tree slabs which gave off a sharp, pungent smoke that made everybody's eyes water.

"It's like a forest the gods have to pass through," Tomàs Moro said to himself, wheezing asthmatically as he bumped into someone he didn't recognize and who let fly with a couple of obscenities. Moro was a melomaniac and opera was his delight. The majestic voices were like a miracle to him; they created the world and the spirits obeyed them.

"Like carbon, the source of life," he reflected, concerned as usual with the modern touch. In Barcelona and Madrid he had observed those fantastic misty stages where singers emerged from the pagan North and the fog: *The Rheingold, Parsifal, The Valkyrie*. He was able to glimpse—in those brief moments of clarity in the vast hall—the breast of a woman, half the face of Arcadi the priest, some children's legs in long stockings.

Yes, rubbing his itchy eyes, with a symphony ringing in his ears, Tomàs imagined those virile Teuton heroes so clearly they seemed to become flesh: huge devilish eyes peering from a wrinkled, hairy black face atop an insolently seated midget's body. Tomàs Moro jumped with a start, feeling suffocated, rubbing his eyes harder, because what he saw before him were not mental visions, but a damnably real beast! It was the Messenger from the Other Side, appearing and disappearing between the crazy swirls of smoke and the roof beams in the hall, as if it were descending from outer space.

Tomàs finally reacted. He realized that was impossible. Waving his arms to disperse the smoke, he was trying to make out the absurd apparition when the shouts from the others erupted, "My god! What's that?"

"It's a monkey!"

"Idiot! A monkey? It can't be!"

"Look at it, then . . . there! It's coming up over the cistern!"

"No, he's grabbing onto a beam!"

"I can't see him. . . ."

"Yes, it is a monkey!"

"How awful!"

"There! The monkey!"

And the wind died down, its howling reduced to a subtle moan through the cracks as if someone were fleeing in fright from a lost battle. The smoke cleared a bit as if it were trying to follow the retreating wind. A gray haze remained, blurring the hall to a vague sweetness, in the center of which a half-dozen people had gathered, all of them from Pula, smiling broadly, carrying a platform above their heads on which indeed a monkey crouched.

The Taltavulls stood there in open-mouthed astonishment. Grandmother Brígida suddenly came to life and exclaimed, "The Pula monkey!"

The people from Pula, grinning from ear to ear, nodded their heads in agreement. "Yes, Aunt Brígida, it's him."

Everyone had gathered around the group of newcomers. Yes, they were carrying a monkey on a platform, a stuffed monkey. Grandmother Brígida, barely able to contain her joy, stroked its fur. She had left Pula seventy years ago to get married at Taltavull Hall. But when she recognized her old neighbors, she tottered toward the group, driven by a sort of senile euphoria. They had not forgotten she was one of them, either.

The Pulans were perhaps more content on that Christmas Eve than they usually were. Their ancestors had been miserably poor, ancient and avid Croatian sailors, some of whom had their origins in Pula and others in distant Adriatic isles. They had fled serfdom's chains and the avalanche of Turks, choosing Majorca as the next-best place to exercise their predilection for coastal trading and piracy. They retained a singular propensity for a rare form of spontaneous joviality, somewhere between authentic and excessive, as well as a cautious but irrepressible cruelty. Both characteristics were undoubtedly traceable to their dark past when their ancestors enjoyed the pleasures of endless treasure earned at the tip of the sword. Dioclecià of Pula spoke to the Taltavulls as if he were chewing a savory piece of meat.

"We wanted to surprise you! The monkey died, but we didn't tell anybody and stuffed him! So here he is, just like he was in real life!"

"May all your goldfinches crash and burn!," cracked Damià, as he spat on the floor and stared irately at the stuffed simian.

"Ugh! How gross!" mumbled Marianna Mas.

Pula was a vague tract of land, or perhaps it might be considered a hamlet, for neither the land deeds nor the family links were all that clear, apart from the anarchistic way the houses and stables had been built. But whatever Pula's problems might be, they never reached the attention of the mayor or the law in Orlandis, for they were always settled right there among the Pulans themselves. Sometimes one of the villagers would disappear, never to be seen again. If anybody was asked about it, they knew nothing. Sometimes one of them would appear with a severed finger or a back full of open wounds. Had they been punished by the community? They would always deny it, as if such a thing were unthinkable.

Access to Pula was by sea, following the sharp-cliffed shore from cove to cove, or by land crossing the inhospitable Camp de les Exèquies, one of the points on the short bay of Orlandis, a wasteland where since prehistoric times the peoples who had disembarked on that rugged coast had dug their own graves. Bushels of burnt bones, broken red pottery, and little bronze statues to the god of war had been found there. The cemetery of Orlandis was also located there, a mixture of tombs, some barely marked by a simple white-washed stone, others intricate baroque monuments to human pain. The sun beat down on that wasteland, converting it into a place of hallucinatory peace. The fog rolled in from the sea and gripped the place, making it appear to float, the last stop for the waiting dead.

In the same manner, the gallows had raised its ugly head at the Exèquies centuries ago in the name of the unknown king and the distant state that had taken over the island. The old folks could still recall, perhaps aided by a touch of fantasy, the last hangings ordered by royal decree, the corpses bleached by the land breeze, pecked to bits by carrion crows, gnawed at by rats. The smell invaded Orlandis if the wind were out of the west.

The little hamlet of Pula had a few good bottom-land fields and a lot of meager terraces built along the sides of some of the wildest cliffs on the coast, at the base of which the Pula folk kept their boats in coves. Their little skiffs were long and narrow, fitted out with lateen sail, as if they had been copied from ancient galleys. They obviously couldn't fish with that kind of boat, for they were too unstable. But their merit lay in their ability to sail swiftly in any waters and still be able to unload contraband on any beach. Pula, with the advent of the Spanish Civil War, had become the most dangerous and ungovernable point on the island.

The soil at Pula was poor, constantly punished by salty sea breezes. The only things that would grow in it were rachitic legumes, a few savory fennel shrubs, a few ashen fig trees. The houses were poorly built, low to the ground, always surrounded by wandering animals: jackasses, chickens, peahens, hogs, geese, calves, and even some exotics such as dromedaries, pheasants, as well as cages full of poisonous snakes, all spectacularly beautiful. The Pulans sold some and ate the rest. They were people who had no fixed jobs and were often accused of robbery, an accusation seldom, if ever, proven. However, they were excellent mechanics. The animals around the houses were always grazing around piles of greasy junked motors which the Pulans also trafficked in. Cackling hens mixed unperturbed with old piston rods, as did the odor of dung with that of grease.

A huge jujube tree rose in the midst of all that scrap, thick and smooth-trunked in all its vigorous splendor. It had been the monkey's tower; he had been chained to its trunk with a slip-ring so that he could run. The monkey would clamber up and down the tree with breakneck agility. If he managed to grab some living thing that didn't belong to the Pula clan, whether person or animal, he would bite it and try to snatch it away as if possessed. The Pulans, both man and beast, usually gave the jujube tree a wide berth and amused themselves with the stimulating antics of the ape.

And thus one stormy autumn day the people gathered to watch as the ape suddenly stood up on a branch and started gesturing with his hands and grunting into space as if he were having a dialog with some invisible being only he could see. Then without further comment he dropped to the ground, dead.

"The most difficult part for the taxidermist was to get the ape's mouth shut, because after that long discourse it had frozen open," recalled Dioclecià of Pula, as if he were sucking c n hard candy. "His tongue was hanging way out, and they had to cut it off. But you don't notice it now. They did a per-fect job!"

The Taltavulls all nodded their heads in dubious agreement, for they were still a bit shaken by the appearance of the monkey which, Tomàs Moro said to himself, looked like an African idol enthroned on his pallet, regal and ugly. Beautiful Egèria started to throw up, Pollònia crossed herself repeatedly, and the retired commander held his nose.

One of the traditions of unknown origin observed at Pula had to do with names: Gala of Pula, Nicomedes of Pula, Constantí of Pula, and so on. They were all names from the period of the Roman Empire. Dioclecià implicitly assumed the responsibility of acting as the patriarch of Pula. He was a large, pot-bellied man with a strong, aquiline nose. Brígida's marriage to Benigne Taltavull had been somewhat of an exceptional event in the annals of Pula and of Orlandis, even though in earlier times a few similarly mixed marriages had taken place.

The racial heritage of the Pulans was not exactly albino, but their skin was fine and lightly pigmented, while their hair was a flaming red. Their skin grew wrinkled at an early age, so that a woman of thirty often looked like an old crone. But there were exceptions, silhouettes of stylish and harmonious elegance. The good blood of Pula had certainly contributed to the molding of Beautiful Egèria.

Grandmother Brígida eagerly continued to pet the ape, at the same time consuming him with her eyes, "Ay, he gives me goose pimples! I've never seen such a cute corpse before!"

8

Carloteta, her big eyes black as coal, her lovely face as beautiful as an angel's, had just sat down on a bell salvaged from a shipwreck off the coast in front of Taltavull Hall a century or two ago. She was sitting on it in a corner of the upstairs parlor with a gutted old sofa, a dark Chinese lamp with colorful tassels hanging from the shade that Joan Pere Tudurí had brought home from Asia, and an oil painting that showed Pontius Pilate washing his hands in a sort of Arab palace.

What had caught Carloteta's attention in the parlor as she was leaving the bathroom was a notebook and pencil lying on the floor amid the dust. That gave her the idea to write a story.

She made an effort to put into words the scenes that had suddenly filled her head, neat and clear scenes through which she seemed to be walking on tip-toes. What might have inspired the scenes was a televised news item she had glimpsed at her house in Orlandis before coming to Taltavull Hall. As the announcer was referring to the hunger in Africa, the TV screen showed a nun ringing a little bell and a little child with very long, fragile limbs, its abdomen terribly bloated, who was slowly sipping a bowl of milk, his eyes crawling with flies.

First Carloteta wrote in large capital letters: I AM LOOKING FOR A FRIEND. Following that, her lines slanted in a minuscule hand, she wrote: "Once upon a time, Mrs. Rabbit had six children, and the youngest of them was simple-minded and ugly, and that's why she abandoned him. He continued on his own, eating plants and getting bigger until he was four years old and that's how the story begins. He was alone in the blue woods and could only see his own shadow and he started to cry. . . ."

The girl stopped writing. She had remembered that the Moro twins had a blue teddy bear Egèria had given them for their birthday. Carloteta became indignant when she thought of it. She reproached Egèria immediately because she had not given her anything. Carloteta felt the urgent need for a little bear like that one. However, she hesitated for a moment and asked herself whether

her birthday had come yet. Was she six or seven years old? She decided it didn't make any difference, but her bear should be pumpkin-colored just like the dress she was wearing. She laid the notebook and pencil back in the dust on the floor and went downstairs, humming a Christmas carol.

9

"I'll go myself," Albert the Younger said.

And so he found himself in that dark room in a solitary wing of the house. From there it seemed that the great hall, the kitchen, and the people were somewhere far away from him. Every step Albert had taken up the stairs and down the corridors toward the other wing had separated him psychologically from the others, as if he had been walking for miles . . . an intense underground passageway that led to another world, just as in a child's fairy tale. Albert was carrying a large cup of chicken broth in his hands. He was taking it to the old man, Dídac Ensenyat, who was lying there somewhere in the dark. Albert couldn't make him out, but a vile stench—almost like rotten meat—reached his nose along with the low sound of slow, labored breathing, like that of a wounded animal. The Taltavulls had picked up Ensenyat from the court house; Bernat and Albert the Younger had gone themselves to get him. The retired commander, Ignasi Taltavull Oliva, also served as justice of the peace. Dídac was the widower of a cousin of the Taltavulls, and apart from his daughter, he had no other living relatives.

Albert didn't know how the old man was feeling, but he imagined him stretched out on the bed, his arms loosely at his sides, his flesh beginning to rot, his gaping jaw drooling, his mind already gone. He was no longer a person, just a defeated sack of guts tossed anonymously into the dark, awaiting his last breath.

Dídac was tall, thin, and deaf, with a haggard look, his gloomy eyebrows large and shadowy. He lived with his daughter Beth, on the road to the truck gardens at the outskirts of Orlandis in a tiny single-story house built atop a dank, airless basement where the previous owner had grown mushrooms and Dídac raised rabbits. Dídac had been a master with the adz; he had had an enviable skill at shaping the gentle curves of the sides of a sailing ship. But his only job now was to walk to the vegetable garden with a sack and gather some cauliflower stalks, some bruised potatoes, an armful of alfalfa for the rabbits and sit in the shade of an apple tree in front of the door to the cellar. He carefully tossed the greens to the fluffy rabbits and watched them as they romped around, at the same time keeping an eye peeled for any women who might be passing by on the road.

And when he discovered a pair of breasts dancing about under a blouse or the aggressive movement of a pair of hips under a full skirt, his eyes would pop out of their sockets as he clucked his tongue and licked his lips. Sometimes he would run up to the road and follow alongside the woman, insolently mumbling indecencies in his low deaf man's voice; she would not be able to understand him and would run off scared. He would then storm down to the basement, catch a young rabbit, knock it in the neck with the back of his hand, then go up to the kitchen—which he took care to lock—and grill it over the smoky fire. And in that heavy atmosphere he would gobble up the rabbit, washing it down with generous swigs of dark red wine. When he had finished, he unbuttoned his fly, and with his mind in a fog, his whole being a jumble of primal sensations, he would begin to masturbate, often falling asleep before he reached orgasm.

His daughter Beth was already seventeen, generously fleshed-out, olive-skinned, with a round, inexpressive face. She took care of the house and prepared the meals, and when the TV programs began, she would slump before the set—the biggest they could find in Tomàs Moro's shop—adjust the color with care and nibble away at peanuts, pistachios, and almonds, washing them all down with bottle after bottle of bubbly mineral water, amused by the gas she burped up. And there she stayed until the TV went off the air. The deaf old man ate alone in the kitchen.

"Just as I'm going to him now with this cup of chicken broth, that night Beth was taking him a cup of chamomile tea," Albert the Younger recalled in disgust as he stopped before Dídac's door. . . .

When he faced Ignasi Taltavull Oliva the judge, the old man still had the good sense to give his testimony with a fair degree of coherence. The daughter remained seated, calmly staring at him. She only opened her mouth apathetically when details were asked of her.

Yes, the old man was apparently in bed that night with a cold. Between his fever and the blankets piled on top of him, he felt as if he were floating in a state of grace. Beth brought him the chamomile tea. She was wearing a tight black smock too short for her. It barely came to her knobby knees, which together with her rosy arms and her firm, well-rounded breasts suddenly seemed to overflow the limits of her smock, invading the closed, obsessive world of the deaf Ensenyat, who felt his whole body going out of control. He drank the tea, and its warmth made him break out in a sweat as he stared at his daughter. And when Beth came over to take the empty cup from him he grabbed her arm, threw back the stifling covers, and flung her onto the bed. She let him do it, lying there limply as Dídac possessed her with unusual vigor.

From that moment on he never let her out of his sight. He would watch her as she ate; he would paw her; he went with her every time she left the house; he took her to bed; he sat beside her and watched TV, always scrutinizing her out of the corner of his eye as if Beth were sick or mentally retarded. And in front of the TV the old man became hypnotized by the images on the screen without understanding any of them, his mind completely engrossed with the discovery of his daughter's existence.

A tumultuous joy overcame the old man; he felt he had been reborn. He had never imagined such a fresh, enticing, and unexpected piece of good luck could ever have befallen him. Sometimes at midmorning or midafternoon while he was seated under the apple tree tossing cauliflower stalks to the rabbits, a burst of desire would well up in him. He then scurried around until he found Beth, dragged her off to bed, squeezed her breasts and bit her thighs and penetrated her, snorting like a pig. When he returned to the rabbits, his gait was unsteady, slow, and halting.

Beth obeyed him in everything without offering the least resistance. She answered one of the judge's questions with, "I knew it was a sin, but it felt like I was the only one sinning."

Instinctively she had continued to consider her father as the only person with authority and prerogative over her life, just as she had been brought up to believe as a child. She cast the idea of culpability only onto herself. Paradoxically, at the beginning of the situation, that idea led her to accede even more to the old man's desires as if she needed his forgiveness, and succumbing to his desire was the only way to achieve it.

In spite of the fact that the concept of sin was only theoretical in the girl, she had tried to explain it to the judge this way: "Yes, a person is guilty of what he does in front of somebody else—I don't know if you understand me or not—or when somebody else discovers you doing what you shouldn't be doing. But if nobody catches you and you don't tell anybody. . . ."

She didn't feel the least bit of sexual pleasure with her father. And she had seen girls on TV who had gone limp with rapture in the arms of a man. She used to study Dídac as he mounted her: he was agitated, blinded, uttering those guttural sounds as if he were being drawn and quartered. She soon learned that she was stronger than he was. She got used to studying him coldly as he embraced her like a drunk. Then, to tease him she would begin to alternately reject and excite him. She learned to manipulate him like a puppet. And then he would get agitated and raise his hand to strike her, but she would counter with a threat to report him to the Guàrdia Civil, the Spanish police.

He would become furious and scold her, but faced with his daughter's inflexibility, he would give in, first with contained rage, and then pleading. When she saw him beaten and sad like that, he reminded her of the beggars who sometimes wandered the streets of Orlandis asking for handouts, people reduced to pleading for a coin or a crust of bread. But that didn't make her feel sorry for him. When she considered him as one with authority over her, she would submit; when she saw him as a raggedy old beggar, she would scorn him. She often refused to let him lie with her and forced him to sleep on a mat at the foot of the bed, where the old man would meekly curl up and doze in the fetal position.

When she spoke to people on the street, Beth felt like an outsider, as if something was wrong with her. The zeal of the others, their gestures and the way they behaved seemed strange to her in contrast to what she was used to at home, that kingdom of aberrant sordidness that she had come to govern so magnificently well by then. She began to distance herself from her neighbors, confining herself within the realm of her own isolated omnipotence. That exultant transformation of pleasure into power became noticeable in her body and behavior, and she filled out even more, acquiring an aura of grotesque defiance.

Men began to notice a sense of heightened excitement surrounding that introverted girl and her repugnant, deaf old father. And so they started loitering around the house, and that drove Dídac crazy. He rebuked them without understanding what they snapped back at him, suspecting desire in their every gesture. Beth observed all this and said nothing, trying to imagine how those men would act in the same naked positions her father took with her and asking herself if she would feel any different in their arms. But she didn't feel the need to pay them any attention. Nothing in her body drew her to males. So she would sprawl out on the sofa, turn on the TV, and drink her bubbly water. . . .

The retired commander, Ignasi Taltavull Oliva, asked Dídac Ensenyat if that whole mess didn't make him feel ashamed. The old man, slack-jawed and quivering, his eyes glazed, shrugged his shoulders imperceptibly and muttered, "Ashamed? Hell, I wanted her!"

One day Beth went to buy an apron at the Flower of Holland Dry Goods

Shop in town. Its narrow aisles were piled high with bolts of cloth that cushioned and muffled every sound. Even though people were talking a few feet away, all you could hear was a murmur. Mr. Alcover, the proprietor, spoke in a ceremonious and barely audible voice as if it were the shop itself talking. He was pot-bellied, and he combed the four or five surviving strands of hair growing behind one of his ears over the top of an otherwise flat, neatly polished bald head. Alcover, with an unctuous air, nodded for Beth to follow him through the labyrinthine aisles of cloth. In the back of the store he chose a dress and put it on her, allowing his hands to run over her breasts, her hips, and her crotch while doing so, repeating over and over that if she were nice to him he would give her the dress. Beth didn't hesitate for an instant: she told him she would be waiting for him at her house, but that the price was three dresses, not one. Then she turned and flew out the door, down the street, and through the vegetable patches as if she were bathed in a shower of gold: she could get anything she wanted!

As usual, that afternoon the old man was squatting at the basement door idly tossing greens to the rabbits. His daughter drew near on tiptoes, shoved him down the stairs, and threw the bolt on the cellar door. And as she wallowed in bed with the shopkeeper above, the weak cries of her entombed father reached them through the floor tiles as he kicked the walls and screamed himself hoarse. But with the television on full-blast, it seemed as if he wasn't even there. The naked Alcover, his sparse hairs dangling, looked like an undressed mannequin.

When the shopkeeper finally left, Beth went down and set free the furious Dídac who, with a swollen and badly bruised back and cheek, wavered between beating her up or saying nothing. Beth paid no attention to him, happily concentrating on the dresses she was trying on before the mirror. Ensenyat stared at her fat and sassy body in her panties and bra and broke out in tears. The old man had realized how old he really was.

"I . . . I suspected what had happened, but I was afraid of something worse: what if she left me?" he confessed to the judge.

Ignasi Taltavull Oliva looked longingly at the girl, desired her vehemently for a moment, swallowed his saliva, and asked her hesitantly, "And you, with other men . . . I mean, if you didn't enjoy it with your father, did you with . . . ? Well . . . well, let's skip that part. Did you . . . entertain others?"

She nodded her head affirmatively, though the judge wasn't sure it was in answer to the first or the second question. And after that afternoon, whenever Beth was expecting any of the many men who appeared at her door, she would lock her father in the cellar. Sometimes she would even lock him up the day before. The old man, by now clearly defeated, got so he would go down to the cellar all by himself at the slightest gesture from her, where he would spend hours in the dark immersed in the stink of rabbit piss.

"And what did you think about down there?" the commander asked.

Dídac moved his head indecisively and answered, "I don't know . . . probably nothing . . . but I liked to touch the soft warm fur of the rabbits."

Standing in the doorway to his room at Taltavull Hall recalling that interrogation of the old man, the scene of a few minutes ago with Brígida, Albert's mother, came to mind: Brígida petting the stuffed ape. He shivered as he thought, "When people grow old, do they find more solace in animals than in other people?"

Flesh . . . just a case of flesh on flesh—whether baptized or not—was what man finally wound up with, because his dreams had become disillusion.

The police had to go fetch Beth from the apartment Alcover had set her up in at Palma. Some neighbors noticed the Ensenyat house had been closed up for many days; they had heard noises coming from the basement—the starving rabbits were lunging at the door trying to get out. And while the neighbors were feeding the rabbits they discovered the old man, huddled in a corner, filthy and scarecrow-thin. They had to drag him out, for he refused to leave the cellar.

Albert the Younger felt he was going to throw up. He opened his mouth and a sour taste rose in his throat. He took a step backward, about to faint. He experienced an instant of sudden revulsion and hurled the cup of chicken broth into the blackness of the dingy room. When it hit and splattered, he turned and ran back to the great hall in a rage.

10

"Oh Lord Jesus! What's that Dídac up to now?" Paula asked her brother Albert when she saw him coming down the stairs.

"Did he drink up his broth?" asked Marieta Verònica.

"Yes . . . everything's all right," Albert stammered.

"I feel sorry for his suffering, but that's God's punishment for him," declared Pollònia firmly.

Ignasi Taltavull Oliva, the retired commander and justice of the peace, made no comment. He observed Albert the Younger, then looked up the stairs as if he were examining somebody who was seriously ill. The trip to take him his broth had reminded the judge of the episode with Dídac and his daughter. While Albert was recalling it upstairs, the commander was remembering the cross-examination in the courthouse. And he recalled another conversation, another set of questions and answers similar in a way to those with deaf old Dídac, which the judge had participated in almost a half-century ago.

Ignasi, the brother-in-law of old Brígida, often asked himself the same question: "What ideas did I have, what did I want, back around 1936?"

It wasn't that he was trying to settle accounts with respect to anything specific, but he was just curious to know who he had been in the years before the war, at the decisive crossroads, for it was his impression that he had not really wished for a single one of the significant events of his lifetime. Instead, everything had sort of fallen into his lap by pure luck; he had even felt enthusiasm for some of them at the time.

And now as he drew nearer death (Do I have two, or seven years left? he would often ask himself), a sweet-and-sour taste would often rise in his throat when he reviewed his past, without arousing the least feeling of frustration or longing for not having taken other paths.

"Why should I have chosen them if in the long run I would have wound up in the same state of confusion? I suppose one's ideals should remain only as projects or misgivings," he meditated with a conviction that wavered between irony and relief, that freed him from all responsibility, that distanced him from all the transcendental convolutions everybody usually embellished things with.

One of his lovers, a precious and incredible woman with an indefatigable spontaneity, had opened her tight and juicy sex to him, her well-rounded haunches arched high, her lips thick and sensuous, pleading with him to penetrate her every orifice—the best lover he had ever had, the Baroness Ingeborg von Nassau-Istrij—and it was she who had started that inner dialog. She had been in Majorca during the Spanish Civil War. One evening while they were making love and listening to the shots of a firing squad carrying out his orders to liquidate some Reds, she hit him with this: "You're a fatalist."

The commander, at the time a mere lieutenant, had been appointed the supreme authority of Orlandis because of the imposition of martial law. He continued tonguing her nipples in short, rapid flicks before he paused to answer her: "Well, so what?"

Words, just words. She had been educated in Northern Europe with a lot of books and ideas. Making love was the only thing that really got her attention. All the rest she had to first convert into cultural concepts. Ignasi, on the other hand, never asked himself questions. Rather, he asked himself only those questions that implicitly contained their own answers in the form of statements he considered basic to life. "Does anything change if you know the name of a thing?" he asked himself, shrugging his shoulders. When she heard the cars stop at the Volta del Carro at midnight under the Penyal del Ca and near the castle of the Duchess of Orlandis where she was staying, the young baroness exclaimed, thinking the cars were near the fortress: "Who could that be at this time of night? My god, what could it be?"

At that moment Ignasi was caressing—marveling at for the hundredth time—her smooth velvety skin, which the baroness anointed with a cream scented with wild strawberries before they made love: "It's nothing, don't worry. Just some Reds about to be executed down there."

"It sounds like it's right here!"

The lieutenant drew her over to the window, to the infinite spring night, and pointed to a place out-of-sight beyond the road. Only the stars spread a dusting of clarity over the broad Orlandis valley.

"It's over there."

"Do you know them, the ones being executed?" Ingeborg demanded.

"Three or four of them . . . well, yes, quite a few."

"So what have they done?"

"They're Reds."

"But have they killed anybody?"

"No. They do that on the peninsula. Here they couldn't get away with it."

"Well, so what did they do, then?"

"You know . . . talk too much, hang around with the Republicans. . . . They're just Reds."

"What do you feel right now?"

Ignasi Taltavull Oliva gazed at her tenderly.

"What do you mean? I like you a lot, you know. Since I received your note I haven't been able to think about anything all day except being with you."

Ingeborg von Nassau-Istrij cocked her head and looked at him.

"No, I mean with regard to them . . . the ones you say are being shot."

It was difficult for Ignasi to find an answer concerning his ties to one of the prisoners to be shot. His name was Pere, and they used to play together as children. Pere was a well-built lad. He always bullied Ignasi, who had been a skinny and timid kid. Ignasi had often been deeply humiliated when Pere brutishly shoved him or made fun of him and laughed at his mistakes when they played ball. So when he saw Pere's name on the Falange list of those to be shot, his first reaction was elation, which quickly vanished. He was repulsed by the fact that he had thought both things at once as if they were cause and effect. But . . .

At that very moment a shot rang out in the dark, then another. Sharp, ugly noises. He erased the image of Pere from his mind, languidly raised his arm, and said, "Ah, I didn't understand what you meant. Well, nothing. I don't feel a thing, really."

"But you must have signed the order, Ignasi."

"Well, I didn't really sign it, but I approved it. The same way I approved the mess hall vouchers so the troops could eat today. The Falangists had brought me the list of those whose turn it was to be liquidated. It was a *pro forma* thing; that's the way it's done."

Several single shots cracked in the night, probably the *coups de grâce,* to make sure the prisoners were dead.

"Could you have opposed the executions?"

"Ah, yes, but what for? We're at war against the Reds. Furthermore—he smiled—thanks to the executions, I had a good excuse to be away from my wife tonight and be with you."

"Do you mean you told her you had to preside over . . . that?"

Down below, car headlights turned on, motors rumbled and the vehicles drove off.

"Yes."

"And what did she say?"

"Nothing . . . that it was all right with her."

"Wasn't she horrified at the idea?"

"Why should she be? That's just the way things are. Do you expect me or my wife, a weak-minded toady anyway, to invent a new war today, in the middle of the afternoon? Which brings me to you: were you horrified just now, when you heard the shots?"

The girl thought for a minute, then said, "No . . . no, I don't think so. But I'm a foreigner. I didn't know them."

"So, if they kill you, I have to accept it calmly because you're a foreigner, is that it? I suppose any man, even though you've never even sat down to have coffee with him, is like any other man to you."

Suddenly the baroness exploded in fury: "Of course he is! And because he is, I'm just a foreign whore who has been lying here clutching your balls while they were killing those other guys! And you're worse because the victims were your neighbors and maybe even your friends! Yes, all men are alike; you just said it yourself!"

The lieutenant didn't want to argue with her, and he couldn't even guess the reason why. He drew her closer to him and ran his fingers through the crinkly down above her sex, saying, "Ingeborg, Ingeborg, one man is like any other of course, but that's only one side of the matter. The other side is that some men kill other men. And there's even a third side, where a man and a woman have this mad desire to make love. And we could find other arguments as well. But they're all the same: different faces on the same old coin that just turns and turns, over and over again. . . . Look, due to pure chance I don't happen to be a killer like the others, but a lover instead, who is going to eat you right here in this bed. But if I have to kill, I shall. And it's almost dead certain that while I'm doing it, others will also be bedding down their women."

"And what about the ones who wind up dead?"

"After you're dead it doesn't matter."

She gripped him with all her might and demanded imperiously, "Give me your tongue!"

Ignasi filled her mouth with his tongue; Ingeborg sucked it in ardently and he closed his eyes, growing faint with pleasure.

The commander smiled. Had the original scene been like that, or had he recreated it that way? It didn't matter. The past was not important, he thought; it was only important for neurotics. The questioning of Dídac and Beth had interested him passionately, for they had answered him as if they were stones, moved only by the weight of the facts. One thing, however, had always intrigued him about his conversation with Ingeborg: did she really believe everything he had argued in favor of, or did she simply limit herself to getting out of a tight spot? It intrigued him because he remembered so well the desire he felt for her that night, in spite of the passage of time and the tricks of memory. At the time he had not wanted to get involved in arguments or introspection. But if he hadn't been convinced of what she was saying, that didn't mean he held the opposite opinion, either. He could have simply refused to think about anything specific regarding those questions. He could have avoided them and remained cozily locked within his own little world, safely distant from what didn't affect him directly.

11

Out of nowhere a furious series of gusts buffeted the house: the wind had brought a downpour with it. The rain beat like hailstones against the windowpanes, the tile roof, and the trees. It had barely rained that winter, and the parched earth drank in the deluge instantly, leaving no puddles. The wind became distorted by the sheets of rain; it came in gusts and oblique swirls. Within the great hall the smoke belched forth from the hearth in tumultuous puffs and dissolved into a scattered, thin haze. The rain had become a swarm of droplets drumming on the house, creating a cozy atmosphere inside. All the Taltavulls experienced a brief rush of contentment. Outside in the dark, the soaked trees and earth shimmered like theater decorations.

" . . . and the sea bashed against Pula. From the cliffs we saw it rise with the first thrusts of wind, like an animal awakening and leaping forth from its lair. When the monkey was alive, he loved that kind of weather because the crash of the waves threw a spray that hit him like a shower," commented Dioclecià of Pula in a ceremonious but barely audible voice to Honorat Moro.

"The storm had flared up so quickly it reminded me of a waterspout."

"A waterspout? What's that?" asked Egèria's brother, Damià, with his usual disdain.

Nicomedes, another youth from Pula, set a sardonic smile on his peach-fuzz face. Dioclecià patiently turned toward Damià and said, "It's a good thing you're a professor at the university. What do you profess?"

"Sociology."

"Perfect! But it wouldn't hurt you to know something about the earth and the sea where you live. The waterspout is one of the facets of water and sky. Sometimes two air masses coincide, one on top of the other, each with its different temperature, barometric pressure, and wind speed, each going in opposite directions. In shallow, smaller seas, this produces a vacuum in the atmosphere which the water then fills. A six-foot or even taller wave can be created in a second. Let's suppose it happens at night. Suddenly, in the middle of a calm, the sea rises and spins a brief, capricious trail consuming everything in its path: boats, people, walls. . . . That's a waterspout."

Damià gave him a scornful glance and started muttering something about pre-history. But Honorat Moro's son Tomàs drew near. He was attracted by the Pulans, maybe because he feared them.

"One day they'll be exposed and everything they've been hiding will surface. . . ." he muttered to himself apprehensively, not forgetting for a minute the remote and obscure ancestry of those people. Adelina Albornoz, the daughter of Marieta Verònica Taltavull and the engineer, drew near when she heard the conversation as she came out of the kitchen carrying the napkins for the dinner table. She clapped her hands and asked, "Since we live in Castile, we don't have the sea as you do here! Go on! Keep telling the story!"

"We had an old aunt who said the prayer for storms at sea," continued the man from Pula, and Tomàs Moro's skin crawled with goose pimples.

"That kind of storm, like a waterspout, swirls vertiginously from the surface of the sea right up to the clouds, sucking up tons and tons of water with it. They used to shout 'Aunt Justiniana!' whenever they saw such a storm building near Pula. And she always knew what it was all about by their tone of voice. We humans don't really have to use words to communicate; we can understand each other with sounds alone, just like the animals. That old Justiniana stood up and faced the sea, looked at the bellowing twister, mumbled the right words as she crossed herself and suddenly you could see the storm break up and fall back into the sea like the stream from a turned-off faucet."

Tomàs Moro waved his arm, overcome by a desire to speak: "I know another—singular—story," he said as he cautiously looked around at the others.

"But I wouldn't want the priest to hear this one, because he doesn't like anything he doesn't understand. I shall relate the events, and I beg your pardon if I don't give names. A friend of mine owns a truck garden here in Orlandis. One fine morning he found it full of flabby little leaf worms voraciously devouring his cabbages, his peppers, and animal fodder. He became desperate, for it meant he would lose his entire crop. It so happened a vacationing seminarian was passing by, also a relative of somebody in Orlandis. He had just been certified as an exorcist, which is one of the steps in a priest's training. He said to my friend, "Take it easy, don't worry!"

He then left and returned in the afternoon with his prayer book and a hyssop. He asked my friend, "What other field is there where these little animals might go to eat? Because one should never abandon a creature of the Lord."

"My friend pointed to his neighbor's garden, of course. The seminarian started to read as if he were rabidly chewing at something and at the same time sprinkled holy water from his hyssop onto the garden. Then my friend invited the tonsured one to a supper of braised sweet potatoes and pork chops. The next morning, my friend's garden was free of worms. But the neighbor's garden was full of them, chomping away like horses."

"We were talking about the sea, Tomàs, not witchcraft," the commander admonished.

"Well, I. . . ."

"How fascinating, Uncle Tomàs. I would have loved to have seen it!" Adelina declared admiringly, imagining how the leaf worms dragged themselves off to the other garden by divine command.

"And the sea gets sorely stirred," Dioclecià said, "about this time of year under the old moon. The birth of Christ signified the triumph of good over evil, the new over the old. The sea is where most of the old evil lies because the sea was the first thing God created. Spending Christmas at sea can be wild, for one of the evils is contrary to the other . . . and now the moon is old, as you know. . . .

"My son was fishing for squid the other night and about a foot under the surface some black shadows appeared before his eyes like giant groupers swimming back and forth around the boat: they were manta rays. They knew the fish would be attracted to the stern light, and the mantas had come to swallow them up. It had been a long time since anybody had seen such monsters in our waters. And anything that eats fish you can bet will bite an arm or foot off people, so be careful!"

"That could be just a coincidence, that part about the moon and the manta," ventured Adelina.

Dioclecià raised his own imperial face and stated rotundly, "No, my chickadee, no. Beast of the sea, antiquity of the evening star, damn it . . . Nicodemes will keep me from lying because he told me how he and his brother-in-law, the lame one, Irineu, were gathering their nets yesterday at dawn out by the little island of Molta Murtra, when they observed in astonishment other little islands emerging from the sea. They were whales—two of them—peaceful and curious, swimming around their boat. Imagine! At this time of year, and in the Mediterranean! They must have lost their wind compasses. The cripple, Irineu, who was a bit mischievous, wanted to harpoon them with a trident, but Nicomedes was afraid the whales might attack and with a swift lash of their tails send the boat to the bottom."

"That's for sure!" confirmed Nicomedes.

"What has disappeared is the Old Man of the Sea, the walrus, *Odobenus rosmarus,*" replied Honorat. Some seamen used to mistake them for mermaids, since they slept in caves and atop the rocks. Sometimes they would be seen resting in the shade, and their bodies resembled human forms, though in reality they are more like a seal's. They were very smart and lived alone. They also got in the habit of robbing fish from the nets instead of hunting for themselves, feeding on the cold-blooded animals by cutting holes in the netting. There was only one solution to that. The fishermen, finally angry and fed up, started killing them, whacking them with their oars."

Dioclecià of Pula sat back more comfortably in his chair and ordered, "Nicomedes, bring me a shot of aquavit."

"There isn't any," answered Marianna Mas.

"Well, bring me a shot of palo then. Come on, get with it, Nicomedes. The last Old Man of the Sea I ever saw was the one Macià Jarreta landed on the docks. That was years ago. He was fishing for squid one fine dark night and suddenly, from beneath the white light of the lantern, the head and half the body of an Old Man of the Sea appeared, like a creature from another world, gabbling and gleaming brightly in the light. Jarreta knocked him in the head with his anchor."

The fat and pale Magdalena, Egèria's mother and the recent widow of Francesc de Borja Taltavull, had apathetically joined the group. She spoke in a monotone, as if she were reciting a school lesson: "One of the last voyages of the *Twelve Apostles,* Uncle Diumenge de La Paret's sailing ship, was to Cuba, laden with soap. Francesc de Borja sailed on it. It was full of immigrants from Orlandis. My husband didn't know whether to stay there or not, and so he only stayed a couple of years. He learned his trade as a cook there, and one of his companions was Macià Jarreta. They used to run a schooner full of blacks in a sort of contraband slave trade from Santo Domingo and Jamaica to Cuba. They rented the slaves out for the sugar cane harvest. The blacks only carried a short machete stuck in their belts to cut the cane, and a game cock on their shoulders, which they would stick in a bread bag at night. When those blacks weren't sleeping, their favorite pastime was to hold cock fights. Francesc de Borja, Macià Jarreta, and the other crew members were always armed with revolvers, hatchets, and knives just in case the blacks got out of line. My husband told me they couldn't even peer down into the hold where the blacks were stowed because the stench that race gave off would knock them over."

Honorat Moro stood up; he was getting restless. He looked gloomy and walked around like a hunchback, wearing muddy old pants and shoes and a torn ski jacket. However, he gave off a strange sense of energy, like a tree trunk or a four-legged animal.

"Did he see it, or didn't he?" he said vociferously, pacing around in great strides. "I speak for my son, who is always probing around beyond reality, or for you, in fact, Dioclecià, and your great and long experience, comparable to none. The combinations between what you can touch and what you imagine you feel are endless."

"What do you mean by that?" demanded Magdalena.

It seems her brother-in-law didn't hear her, for he continued, head bowed: "I suppose you have all observed the passing of time out in the country. Out there in that hot plain where I live, I feel like a seed sown in the ground. The grass grows like a funny, slippery little animal. You see it everywhere you turn. Or the light . . . dawn seems like it's never coming; then suddenly it's there. Then at midday you want to shout and hear the wild echo of your voice. At night—even though you don't believe it—any kind of enchanted and terrible animal is likely to appear. The sea splashes and plays and sucks through the depressions on shore, making holes and covering them; it's like a surfacing female demon from the sea, a night-mare. But you can't grasp it . . . it escapes you. And then it grips you, accosts you . . . yes, like a nightmare. The clouds are like towers of the spirit. A kestrel flies off, a weasel sniffs about . . . you live it all, vibrate with it, because the earth throbs and the taste of tree sap has as many variants as there are stars shining in the sky. I lie down in the grass and hours go by. The cool stones saturate my being, the outline of every leaf enchants me."

The patriarch of Pula listened with extraordinary interest, his brows knit. Adelina had dragged the priest and Beautiful Egèria over to the group. Egèria whispered, "Uncle. . . ."

"Yes, Egèria. That thing about the hedgehog caught me off guard. It's not that I don't see them, as I said. But I also consider them to be part of the world, the one I'm explaining to you now. Because by living like that, is it a miracle, or is it a mantle of horrors you discover? When something arrives unexpectedly where I live, when somebody comes up any of the paths, it could turn out to be very innocuous or very terrible. I'll give you an example: forest fires . . . the crazy beauty of the flames, their cruelty. Neither good nor evil is inherent up there . . . it just IS!"

Arcadi Frau Taltavull opened his mouth and started to say, "What I mean to say is. . . ."

"Shut up, priest!" said Honorat to silence him, then continued. "The fires or the storms at sea. For days now, regardless of whether it's an old moon or a new moon, the weather has been driving hard out of the north . . . heavy waves, their roar rocking the coast. The other afternoon I was walking along the rocks, gathering fennel to pickle some olives when I saw a small boat caught in the middle of the channel, being buffeted violently in a hopeless battle, as if it had lost its rudder or there were no men on board. It could have been a catboat, though it was higher on the bow and shorter in length. Now, with all the tourism they make some truly fantastic craft. But I think you could find wood like that in Turkey or in Greece. How many days had the storm been battering her? It was being tossed to and fro, in a zigzag line. Tattered sails snapped against its only remaining mast . . . a miserable flag it was.

"She was standing on the deck, hanging onto the mast, frozen in fear, her splendid hair lashed by the wind, which billowed out her dress, then collapsed it, inert against her slim frame, a white tunic and . . . and it was impressive. No, not really. . . . I don't know how else to say it. Illuminated? I'm sure I saw the desperation in her eyes. Her face—its high cheekbones, eyes as sharp as tridents, her swollen lips parted—is graven in my memory. It was as if her face were projected toward me over the roar of the storm. Or did I imagine it from staring at her in fascination so long? Or perhaps the intensity of my thoughts about it afterward has left it stuck here in my head. . . .

"Two abrupt turns and a funny zigzag brought the boat closer to shore. Then suddenly the bow dipped into the sea, and the woman flew up in the air, her arms flailing, her dress billowing in the wind. And I swear she stayed suspended there for a second or a minute, looking like an apparition about to take over the planet or a blessed little statue, like a saint, that would look good atop a writing desk. Then she dropped like a rock, and the waves swallowed her up. The catboat bucked again, did a complete turn-about and headed for the bottom without leaving a single survivor in that vast, inclement sea.

"I jumped about on the crags for hours—all night in fact—looking for the woman's body. What enigmatic and capricious destiny had brought her to me, only to leave her dead? The waves broke over me, soaking me, thundering in my head. I felt drunk with the roar and the fury of it all. Then a few stars broke through the storm. Their vague bluish brightness turned the sea to a mineral crispness, and I kept imagining, obsessively, that lady's face emerging like a pale ghost from the sea, her hair sticking out like tentacles. The water weighed on me, driving me closer to her. . . ."

12

The table had been set with care, plates arranged in triumphal symmetry like the rainbow hues of a peacock's tail, bottles with their noble labels, succulent pyramids of fruit. The dense odors drifted in heavy clouds from the kitchen, dark savory roasts blending with vegetable dishes and hearty sauces. The delicate aroma of dessert sweets lingered over the platters of pastry.

The justice of the peace and ex-commander Ignasi Taltavull Oliva was reminded by this brilliant display of culinary prowess and his recent memories of Ingeborg von Nassau-Istrij of the splendid banquets—a triumph of the baroque—the Duchess of Orlandis had given during the Civil War years . . . years of great happiness for Ignasi, years of great promise.

The late-evening dinners at the castle offered game and caviar, lobster and truffles, Viennese pastries, wines from the Rhine, and French champagne, all served by white-gloved waiters. A violinist and a pianist ceremoniously played their instruments on a raised platform in complete self-absorption. The food, apart from what was caught or produced in Majorca, was imported from Germany—or in some cases even from Italy—by the very powerful Nazi and Fascist advisors who had been incorporated into the military and political organization of the island, which supported the solid and ever-growing revolt against the Spanish Republic.

The salon of the castle was filled with dignitaries of the new regime established on that mythical eighteenth of July 1936. Their uniforms were a shiny black: high-sounding Roman consuls and grim emissaries from Berlin; the important upper crust from Palma, who assented to everything with circumspect nods of their heads; colonels who wore their medals with pride, evidence of their heroism; unctuous priests, maximalists at their finest; local ladies with their inquisitive eyes and trim figures; grandes dames with opulent breasts and wholesome, ruddy cheeks; determined foreign ladies. . . .

Ignasi had studied business accounting and had gotten his first job in the Orlandis grain shop working as an assistant to the accountant, Mr. Arguimbau, a dandruff-plagued little man with a rotund belly who had three daughters and rejoiced with satisfaction at midmorning and midafternoon when he would pause in his work and drink a *carajillo* of espresso and brandy that Ignasi himself fetched for him, after which he would smoke a cigarette. And Ignasi knew that if he were both diligent and respectful he would replace the old man in twenty years or so.

But in the meantime Ignasi had married Roseta, one of his boss's daughters.

"Why did I ever do that?" was one of the many questions the retired commander often asked himself.

And he had an answer, although it lay at the very bottom of his heart of hearts. He had gotten involved with her one wintry Sunday afternoon. . . .

Ignasi was at home alone with nothing to do. His parents had gone to Taltavull Hall to visit Grandfather Bartomeu, the one who had killed the Cordovan. Young Ignasi was seated at one of the windows in the parlor, staring out at the ashen, leaden-gray winter clouds. Swallows, stiff with cold, pecked vigorously at the ground then rose on the wing in swift flight, only to land all in a row on the icy power lines. Ignasi couldn't figure out how to spend the remaining hours of that Sunday afternoon. He would have liked something to look forward to, but he had no idea what.

Then the little Red Riding Hoods appeared out of the alley. Two girls wearing purple smocks of a rough material cut too long for them, walking along like robots, their jaws firmly set, their large eyes silently accusatorial, their hair severely scissored in bowl cuts. . . . An austere doughy-faced nun accompanied them, who would melt into honeyed smiles whenever she met anyone on the street or appeared at someone's door.

Ignasi's door knocker reverberated through the house. Instead of going to the door, he remained behind the window curtain and observed the three little women. They knocked again. Suddenly one of the little Red Riding Hoods whispered something in the other's ear and giggled, shielding her mouth with her hand. The nun turned to them irately and with a rapid movement pinched one of them on the arm and the other on the neck. They remained standing there, unmoving, paralyzed with fear. A drop, then a second drop of blood ran down the child's neck. A married couple passed by, and the nun greeted them obsequiously, and the little Red Riding Hoods, their eyes cast to the ground, held out their hands as they had been taught to do.

The little misses in their reddish smocks, inmates of the poorhouse, had to walk the length and breadth of the island begging for alms. Ignasi became uneasy and as he turned away from the scene knocked over a vase, and it crashed to the floor. Poor little Red Riding Hoods, who had known neither father nor mother nor a home. ... He would have gladly given them his house and everything in it, but he remained in his hiding place instead. After they left, he ran outside and walked aimlessly from one street to another. That was perhaps the only time in his life he had felt guilty—very guilty—without knowing why, unless it was for the sins of the world.

Rough whitecaps were building on the sea when he got to the port, and there he met Roseta Arguimbau, who was on her way to church to attend the forty hours of the Most Holy Sacrament. He asked if he might accompany her. The church was packed with people, standing room only at the back. They stood there in the shadows of the portal, pressed together by the crowd.

Ignasi felt an irresistible desire to touch the girl. He became alarmed when he realized he shouldn't, especially there. She was praying out loud with the rest of the congregation. He cautiously slipped his arm around her waist. Roseta stopped praying for an instant, then continued the Ave Maria, and with her elbow covered his hand so the others would not see it.

Young Ignasi did not consider what he had done as either good or evil. That was just the way things had happened. He even remembered how he had imitated his boss by drinking a *carajillo* twice a day, followed by a cigarette. He had looked forward to that delightful moment—the strong coffee, that first deep drag filling his lungs—as a relief from working among the dusty sacks in the grain warehouse.

When the war started, he signed up for one of the training courses for reserve officers when one day he saw his name on the list of pre-inductees posted at city hall, where Arguimbau had sent him to find out whether prices were being quoted on almonds the government had commandeered.

The uniforms, the parades, the singing, and the authority that his position gave him made him feel successful. The war, on the other hand—except for some isolated local skirmishes—remained very far away on the strange and distant peninsula of Spain. They could have capriciously failed him after he completed the training course, but they passed him instead. And the lack of officers in the isolated Majorcan army allowed him to rise rapidly to the position of commander of the Orlandis zone. It was then that the duchess began to invite him to her dinners.

The priest of the aristocracy—Monsignor Estopañán, the local representative of His Holiness—during a sermon on an auspicious holy day had preached something about "a life with a higher calling." That expression caught the young lieutenant's attention: the atmosphere at the castle made him feel there was a life beckoning him out there, a vague but powerful higher calling. Or at least that was what he thought, he for whom a new experience was still the discovery of a truth.

The spiral of luxury surrounding the duchess seemed a door the generous fates had opened for Ignasi onto a garden saturated with voluptuous promises. It wasn't that he had a special predilection for luxury, but if that were to be the first step toward acceptance, then it did indeed interest him more than the warehouse and the *carajillos* with Arguimbau. But would he be able to enter that garden? He felt confident he could, and so he explained to Roseta that the meetings he was called to at the castle were of an official nature and that she was to stay at home. Roseta had been the first flower of spring. He didn't even think of her any more. That was Destiny, what Honorat Moro had just described as occult and oppressive. "But Moro," Ignasi Taltavull Oliva reasoned to himself, "thinks he has developed a philosophy of life just because he lives alone among the trees, when what really lurks inside him is his huge pride. He has seen—or claims to have seen—that sea maiden on the foundering ship. That's all well and good, but all he had really seen was her drowning. A moment of suffering for her, at most a day, a week? But maybe she had lived a very rich life before that fatal moment . . . and we all have to die, some in more pain than others. The trouble was that Honorat confused the woman's entire life with the few moments of his coincidental meeting with her."

Ignasi had first met Ingeborg under the archway of a French door opening onto the perfumed garden of a summer evening, its flower-covered walls serving as a gallant cortège, and the dragonflies as a snowstorm of light. She was rather tall—about Ignasi's height—wearing a very simple, long, lemon-yellow dress, a large magnolia pinned over her heart, pearls around her neck. Her thick braid drew her hair back and accentuated her facial features, resembling a sculpture. What was the name of that head of an Egyptian queen exhibited in a Berlin museum, the granite reproduction of which Ingeborg kept on display in her bedroom because it resembled her so much? Ah, Ingeborg. . . .

"Do you like our island, Madam?" the lieutenant had asked courteously.

"Oh, yes. I come from a nation of woodlands where it seems heartache is always ready to befall us. That is why these low, stubby, sun-broiled hills are like a drug to me with their sparse but fragrant grasses. How I love to walk through them!"

And on that hilltop, exultant in the sun, its brilliance crackling in the air, amid the hot, monumental gray rocks, the rockrose and reeds as stalwart symbols of resistance, they had begun their adventure of love.

He was wearing army boots and a khaki shirt, sweating profusely, accompanying Ingeborg as she scampered like a goat up the mountain. Between leaps from crag to crag she shed her blouse and skirt, revealing her small, cinnamon-colored breasts and svelte thighs. Beyond the peaks all they could see above their heads was the vast blue of the sky, as if their world had become a grandiose, endless space where nothing else existed.

Ingeborg drew Ignasi over to her, looked him mockingly in the eye and at the same time with an air of capitulation said, "Do with me what you will; I am yours. A woman should serve her man in whatever he wishes."

Blinded by the light, confused by the blazing heat, driven by a frenzied devotion to that girl who had become the first momentous discovery of his life, Ignasi embraced her and laid her down on a heavy bed of fescue still cool from the morning dew. He possessed her slowly, holding her tightly, for the mere perception of her delicate but solid flesh had already seduced him. And she, sure of herself, concentrating on her every sensation, absorbing him, letting him do as he wished.

They were able to be together often. Her husband, Baron Rolf von Nassau-Istrij, one of the German officers stationed on the island, a well-proportioned ruddy blond, was obliged to remain in Palma many nights. So Ingeborg and Ignasi often returned to the mountains, for she loved them ecstatically: "I would love to be a lone explorer, always trekking over deserts, over the peaks of the sun!"

Whenever Ignasi received word of a tryst from the baroness, that night he would leave the barracks when the town hall clock struck eleven, cross the fields submerged in darkness, climb the trails along the edge of an old olive grove where a flock of sheep usually grazed, wraithlike blotches in the night.

He would sit and wait in the garden at the castle, shielded by a clump of oleander until Ingeborg, naked and graceful, opened the balcony doors to her room. As he waited, he contemplated the brilliance of the sea against the blackness of the night at the end of the valley; he listened to the vagabond tinkling of the sheeps' bells and the fragments of conversation that reached him in German, Italian, and Spanish from the great salon of the duchess.

Sometimes he would drowse and dreams would come to him in which the reality of the moment never completely disappeared, but in which absurd, surreal elements freely mixed. He could never forget one of those dreams: the outlines of the oleander and the garden slowly disappeared, transformed into little soldiers marching back and forth carrying huge musical notes while he looked on, laughing and crying at the same time. Sometimes he would be awakened by a fat tiger-striped cat that jumped into his lap and rubbed its nose against his face as if it were kissing him.

And then there were Ingeborg's kisses. She received him calmly as if he were performing some routine function in her life. And he would throw himself thirstily upon her, for never in his most unimaginable fantasies had a female like her ever existed.

But as he continued to possess her over time, his sexual drive and his pride began to subside: Ingeborg's kisses came to feel as innocuous as they were agreeable. "Every candle eventually burns out," Ignasi would muse as he immersed himself in the thousands of details of his daily wartime routine. Incapable of considering life itself as a passion, all his feelings seemed to melt into an indistinguishable sameness.

"You're as cold-blooded as a snake," people had censured him at times. He knew that was not true, but if women were attractive to him, he was even more attracted by their novelty. If he could have gotten away with it, he would have reared up, snorted, and drooled in the middle of the street every time he saw a woman whose gaze or waggling hips pushed the hidden buttons of his libido. On the other hand, women whose gestures and tone of voice had become familiar bored him.

And Ingeborg had been for him like the shot at the starting gate: her beauty, her social standing, her attractiveness had awakened him and given him confidence in himself. He now approached other women with the hardened self-assurance of experience. The disruptions and distortions of the war only made the ground around him more fertile.

But Ingeborg's experience had been quite the opposite. She had cheated on her husband from the first moment of their marriage, or rather, she continued having the same indiscriminate sexual relationships she had been having since adolescence. Her only desire was to have a naked man at her side, to feel his weight upon her body.

Her parents were always away traveling when she was a child. When they were at home, they were out to dinner every evening; they barely saw the girl for days at a time. Ingeborg had grown up and been educated in the stellar solitude of the family castle, deep in the wooded hinterland of Bavaria. She read nineteenth-century novels about poor abandoned orphans like Genoveva de Brabante and wept in miserable self-pity.

Those lost, fog-shrouded valleys became an erratic but persistent threat to her. The intense brilliant green of the forest was a foreshadowing of the deep and repugnant gloom of the gorges below: the solemn fir trees, the ancient oaks, the ravines over which the echoes of her voice flew like a screeching flock of birds. The rushing torrents of water, sparkling clear and freezing cold, seemed to be dictating a sentence. The stone-gray eyes of the wolves, the sprightliness of the playful otter, the invisible bear, lethal in his silent lumberings along the trails—all lurked there in those woods. And there were the endless afternoons when at dusk the rain fell with a metronomic drumming intensity. She did not want her eyes to roam within the castle, so she would gaze through the windows at the dreary weather beyond. She felt desolate; she derived her only hope from the landscape, where the rumblings of heaven and earth at least gave her a sense of movement, of change, messages of life and death.

The bone-chilling rooms of the castle, its infinite corridors, the murky paintings on the walls, the stiff servants smothering her with their officious presence, only reinforced the message that her parents were not there. Other people became a threat to her, for the only people who should by rights have loved her were never there. She needed human warmth, the intensity of contact with another human being. She discovered she could get that warmth only with men. And she did not tarry in finding them.

Then the change of scenery in Majorca, its hypnotically brilliant light, its dry mountains, the jolly seascape, reversed her registers: now nothing was ever sad, nor did she reject anything; her ghosts had remained buried in the Bavarian fog. The summer and the new landscape were no longer an inert substitute for her past, but instead a lashing flame within her blood.

And Ignasi, whom she had taken as her male refuge, had grown up on this island and in this atmosphere. Ingeborg had progressively given more and more of herself to this man, as she had done with all the nature surrounding her, of which Ignasi was an integral part. Ingeborg adored him because she needed him.

When she suddenly told him she had to leave because her husband had been transferred to Germany, Ignasi felt relieved. Not only did he no longer attract him as much, but in her increasing ardor she had become more demanding of him. Ingeborg, despairing and collapsing in tears, promised to write him, get a divorce, and return to him. Ignasi answered yes to everything she said, agreed with her completely. But he didn't believe he would ever see her again because of the war in Spain and the greater war yet to come. Germany to him was at the other end of the world.

And that's just the way things turned out: Ingeborg had written lots of letters at the beginning of their separation; later they grew less frequent, then stopped altogether. Ignasi did not open a single one of the letters. He left them lying around everywhere, forgotten. If he had read them he would have become uneasy, for just thinking of her was now a disagreeable chore. He never had the least interest in discovering what had happened to the girl who now appeared in his old man's mind as the most beautiful woman he had ever had. But that did not worry him overly much, for just as with the other things in his life, there wasn't anything he could do about it.

13

When he finished unloading the grandfather clock, Ramon Consolat drank a glass of sherry and ate a bite of Christmas candy. And smoked a fat Havana cigar. Afterward, Bernat Taltavull amicably said good-bye to Ramon in the van. In spite of the blustery weather, Bernat felt good standing there outside, listening to the wind lashing the trees in the pitch-black valley. Nature was always present in both visible and invisible movements; it reminded him of clocks and their constant ticking.

Bernat the Wise was never ill at ease anywhere or with anybody. He was a person who invariably went around unshaven, in baggy-kneed trousers, with a relaxed and cordial smile on his face. As a young school lad—before the astonished faces of both teachers and students—an inspector from Palma had awarded him a diploma that carried a picture of Minerva, the goddess of wisdom, wearing a pointed helmet. He received the award because he had recited from memory and with his eyes closed the many different lessons required by the difficult examination, covering the European lake system, the human circulatory system, the prayer that began "I am a sinner. . . . ," the mathematical rule of three, the poem "The Second of May," a song in praise of domestic animals, and more. Bernat had become Bernat Taltavull the Wise.

Almost surely because of that passionate and stubborn ability to assimilate culture within a scheme that allowed for the calm coexistence of everything in one uniform and aseptic space, Bernat contemplated creation and its vicissitudes as if they formed a harmonious unity, free from all absurdities and secrets. Had he in this way come to a closer understanding of the mysterious and wise mechanism that controlled the universal order of things?

So it appeared, for he made a success of everything he touched. From his very early years he had run risks with daring coolness—even though he lacked the lust for material wealth—in a series of businesses that had turned a handsome profit for him: seine fishing, hand-embroidered linens, insurance, swimming pool construction, truck gardening, a discotheque, and the management of the family alarm clock factory. He had become a wealthy man without trying, almost indifferently.

"You probably captured a little Moorish dwarf," people would say.

From the olden days of the lightning Christian reconquest of the island in 1229 that had defeated and expelled the intolerable Infidel—those Islamic hordes, their scimitars tempered in the torrid deserts of Africa—the legend of the Moorish dwarfs had persisted. In inaccessible mountainous caves, in remote oak forests where only the breeze whispered through the wild luxuriant vegetation, in coves hidden among sharp cliffs where the sea was always calm and green, by springs that sang and wept in the canebrakes, was where the legends of the Moorish dwarfs—their eyes like burning coals—lived on as they guarded the subterranean caverns where fabulous treasures from *The Arabian Nights* lay hidden.

Many homes still treasured old editions of the book in which so many tales about that heretical and vanquished civilization were told. Rather than just a volume of *The Arabian Nights,* they were in fact more often just a bundle of poorly-printed, moth-eaten pages written in strange languages and tied together with string, brought back from the far corners of the Mediterranean by Orlandis sailors. But that didn't matter, for despite having had either the book or the knotted bundles of pages, almost nobody had ever read them. Alas, the book had become a sort of act of faith, something certifying the existence of all those Moors and their deceitful, magical charms.

If someone from Orlandis or anywhere else on the island were one day able to capture a Moorish dwarf, which was possible only through the use of obscure incantations from a time long ago that nobody remembered, the dwarf was supposed to bow in reverence before his new master and guide him to the hidden chests of gold. Bernat the Wise, when he heard people accuse him of having caught a Moorish dwarf, would shake his head no: nobody, neither he nor anybody else, believed in those childish tales of Moors and treasures of gold. So he would raise his index finger and accuse them in turn: "When you refer to that mysterious dwarf, what you're trying to do is scorn me, lower me to the status of a miserable clown, a fluke of nature. You don't believe in little Moorish dwarfs and so you become imbeciles by not bothering to verify the only proof that they don't exist, namely that the world is constantly changing. Hasn't the world advanced since the invention of the wheel? Well then, get with it, heart and soul!"

Between the gusts of wind a dull, mechanical humming reached Bernat's ears. "It must be the pump," he thought, as he tip-toed along the flagstone path over to the well. The wellhead was round and low to the ground, covered with a steel door, right beside the apricot grove.

A submersible pump raised the water from a depth of a hundred and fifty feet. It was capable of pumping over eight thousand gallons an hour, an absolute gusher as thick as a man's leg.

"Now it's easy to say the word water here, but back then . . . ," he chuckled with sarcastic affability. It had been Bernat who had decided to drill the well two summers ago. Bernat's mother Brígida lived at Taltavull Hall only half the year and spent the rest of the year in town. Her children and grand-children came and went from the old family house which served as a focal point for all of them, an ironclad human link between them and all their dead ancestors. Bernat had taken a week's vacation that August and together with his wife, Marianna Mas, he had come to stay at Taltavull Hall with his old mother Brígida.

It had been a very dry summer, flecked with golden light as never before. The valley was flooded with the toasted odor of grain stubble and dust in the fields under the bright heat of the broiling sun. The dry spell caused the clay soil to shrink and crack, opening fissures next to the house foundations. Then the walls would groan, and cracks would appear in almost all the rooms as if the old house had been shaken by an earthquake. And every year as time moved on toward the first rains of autumn, they had to call the mason to repair the cracks.

That summer Brígida repeated the same old whining Bernat had heard ever since his childhood, his mother appointing herself the trumpeter of the people's lament: "Just look at those fields! Not a drop of water! This year all the begonias and a plum tree have already died. The leaves are hanging limp on the almond trees. We'll see if they give almonds or empty shells this year. Your father and I used to have to take the cart to the Spring of the Angels to haul water in jugs. I was younger then. We got exhausted loading the cart and exhausted again pouring out the water. Once one of the glass jugs broke on him and he looked like Saint Sebastian, all cut up. They were so heavy; they weighed as much as the family debt. But if we wanted to grow a few cab-bages and parsley and to water the animals, we had no choice but to haul the water by cart. Today you have cars, and you can transport everything that way, and besides, we don't live off the place any more. But back then, things were different. Ay, look at those terraced fields: they look like they're going to burn up, what with the sun and the drought. I've begun to find dead birds lying around just like every hard, dry summer. It gets to the point where they can't fly very far to drink and they just drop from the sky like rags."

Bernat the Wise, tired of her tirade, had answered, "And why didn't you drill for water?"

His mother looked at him, stupefied: "Because there isn't any, that's why!"

"And how do you know that? "

"Well, where do you see any, my boy? We've never had any water here. My father-in-law used to say his grandfather always complained that summers here were a living hell."

"Instead of whining so much and wasting hours hauling jugs, I think you should have . . ."

Brígida interrupted him, saying, "What do you mean, hours? It took us days, weeks out of each year!"

"Well, instead of doing so much useless work hauling water only to use it up, if you had used your heads, we would have had water long ago. You should have started digging a century ago, five centuries ago, until you found the underground vein!"

"Don't you touch the tombs of the past, my boy! You'd just love to shake things up around here, the earth and all our ancestral bones in it!"

Bernat jumped up as if someone had stuck a needle in him. He had decided he would move tombs if that's what it took. He always recalled a little tale he had heard as a child: a man was walking through the woods when he discovered an old lady as ugly as sin collapsed on the ground under the weight of a bundle of firewood. The man helped her get up and then carried her burden to the miserable cabin where she lived. And before the cabin door the old hag turned into a beautiful, delicate, and noble fairy who said, "My good man, you helped me while I walked the world in disguise testing man's kindness to his fellow man. You are of noble heart. Make two wishes, and I will make them come true, however extravagant they may be. But only two, since you have done me but two favors."

The man didn't hesitate a moment, "I want a bowl full of water."

"Done," said the fairy, "although you're very modest in your wish. What about the second?"

"That the bowl never run dry."

The fairy looked at him even more surprised: "You'll always have your bowl full. But I don't understand you, my good man. I could have given you sacks overflowing with gold coins and a many-colored marble palace."

The man replied, "What would I do with all those riches if I died of thirst? With the water I have the key to life. And with life, I can achieve anything."

The tombs of fatalism would be what Bernat Taltavull the Wise would tear open and then cast their ashes to the wind and throw their bones to the hounds. If the womb of the planet still sheltered its original sources of water, he would discover them and control them. The world was meant to be conquered.

Bernat went to fetch the water witcher Borrassà—the uncle of that Algerian from La Paret—and set him in the middle of the fields at Taltavull Hall one muggy afternoon when the earth was burning up. The stench of the old fish peddler's clothes seemed to saturate the whole valley, disturbing the peace of every living thing, from plant foliage to human skin. The cats, exhausted by the heat, their eyes glazed, lay among the little purple flowers of a thick bougainvillea vine until they caught the whiff of fish on the witcher, which snapped them wide awake and sent them excitedly yowling and running after Manuel Borrassà.

"That son of mine has a screw loose," declared Brígida, perhaps uneasy about Bernat's health, but of course deeply satisfied at the thought of his approaching failure: the forces of fate were never to be discussed.

Bernat on the other hand gave the order to old man Borrassà: "Find water!"

Manuel Borrassà carried a wild olive switch and two pendulums, one a silver rectangle and the other round and of steel. He gripped the olive switch with both hands, walking from one end of the field to the other. Suddenly at the edge of the apricot grove, its overripe fruit swarming with bees and wasps, the olive switch bent tensely toward the ground. The old man knelt down, sweating profusely. He held up the rectangular pendulum and in one place it started swinging in a circle; in another, it did nothing at all.

The cats sniffed their way closer as they observed the fish peddler kneeling on the ground. One of them even batted a paw at him to see if he were made of fish. Borrassà paid no attention to the cats but instead drew out his other pendulum, which immediately began a feverish rotation. Finally the exhausted fish peddler stood up: "You have eight thousand gallons an hour at a hundred and fifty feet," he decreed.

An ancestral sense of disbelief invaded Bernat the Wise. Mentally he imagined the pained and confused procession of his forebears wandering around the dusty and barren Taltavull lands . . . all of them were staring at him—for he was just one and there were so many of them and they came from so far back in the past. The very fibers of Bernat's being grew weak as if he were being slowly and inexorably sucked into the landscape of his silent, staring ancestors. . . . He was about to say, "Let's forget it." But his convictions—that tenacious rebellion against his roots—won out, for he truly believed he could find water and mark his new destiny. So he gave the witcher another order: "Let's bring in the drillers!"

The gigantic machine came rolling up with its chimney-like tubes and its roaring compressor. And they drilled. It felt like the valley was about to collapse under the perpetual hammering of the drill, until an eruption of muddy water broke to the surface, having passed through layers of bluish then brownish clay. Then there was a shrill, squalling, grinding noise as the drill bit hit bedrock and sent off sparks . . . until the breakthrough when the dirty silvery gusher burst to the surface in a glorious roaring plume.

Brígida, her forewarnings completely forgotten, jumped into the middle of the great shower and danced in the mud, drunk with joy. Bernat stood off at a distance, in silence, as if he had been stunned by a club.

"What else must the earth be hiding in its depths, and heaven in its infinity?" he asked himself timidly. Yes, he had won because he had believed in modern ingenuity, in willpower, and in progress. But it also bothered him to have discovered the long-hidden secret of the water, unknown to all his thirsty ancestors. He feared—irrationally—that he had gone too far with his challenge to the nature of things.

"But a challenge against whom or what?" he asked himself at the same time. He felt an atavistic anguish writhe in his gut, anguish at the realization that man is nothing.

Not so, for that day the prodigious plume of water had made him finally understand—and he reaffirmed it on this Christmas Eve out there in the wind as he listened to the subterranean humming of the pump—that if the dead were to raise their heads, they would learn that only they were eternal, that only they were the immobile ones.

14

Adelina, Niní, Sebastiana, Tina, and Joana Maria burst into the hall—nobody knew through which door—as if they were some bizarre handiwork of the wind and the smoke. They were laughing, screaming, pushing each other, and singing. A tangled mass of skirts and long hair out of which a voice proclaimed, "Uncle Albert! Uncle Albert!"

And all the girls, clapping and shouting, started to dance around Albert the Younger.

He looked up in surprise, for he had been dragging his ill humor around with him ever since the episode with Dídac Ensenyat. Practically anything could upset him, and that's why he needed an immutable base for his being so that he would not slip into the abyss of indescribable turbulence that besieged his inner peace and that he neither understood nor wanted to accept. That's why he instinctively rejected anything but a minimal relationship with reality, nothing that went beyond the purely conventional. The story of deaf old Dídac was, of course, the story of someone who had risked throwing himself headfirst into a pit with complete disregard for the consequences. The girls swarming around him alarmed him: with their outrageous whooping and hollering they could offend him, confuse him, turn his mood even uglier.

"How young you look, Uncle Albert!" exclaimed Tina.

"And as elegant as ever!" added Sebastiana emphatically, as she adjusted his silk cravat.

"I would love to have a lover like you!" Adelina said, teasingly licking her lips with the tip of her tongue.

"Hey! Hey! What will Alexandre say?" Sebastiana squealed as she poked her.

"Hey, quit it!" shouted Adelina, alarmed.

"And how handsome you are, Uncle Albert!" said Niní as she planted a wet kiss on each of his cheeks.

"You have to tell us how many hearts you've broken!" demanded Joana Maria.

Albert grew calmer. They were just saying what they had to say. A breath of optimism invaded his inner being. Yes, he knows—friendly joking aside—that he is very young-looking, that he dresses like a fashion model, that he is a fine catch for anyone. And he cannot—nor does he want to—become vain over the fact, for to him it is just his natural way. He smiles with affected and condescending modesty, for he is Albert the Younger.

He moves as if he were being filmed in slow motion. His gestures are courtly; he bows ceremoniously. He arches an eyebrow as he speaks. He wears those elegantly pleated silk cravats. The creases in his trousers have been ironed to perfection. His sweater is knitted of undyed wool, interrupted by a broad red stripe, like that of a salon sportsman. His agile frame is a miraculous proclamation of youth. During the past forty years, nothing would have changed in Albert the Younger had he not just celebrated his sixtieth birthday, and if he did not walk quite so stiffly and if, up close, his eyes did not appear milky like those of a rotting fish, and if his face was not a wan network of fine wrinkles.

The only person in the family who had ever spoken ill of Albert was his father, Benigne Taltavull. Everyone seated around the vast table appeared truly young as they ate and listened to Albert, who was explaining something in his deep voice with deliberate circumlocutions. Benigne, who was sometimes overcome by fits of sardonic bitterness, as if he had been the victim of a swindle, suddenly banged his fist on the table like a hammer, shouting: "You, Albert, are more indigestible than a cream puff! You have never said anything that was not the voice of reason. Ugh! And you've probably never stained so much as the front of your shirt! When you go to take a leak you probably hold your pecker with a cigarette paper!" Albert's father slammed the door behind him as he stormed out of the hall.

But his mother Brígida looked at him devotedly. Albert was the best-dressed, the most well-mannered, the best-educated in all Orlandis. She had combed his hair as a child; as a youth she had touched up his suit with her iron when he was invited out; she melted before his affected language. And she noticed, subtly pleased, the admiration he awoke among the young ladies. How many would not have willingly fallen in love with Albert the Younger? Her niece Joana Maria had just asked him that with a smile on her face, for the thousandth time.

Albert blushed ever so slightly, proudly, "Oh, no. I don't. . . ."

"Come on! Come on! Let's have their names!" the girl demanded. Tomàs Moro's wife Càndida appeared from the bedrooms, where she had been making the beds for those who wanted to sleep over and celebrate the rest of Christmas at Taltavull Hall, and said, "At least two of my girlfriends—when

Tomàs and I were engaged—were running after Albert: Catalina Balança and Noemí Borrell."

"And my sister, Margarida!" added Marianna Mas.

"Olé! Olé!" applauded the girls.

"And then there was that one from Palma—Mercedes was her name—who used to spend her summer vacation at Carrer del Nord. I used to chase after her, but she threw me over for Uncle Albert," Joan Pere Tudurí stated in all seriousness.

Albert the Younger, as if he were ascending into Heaven on clouds of incense, protested rhetorically, "Please, my dears, please. . . . A gentleman mustn't betray. . . ."

"And what do you say about the Rosales and the Lyric Theater, eh? What do you say to that?" asked Bernat the Wise with a malicious grin.

Damià, Egèria's brother, broke up in peals of laughter, "He always says he goes to bed early, but what he does is take the car and drive to Palma, and then it's champagne and women!"

"Damià, be careful," pleaded Egèria.

Albert the Younger became at once solemn, confused, and pretentious, "Quiet, please, Mother might hear you . . . don't overdo it. Doesn't everyone have a right to his amorous intimacies?"

The Rosales, the cabaret with the Brazilian stage show, and the Lyric Theater with the review: la Chelito, la Natacha, the chorus girls with their derrières in the air. . . . The first place had been turned into a garage over thirty years ago. The second had been demolished in Franco's time and replaced by a park. But Albert the Younger had never noticed, or his subconscious mind had erased the fact. For him, the Lyric and the Rosales continued to be the caverns of debauchery he had known as a younger man. . . . Oh eternal memory!

To tell the truth he had been in them only once, while he was in the army. He stumbled out of the Rosales dizzy from the glass of eggnog liqueur he had drunk, and from the plethora of female breasts he had not dared rub against as he danced. He had sat in the balcony at the Lyric, and since he was near-sighted, he was only able to make out lighted blotches of color moving around the stage. As for the showgirls, all he knew of their exuberant curves was what he had seen painted on the posters in the theater lobby.

And if Catalina Balança, Noemí Borrell, Marianna Mas, and Mercedes from Carrer del Nord had ever been in love with Albert, neither he nor they had ever been aware of it. Whenever any of the Taltavulls saw Albert speaking casually with a girl at a bus stop or during the intermission between movies at the Orlandis cinema, they always merrily decreed as a family that it must be her burning passion, like a bell tolling the last call to mass, which drew her to Albert the Younger.

One of the girls, however, had certainly loved him: Vicenta Espriu. She was still an attractive woman these many years later, with her tall frame, dark complexion, and decisive manner. She had married Orlandis's pharmacist and had had three children, one of whom was already practicing medicine. But Vicenta, a svelte youth with a dazzling Gypsy beauty, had adored the very air Albert the Younger breathed, back when he was truly young . . . a night in June, a field of wildflowers, the moon full. Vicenta, naked and poised in sweet surrender before him, incarnated all his heart's desires. Vicenta, languid upon the grass, love in her voice, murmured, "Oh, Albert, my Albert. . . ." And he, his voice suddenly grown hoarse after removing only his shirt, moaned pathetically where he stood and averted his eyes from that feast, nervously knotting his silk cravat. Vicenta suddenly and abruptly rose and stalked off through the enchanted fields into the solitude of the night, naked and irate.

Albert had returned home upset that night, his shirt still unbuttoned. He felt helpless, humiliated, and confused, as if he had fallen into a deep chasm. Brígida as always was waiting for him in the kitchen with a glass of warm milk. When she saw him, she spat harshly, "Women are filthy beasts!"

He nodded affirmatively, not quite reaching for the glass of warm milk. His mother continued, "You have to overcome them!"

And then a light bulb lit in Albert's head: beat them! He had just beaten Vicenta. And with that, the chasm disappeared. He puffed out his chest and drank the milk with his accustomed delicacy of movement. Brígida lay a cotton counterpane at the foot of her son's bed that night so that if there should be a chill in the early morning air, Albert would not catch cold.

It didn't take Vicenta long to forget about that night and the couple of months she had gone out with Albert the Younger. When they met on the street she always accosted him with her warm smile: "Hi, Albert! You look so handsome today!"

Albert would gaze at her with half-closed eyes, practicing his most seductive pose. She must have still been crazy about him—even more so because he had conquered her, had risen to an inaccessible peak high above her. He was Albert the Younger.

"I want you to sit beside me at the table," Joana Maria demanded, taking her uncle by the arm.

"Eh! And what about me?" Tina exclaimed, grabbing him by the other arm.

Albert wilted and allowed himself to be escorted, remarking, "Confidentially, dear girls, and because you're both grown-ups now, I want to tell you that once—ahem—I sent a huge bouquet of chrysanthemums— as big as that vase over there—to a Brazilian girl who was one of the vedettes—ahem—well—ahem—without the slightest bad intention, of course, then . . . what did you say? Ah, yes, the dressing rooms. . . . The Lyric offers one of the specialties in the arts, don't you think?—that of Terpsichore the Muse . . . because . . . well, a gentleman never. . . ."

15

The downpour continued. It soon turned to large leaden drops, leaving the air clean and free of the driving wind that had turned into a rush of warm air filtering through the humidity. A subtle mugginess filled the valley, cleared rapidly and was replaced by dryer air charged with electricity. Lightning scored the sky; thunder rolled and surged.

On the mountain peaks prongs of fire crackled as if battling furious gods foreign to man. The almond grove, the pines, and the mountainous outlines of Taltavull Hall appeared in the bluish flashes, then darkened in the pauses between the spectral lashings of light. Everyone in the great hall looked out the windows at the show and felt an intimate and improbable conviction that they were gazing at a new and unknown landscape.

Suddenly a brilliantly contorted bolt of lightning struck a pine tree on the hill directly beside Taltavull Hall with demonic fury, as if it had been a chosen, premeditated target. The tree trunk exploded with the crack of a cannon shot, followed by a rumbling echo, becoming a tongue of fire, a billowing flame. The crown of the tree burst into a ball of red and orange, creating a moment of euphoria before it was extinguished by another sheet of rain. The lightning passed and was replaced by a soft whispering breeze, and the winter night—the only one there was—went on.

16

It was Marianna Mas who called everyone to the dinner table and announced the menu with great fanfare: "We have platters of grouper, and what wonderful grouper it is! The finest in the sea . . . what those folks from Pula haven't caught doesn't exist! Dioclecià brought them. Three cheers for him!" Everyone cheered. "And . . . we have chicken! Not only are they round and plump, but they have been grain-fed, right here at Taltavull Hall, no less. We are the cocks of the walk when it comes to fine chickens. Compared with those tasteless, odorless mass-produced birds the rest of the people eat, ours taste like game hens. Not to mention the nougat and other side dishes in which the almonds—also harvested here—are a major ingredient. Not to mention the wine, my God! You won't find a better wine around, not even on the king's table at Marivent!"

Just then her son Pere marched into the hall frowning and distressed. He had been playing with a small but powerful computer in the coach house with the other Taltavull boys, Alexandre, Carles, and Andreu. Joan Pere Tudurí had bought it for his brother Alexandre at the International Airport in Zurich.

"You kids sit down to dinner!" ordered Marianna Mas as she looked at her son, who always irritated her. He had come very late in her life, just a few years before her granddaughter Adelina was born.

"We've called you several times! Don't let your father have to tell you again!"

The tall curly-haired youth, wiry and athletic, stammered, "Yes . . . of course, but . . . there's a man out there. He said something about dinner . . . he . . . well, he's right outside. . . ."

"What's he mumbling about?" inquired Honorat Moro.

"An old man just arrived. He's right outside! Cristòfol Mardà he says his name is. 'Don't you recognize me?' he said. 'No,' I said. 'Then tell them Cristòfol Mardà is here,' he said. He came in a taxi, and he wants to talk with somebody. Oh, yes, I don't know what he was saying about whether we were having supper yet or not," replied the young man.

"Cristòfol? What could he want? That man scares me," said Pollònia with alarm.

The hall fell silent. Everyone looked at his neighbor. Magdalena, the recent widow of Francesc de Borja, was the first to react, "Hasn't he already spoken with you, Pere?"

"Well, I'm not . . . Well, one of you . . . ," Pere said as the sweep of his eyes included the Taltavull siblings and in-laws: Magdalena herself, her mother and Bernat, her father, the Tudurí widow Pollònia, Albert the Younger, Paula Taltavull, and her husband Honorat Moro.

All of them turned instinctively toward their uncle Ignasi Taltavull Oliva, the retired commander. He avoided their stares, concentrating his attention on stirring the fire. Bernat appealed to him, "Uncle . . ."

"Are you talking to me? What do you want, Bernat?"

"No, I just wanted to ask you what you thought of Cristòfol Mardà, standing out there."

"I haven't seen him in over forty years. I heard he came back a couple of months ago, but that's all I know."

"Well, since you wore the same uniform during the war . . . ," suggested Pollònia.

"The war. . . . It's as if it never happened," responded the commander indifferently.

Bernat the Wise reflected a moment, then motioned to his sister Paula, "Let's both of us go. Don't get mad if I say this, Paula, but you've got a temper and maybe we'll need it. You never know what to expect from that Mardà fellow, and sometimes I'm a little too easygoing. Come on!"

They went outside; the wind was whispering softly, gently. The lanterns along the terrace had become simple orange blotches, strangled in the murk. At the roadside a car had halted, its motor idling, its parking lights on. A stocky man stood in the shadows of the car, breathing heavily.

That scene was almost a repeat of another which took place the autumn before when that same figure, Cristòfol Mardà, had emerged from another taxi and stood there in front of his own house as the sun was setting, trying to come to terms with his dull, stubborn restlessness.

Mexico, Peru, Bolivia. . . . Petulantly, Cristòfol Mardà Taltavull had traveled half of Latin America. Six months before that Christmas Eve he had been running a gasoline station in a town where a gang of guerrillas had taken him captive. They had emerged cautiously from the thick jungle of banana trees. They were very young, very brown-skinned, wiry, and hostile and carried short, gleaming submachine guns. They asked a lot of questions and wanted provisions. People obeyed them with alacrity. Mardà was with a group they had ordered to stay put beside a pile of brush.

He was getting irritated. Those kids were punks. One of them laid his submachine gun carelessly on the table; the others wore theirs slung across their chests. Mardà felt his dormant energy and instincts awakening. Armed revolution was a part of him; it was really his whole being. Cristòfol Mardà, the veteran. He who had wound up as the lord of terror on the Nationalist side in Orlandis during the Civil War. They had decorated him, a blueshirt, for the physical valor that had been part of him all his life.

He was sure that with an audacious move, he could overwhelm that rag-tag troop of scraggly kids. One of the guerrillas came over to Mardà, demanding jerry cans of gasoline. Mardà rose slowly, calculating how he would jump him from behind and grab his submachine gun, how he would force the others to.... When the guerrilla came within reach, Mardà lunged at him, his forearm a stranglehold around the kid's throat, and . . . something erupted in Mardà's head and he dropped like a stone.

Some time later he awoke, groggy. He lay splayed upon the ground and, furious with himself, tried to get up. A swift kick dropped him to the ground again. Finally pacified, he obeyed the orders they gave in the form of pushes and shoves, his once-proud head sunken to his chest during the five days the insurrectionists held him captive.

Cristòfol realized something that revolted him: they had beaten him in a flash and continued to crush whatever resistance he put up. Those men were young and agile, with muscles of steel compared with Mardà's aging bulk. They operated with modern arms, which confused him, and which he had no instinct for, accustomed as he was to his ancient rifle. They were also excellent at hand-to-hand fighting, which Cristòfol had seen only on TV.

Mardà filled the gasoline cans mechanically, carefully guarded by the guerrillas. All his paralyzed brain could do was repeat that everything he had been, his body and his life, his ideas, his knowledge, and his image of himself had all collapsed in his old age. Up until that moment, anything he had ever planned or struggled for he had been able to achieve because his fiery temperament demanded it and he knew what it took to do it. But as a consequence of the unexpected episode with the guerrillas, his thoughts and schemes were now in disarray. They had struck at the core of his pride, that vision of himself as a strong, tenacious man, a fighting man. Now he was nothing, a nobody.

But he couldn't resign himself to that. After several weeks of drinking whiskey in his tarpaper shack, unshaven and sweat-sodden, ignoring the honking cars demanding gasoline, he decided to return to Orlandis. It was the only place where he would never be thought of as beaten. Tangled up in his dirty sheets, swatting bugs with his shoe, he discovered that in all those years of wandering through the world he had been wrong in thinking he was a personality, a singular individual, daring and hard. What had really characterized him in his own eyes, what had acted as his motivating force was Orlandis, the memory of Orlandis.

He was like a camel that could plod the Saharan desert trails for weeks with not a well in sight, living off the water in its hump. Not only had the acts he had committed in Orlandis during the war molded his personality, but he was secure in the knowledge that the town had not forgotten him. They even feared him, ever-present in their memory. These thoughts formed a scaffolding that supported the rest of him, especially his façade, a façade that had just collapsed. But he felt confident he could get it all back in Orlandis.

Why had he left Orlandis after the war, anyway? It was all too clear to him now: because he couldn't adapt to peacetime conditions. He had felt locked in a glass cage too small for him to even stand up in. And the cage would shatter every time he moved. He had been named the local trades union representative in town. That meant spending endless hours cooped up in a small flat that served as his office, among wobbly pine tables and endless paperwork. And even though Cristòfol Mardà was someone in that office, that someone was but a modest cog in a larger wheel he didn't even understand. He was an address for that sector of the state he represented, and his awareness of what he was doing only confirmed his suspicion that it had nothing to do with the forceful principles shouted on the streets during the war, which had breathed pride into his will and spurred his sense of adventure. In reality they existed only as fine print smelling of fresh ink, an intricate rosary of laws, a tentacular bureaucratic chore.

At least Cristòfol had something to keep himself busy in that little postage-stamp flat. But when he closed the door on those miserable rooms and left for the day, he felt lost and frustrated. He was free but trapped in a void. He would brag in the café. He conspired to appoint a new mayor, but everything he did seemed artificial; there was nothing dynamic about it that motivated him. The world no longer inflamed him or sizzled within him. It had become a world of exhausting and useless attempts on his part to create his own ideal space.

Back then the excitement of the war had been never-ending; it went on day and night, saturating heaven and earth and all the spirits. For Cristòfol it had been as if he were finally flying around on one of those magic carpets that glided over Baghdad in *The Arabian Nights,* which his grandmother had told him about in her evocative, mellifluous voice. The catastrophe of war, all its unexpected ups and downs, had excited him and made him proud. With the collapse of traditional social structures, Mardà felt his individualism emerge magnificently, while at the same time he proudly observed how the gray existence of the masses was effaced as they became an anonymous flock of sheep.

Those who thought Cristòfol had left Orlandis pursued by remorse or out of fear of retaliation for the killings were wrong. He had taken part in the shooting of more than two dozen people: either directly, by pulling the trigger himself, or by giving the order to fire. All kinds of crazy things had happened. But not one of those dead bodies worried him now. Rather, those corpses infuriated him as much as the people of Orlandis hated him.

Cristòfol had gone to his first execution by firing squad one night feeling fearful and unsure of himself. Until he saw how his victims looked at him, how the townspeople looked at him the next morning on the street: a silence overflowing with recrimination lurked in their eyes. They actually considered him, Cristòfol Mardà, who was just beginning to feel the exhilaration of war, as an evil beast! He felt indignant. He squeezed the trigger because the war demanded it, because no inner repugnance on his part stopped him, and because he noticed he grew in stature and strength in the midst of that swelling tide, in the same way that grapevines in spring began to sprout with new life in preparation for the juicy autumn harvest. And as a concomitant of that luxuriance came the need for people to impose themselves on each other.

It pleased him to think that the concept of evil, in spite of what had been preached to him, did not exist. Evil was only a word through which the defeated and the resentful sought solace. At each new execution his anger toward his victims grew. Mardà, with a glass of brandy before him on the bar, shouted himself hoarse explaining his motives. Those men—those Reds— had misunderstood life, an error that had led them to their deaths, ignoble and stupid deaths. They had misunderstood death too, committing their lives to leaders who had stirred up their enthusiasm for new ideas and new times.

"Yes, that's it!" he insisted.

And he wanted his revenge because the others were constantly pestering him, trying to make him hate himself as much as they hated him. Everything became complicated when he had to deal with people. His enemies confused him and made him feel dirty. Those imbecile corpses up on Penyal del Ca in the dead of night, who in their last moments still imagined themselves cloaked in accusatory dignity!

However, one evil did exist for him: adults were responsible for children and animals, but not for other adults. It was their fault if they didn't dare defend themselves, poor devils! Cristòfol became exasperated: each person had to bear his own cross! So what was the sense of blaming others for one's own failures? But he couldn't stand people who inflicted pain on children or animals.

Cristòfol had never had children. He had never caressed a child. Cats and dogs, yes; they had always been around the house. He would have felt ashamed if he had playfully tweaked the nose of a child on the street. That was a thing women did—or weaklings—and he didn't do it. But he always felt pleasure when the cat and the dog would jump up on his bed at night and snuggle down close to him with their warm bodies. What upset him and touched him deeply about a pet or a child was their lack of rationality, which made them seem like toys, the purity and simplicity of their minds uncontaminated by . . . by what? Cristòfol thought for a moment. By man's egotistical self-interest? Maybe, he half-believed.

No, it wasn't that exactly. Was it the secret sense of brotherhood he felt toward them? If it were that, then he felt it even more for animals than for children because a child grows into an adult human being, whereas an animal is still an animal all its life, physically glorious but morally oblivious. Men became rivals, enemies of each other. In the long run, the only solution was to fight and conquer.

"Unless you want to be the one who is destroyed," Cristòfol, heir to a maze of primitive mental jungles, remarked to himself. And when men grew old, he considered them to be obscenity itself. He loathed the spectacle of an old geezer stuffing himself at the table, his only purpose being to sustain his useless, ugly body; his shrunken, one-track mind concentrated only on protecting his degraded and decaying ego.

Children, on the other hand, only asked for love, egotistically, but gracefully. And animals were always clean, quiet companions. Did Cristòfol recognize in them a stage just prior to adulthood? Did he intuit from them his own authentic origins?

"Yes, I see myself in their eyes; I feel as their hearts feel," he exclaimed to himself.

That's why he was repelled by the story about the she-ass. He even enjoyed being irritated by the thought of her after so many years, for he held the absurd but comforting opinion that in this way he was prolonging the distant possibility of redeeming the poor animal.

His father had a very old and very tall she-ass, gone white with the years. Old Man Mardà suffered from rheumatism, and without the animal he wouldn't have been able to get around. He would hitch her up to his cart and drive it around Orlandis, visiting relatives and caring for his scattered fields. He would loan the she-ass out to his neighbors for their plowing in exchange for their coming over and doing his plowing and threshing. He used to brag to people about his she-ass as he stroked her back.

Until one day the she-ass began to limp and go weak in the knees on the hills, panting and unable to pull the cart. At first Old Man Mardà tried to coax her on, but soon he started lashing her with his whip, which the poor beast stolidly endured, with raw running sores on her haunches, clotted with blowflies. Then the old man cut down her rations. He stopped giving her carob pods and sold them in town instead. All the ass got was straw.

The old man finally didn't even bother putting her in the barn at night. He staked her out back in a ravine, between the myrtle and the canebrake. Winter came, and with it the rain and the cold. The she-ass endured, immobile, skinny and shivering, a watery membrane veiling her large, tired eyes. One day she slipped off the edge of the ravine and fractured a hip. She spent days there lying in the brush, the mud, and the thorns, unable to get up, unable to eat.

Old Man Mardà didn't even want to look at her. When he spoke of her, he became frenetic. Cristòfol, by then a young man, observed all this in silence. Until one day his father, cursing fiercely, went up to the she-ass with a sledge hammer and bashed her in the forehead. The beast, without a sound, lowered her head and rolled over, belly up, her legs twitching weakly.

The old man called for his son to go get the neighbor's mule. They loaded the she-ass in a wagon with a block and tackle. She was still moaning and pawing the air. They drove the wagon out to an abandoned dirt bank, dug a hole, and dumped the ass into it. She hit with a dull, heavy thud. They started to shovel dirt into the hole to cover her up, but the hole wasn't deep enough: two of her legs were still sticking out. Old Man Mardà raged as he cut one of them off with a pick-ax and buried it. Then they left. Cristòfol observed from a distance how the remaining leg, still with a trace of life in it, twitched in the air. Back at the house Cristòfol packed his clothes in a bundle and sneaked out the window of his room in the early morning hours. He never returned until after his father had died.

During the war, Cristòfol often dreamed of himself as a giant, a long cat-o'-nine-tails in hand, euphorically lashing and driving exhausted masses of human wretches through a desolate land. And someone he couldn't see, like an immense white light in the sky, drove him on. At the end of the war, he would often wake from an anguished dream: in it, a car stuffed with dead and near-dead bodies drove around an olive grove in endless confusion. Cristòfol was unable to determine whether he and his father were among the bodies. With the coming of peace, the nights had become hostile to him. Time, too, was different during the war: a dynamic destiny helping him overcome his limitations, commanding him.

At the end of the fighting the gray people returned and patiently reconstructed their gray lives. At the same time, with repressed impartiality, they bitterly looked askance at Cristòfol Mardà as he slowly suffocated. When he sailed for Latin America, he wasn't looking for anything out of the ordinary, nothing specific, nothing more than what he did when he got there: substituting his old routine and ambitions, his old ties—what Majorca had become for him—for mere movement itself, for a vertiginous lack of conscience, for an exultant lack of solidarity with his fellow man. Paradoxically, that new, vast, and chaotic continent seemed made to measure for him in that it empowered and encouraged human individuality with a vengeance.

Old Man Mardà had lived for many years in Cuba. Once, Cristòfol had asked him, "Father, what did you like most about it over there?"

Old Man Mardà answered between clenched teeth, bitterly, as he glared at his wife and everything around him: "Over there you could be a nobody if you wanted to."

Cristòfol had no trouble abandoning his wife Francesca. She was long-suffering, perhaps had even been attractive at one time. Mardà had married her with desire in his eye, desire that disappeared after a couple of years of sleeping at her side. If a wife couldn't bear children, why keep her around and have to respect her when screwing females on the wing was more fun? And that's what Cristòfol thought and did without any further consideration for his wife, who finally heard from others that her husband was about to leave her.

"Tòfol, people are saying . . ." she told him with a knot in her throat.

"What's that you say?"

"They say you're leaving . . . for America."

He nodded his head indifferently. "Yeah, the day after tomorrow. And I won't be back. After I've left, you can do whatever you like."

"But, Cristòfol, think of the. . . ."

"Forget all that shit. Oh, I've left you a signed power of attorney. Those four little fields and the house are yours."

As he changed trains and planes on his way back to Orlandis, he thought about the people, the families whose lives had been irremediably changed because of what he had done during the war. He had acted, Mardà said to himself, as the priests claimed God acted: deciding the fates of other human beings. When he walked down the dock, people would become quiet as they used to years ago, and they would point him out to their children, murmuring, "He's the one you've heard about who. . . ." The poisonous claws of terror come from far beyond reason and surpass it.

It was noon on a gray autumn day when he arrived in port. The sea was frothy from the southwester blowing up the bay of Orlandis. He paid the taxi in front of his house. It was the dinner hour, and the streets were deserted. His one-story house had a backyard full of fruit trees and a vegetable garden. Cristòfol was about to knock on the door when he noticed it was ajar, so he went in.

In the living room there were two rockers upholstered in colorful Majorcan fabric, a table between them with a small figurine of a dog and a conch shell on it, the picture of the deer and his wedding picture. In the dining room stood the marble-topped table with its basket of wax fruit, the Last Supper cast in plaster on the wall above the chest of drawers that had been made into a sideboard. He stuck his head in the bedroom. The bed was made, the comforter decorated with tiny embroidered fairy roses. The wardrobe still had the same scratch on its mirror from the day they had moved it in; a framed color print of the Good Shepherd hung on the wall. Nothing had changed. The house looked unlived-in, as if a tenuous layer of dust had settled on everything, on the furniture, on the atmosphere itself.

For the first time it occurred to Mardà to wonder whether Francesca might have died. Everything seemed so unreal. . . . It had never occurred to him in all those years, nor even on the return voyage, that his wife might have changed, grown older or died. She simply existed in his mind as a concept, a fact, like a mountain or a street in a town he didn't have to think about.

"Hell, if she had died, someone would have changed things around in the house," he reasoned to himself, relieved.

He continued standing there, surprised. Was he expecting to find Francesca there; was he afraid she might have disappeared? "Of course not! But I don't know . . . I had imagined my arrival would be different." He opened the French doors that led to the garden.

Francesca was seated there on a bench, eating a pomegranate. Mardà recalled the beginning of a song he had learned as a child:

The devil Cucarell
was born in the season
of pomegranates. . . .

His wife recognized him immediately: "Tòfol!"

Then she fell silent. He said nothing either. She had become a weak-voiced, bony old lady, in whose eyes flickered the acceptance of eternal exhaustion. His father's bony old she-ass flashed across his mind when he realized in dismay that he might well be reflecting the incarnation of ruin in her eyes as well. He felt a wave of nausea rising.

"Do you want a pomegranate?" she asked, pushing the fruit basket toward him, full of rotund, rust-colored pomegranates.

Cristòfol shook his head, opened his mouth and said in a hoarse voice: "It's me."

He immediately realized he had said something quite stupid: that was what he should have said at the door when he knocked, while she still didn't know who was outside. Francesca's eyes reflected a certain surprise. Confused, Cristòfol sat down, took a pomegranate and began to peel it. She continued to stare at him, dumbstruck. Her eyes, her spirit had not experienced such intensity for years. He sensed Francesca had begun to see he was acting a bit unsure of himself, like a disoriented animal set loose in the woods. And Mardà was startled when he asked himself another question: "Am I really floating, adrift?"

He put down the pomegranate, hurried into the house, went straight to the bedroom, and lay down on the bed. When Francesca came to him, he would yell at her . . . but his wife didn't come to him. Cristòfol, suddenly overcome by exhaustion, fell asleep.

He didn't leave the house for a month. He barely spoke to Francesca. She had served him his dinner at the table and that first night, like a ghost in her floor-length white chemise, sad and lost in thought, had lain down beside him in bed. Cristòfol sat on the bench out back, morning and evening, watching the foliage in the little garden fade a bit more each day. Autumn was getting on. In a gust of wind the leaves would suddenly swirl up from the ground. His old comrades would come to visit him. Orlandis would know by now that he, Cristòfol Mardà Taltavull, had returned . . . Orlandis at his feet.

But nobody came to see him. Finally, one night he asked Francesca: "What are they saying about me in town, now that I have returned?"

"Returned? Who returned?"

"Who else, you blockhead! Me!"

"I don't know. . . . They don't say anything."

"Nothing?"

"Nothing."

"But aren't they afraid because I'm back?"

"Yes. . . . I mentioned it at the butcher's, and to some Taltavull cousins and some others."

"And so?"

"And so what?"

"I'll shit on your very soul, I swear, Francesca! What do they think of me, what are they saying about me, about the fact that I'm back in Orlandis?"

"They say, 'Well . . . Hmm . . . ,' things like that."

Cristòfol was seized by a trembling rage. He wanted to strangle the woman. He downed two glasses of wine one after the other. He asked her again, this time about some of his Falangist friends, "and Serafí, and Macià Simona, and Mitger, and the two Puigdorfilas, and Telm, and Baltasar Prim, and . . . ? Haven't any of them asked about me? Why haven't they come to visit?"

Francesca answered him as she said her rosary, her mind quietly functioning on two levels, "Telm died. Mitger, too. One of the Puigdorfilas lives in Palma and the other, Eusebio, is all crippled up in a wheelchair and can't walk. Sometimes I run into Serafí. . . . Who else did you say?"

"Baltasar Prim, Macià Simona, Antonio from Sanàbria, the two Cantós, father and son."

"Oh, I see Simona's wife quite often. Old man Cantó died, too. The one from Sanàbria . . . I don't know . . . he used to rent chaises lounges to the tourists on the beach down by Les Exèquies."

"You mean they haven't asked for me?" He got up with a menacing look on his face. "Did you tell them I didn't want to see them?"

"Tòfol, I haven't said a thing, nor has anyone asked me anything. If you don't mind, let me finish my rosary."

"Go get Macià Simona tomorrow and tell him to come over right away! And that's . . . an order!"

"Yes."

Macià Simona arrived punctually. He walked with difficulty, his legs terribly swollen; he was being helped by a grandson, a robust and energetic lad who shook Mardà's hand heartily: "Glad to meet you. My grandfather has spoken often of you. Now that we finally have a democracy here in Spain, this is the time when Orlandis needs people from the war who know how to run things. We admire them."

Mardà was taken aback. Did that young man mean they had to break up the republic or the democracy again, or had he grotesquely confused everything? He turned his head questioningly toward Simona, who vaguely shrugged his shoulders and said to his grandson, "Of course! Hey, come back for me in a couple of hours." Once they were alone, Macià Simona broke into a crying fit: "Tòfol! Tòfol!, what a joy to have you back! Tòfolito! Tòfolito!"

Mardà stomped his foot on the floor impatiently, "Quit that crying! Your grandson, what does he think, what does he say? Why exactly does he admire me so much? Who is he speaking for?"

"Tòfol, my son. . . . Fifty years have passed between us since the war. He's the best grandson I have. A very well-meaning lad. Today's youth are like that . . . if they're not on drugs. You can't ask any more of them. He knows about you and then he doesn't," and his tears welled up again. "Tòfol! You have no idea how happy I am to see you, Tòfol!"

"Damn it Simona, stop pissing through your eyes! Why didn't you come to see me before?"

"Oh, I didn't know you were back. And since you didn't let anybody know. . . . I thought maybe you wouldn't remember me. And sometimes I watch TV in the afternoon, and sometimes I go to see if there are still any figs on my trees, and the days just seem to fly by. Cristòfolito! Seeing you is the happiest thing that could happen to me before the Grim Reaper comes to get me!" Again Simona broke out crying. Angrily, Cristòfol Mardà started pacing up and down the room.

"Stop that, Macià, stop that bawling!"

"Ay, my boy . . . you have no idea how many times I've asked myself, 'What must Cristòfol be doing, way off in some foreign land? What must he be up to?' And not a single word from you!"

Cristòfol interrupted him: "What about the others, our comrades? None of them has come to see me. Do you ever get together? What do you do?"

"I don't get what you mean," said the fat, sweaty old man as he stared at Mardà, his mouth agape.

"I mean our gang: Prim, Sanàbria, Serafí, Puigdorfila, all of them. Have you had any trouble since Franco died? What do you think about now? This new king we've got is a traitor! Is anybody making plans to do something about it?"

Mardà Taltavull then realized he had made a mistake: nothing like that was in the works at all. It was his old wartime self that had stubbornly insisted on asking the questions, the self that had planned his return to Orlandis, not the self that was in Orlandis, alone and forgotten. Macià Simona scratched the back of his neck, musing: "You put me in a difficult position. Some of our comrades are dead; others come and go. And we've not been bothered by anybody from the other side at all. Why should they? Our lives go on just the same, with or without Franco. My father had even said times were better under King Alfonso. As for plans, what plans do you mean? I see that fellow from Sanàbria sometimes in the café, and we play dominoes together . . . or do you mean the plan to collect social security?"

"What?"

"The old age pension. They pay me thirty thousand pesetas a month. You should apply for it too. You are probably on the qualifying list from the time you worked for the union. Even though you didn't pay anything into it while you were in America, you should at least get the minimum . . . and every little bit helps me bear my cross . . . or have you returned with your pockets loaded?"

Cristòfol didn't bother to answer, but instead tried for the last time to probe into the vast hole that was opening before him, deeper and deeper.

"Do they hate me? What do people say about me? I'm ready to face up to them; you know me!"

"Cristòfolito, I don't know how to say this. . . ."

The old man's gaze wandered off to one side, as if he had lost something.

"Some families don't like you, that's for sure, and that's understandable. But nobody's doing anything about it anymore. Anyway, we did what we had to do during the war: clean the scum out of this town. I don't think I've heard more than two comments about your return, and that from people like me, who can still remember their youth. Ah, Cristòfol, what a time that was! Aye, I sit here looking at you and I can't believe it's really you! Oh, Cristòfolito!"

Cristòfol Mardà didn't get together with Macià Simona again, but he did start to get out of the house more. He didn't notice much that had changed. A lot of yachts bearing foreign flags were berthed down at the port, and a lot of new apartments houses had been built and rented out to foreigners. The streets had been paved. He ran into a few people he recognized, but not many. Some of the aged faces reminded him of other, younger faces, but he couldn't put a name to them. Then there were young faces in whose eyes he caught a glint of some friend or family from his past.

"What the hell am I going to do?" he asked himself in anguish, looking cautiously around and thinking of himself.

"What will I do? Where will I go if I leave here?" was the next, even more unfathomable question.

A few people nodded their heads to him in a casual, superficial hello, out of curiosity. Others whom he recognized looked past him with indifference and kept on walking. He saw surprise sketched on two of the faces.

"Were they afraid of me?" he pondered, but abandoned the thought. He was standing before a shop window and noticed his reflection in it: he still looked robust, but heavy and pudgy. Cristòfol didn't feel like visiting any of his relatives. He wouldn't have known what to say to them.

He felt moments of cold fury, of anger at himself and everybody else. And then there were the moments of depression when there didn't seem to be any way out of his predicament. He still had some money left. He started giving Francesca a certain amount each week; she accepted it without a word. In the late afternoons, he took long walks along the wharf and through the narrow, porticoed streets. He sat on a hotel terrace, sipping an espresso as he watched the waves gently lapping the shore.

When had Cristòfol started playing this delirious mental game? While on his walks, while drinking coffee, and especially when he felt consumed with irritation and blamed everybody else for his woes, he would feel swamped by it all and swear to himself that if they didn't hate him, he would hate them instead—specifically his old comrades, the ones who were no longer the gritty characters he had known in the old days, and especially the only one he had talked with, that idiot Macià Simona. It helped him to release his pent-up tension by having a target to unload on. The town was only an abstraction, inaccessible to him.

As a child, Mardà used to invent jolly tales of pirates and the far west with himself as the hero, reliving each fantasy in all its savory details, oblivious to everything around him.

During that autumn of his return he subconsciously began to blame his old gang: they were responsible for the present disastrous state of things. And when his mind rebelliously raised the question, "What disaster?" he pushed it impatiently aside. He could no longer remain objective in these, to him, surreal circumstances. He had lost all sense of perspective because Orlandis— and he on his return to Orlandis—now formed a reality and a personality that, viewed calmly, scared him because he neither recognized the town nor himself.

Francesca tried to get his attention by saying, "Cristòfol, you have to decide what we're going to do, or what you want to do."

Mardà Taltavull didn't bother to answer her, for other thoughts were running through his mind: "That pack of idiots and deserters. . . ." His old gang were no longer his comrades. They had become something else: "Renegades! They deserve to be punished. They'll find out what's good for them!" He would settle accounts with them: "They'll beg for their lives on their knees!" He needed to feel someone opposing him in order to reaffirm his own identity; he needed to struggle in order to exist. The others were his prisoners since they had not declared him theirs. He would kick up a fuss with every one of them.

He neither saw nor heard anything; he would walk for three hours feverishly plotting. Soon the rainy season would arrive. He well remembered those dark afternoons with Orlandis under leaden thunderheads, the sea riled, showering the town with its salty spray, nobody on the streets. Macià Simona would probably be at home, alone. His daughter and son-in-law would be working at their pastry shop. The old man would be sitting in his kitchen, nodding in front of the TV. The door wouldn't be locked, and if it were, it would be just a hook that wouldn't resist a stout push. Cristòfol would put on a ski mask and go in.

And he would chop off Macià Simona's right hand with a machete blow . . . the hot stream of blood, the nerve ends wriggling like snakes. When Simona began to wail, he would kick his face in, crushing it. Would he bleed to death, or die of gangrene? Wasn't Macià a diabetic? If he died, so much the better. But it was all the same to him because if he didn't die, Cristòfol would see to the *coup de grâce*. Then he would scrawl FASCIST! on the wall in Simona's own dark blood. The outrage would leave Orlandis in shock.

He would get back into action soon. He would toss a can of gasoline and a lighted rag into another old comrade's house. The blaze would light up the night and devour everything in its path like a famished beast. Then Cristòfol would send an anonymous letter to that old turncoat judge, his cousin Ignasi Taltavull Oliva. He would write, "Every fascist shall be punished!" All those old geezers would piss their pants in fear! He knew them all too well. Cristòfol Mardà laughed as he thought about it. And the whole town would be undermined by suspicion, confusion, and guilt, just like in the old days. Mardà rubbed his hands together, anxiously pacing around in a circle on his back porch, a driven man. He started to snicker as he drummed his fingers on the window pane: he would stone his own windows and report it to the police to divert suspicion from himself.

That's the way he would make his statement; he would take over center stage! "That's Cristòfol Mardà!" the whole town of Orlandis would exclaim in fear and awe. Mardà would preside over the funeral of Macià Simona, the crested imperial flag draped over his coffin, Mardà looking defiantly from side to side at the crowds gathered along the streets as the procession passed, the masses duly impressed, as he. . . .

The voice of his wife, who was staring at him from the bedroom window, snapped him out of his reverie.

"What on earth are you up to? Why are you walking around like that, laughing to yourself? It's eleven o'clock. You look like a stubborn old bull, head down, ready to charge! You're going to go crazy, Tòfol." And Francesca carefully closed the blinds and crawled back into bed.

He stood there, confused. He took a closer look at himself: he had been marching around the back porch like a soldier on parade. And yes, it was eleven o'clock at night. A weak light bulb hung from the porch ceiling, a moth fluttering around it. A mosquito bit him. The muffled rumble of a distant motor boat reached him from the port. There was no funeral, no cheering crowds. Suddenly the world seemed an immense exhausting void to him, with no road for him to travel, however hard he searched. Nobody even knew he existed. Except Francesca. Cristòfol and Francesca, two doddering old wrecks, exhausted flesh.

Barely able to lift his feet from the floor, Mardà shuffled off to the bedroom. A few weak rays of light filtered through the blinds from the porch. Francesca was asleep in the shadows, her breathing barely audible. Cristòfol could smell her, the rank odor of a tired old body. He pulled back the covers and stared: this woman resembled just another rag among the sheets, her wrinkled white nightgown barely outlining the skeleton beneath it, her legs as thin as sticks. And her face was a dark, amorphous mask, her hair in disarray. He stared at her in utter amazement; she was the last port of call on his voyage; she was the only person to whom he still meant something.

Cristòfol Mardà straightened up, his muscles tensing as he noisily sucked in air through his nose. He was somebody! Yes, he was! He grabbed his walking stick from the coat rack. He was somebody, and he would impose himself on others, and then the whole world would know who he was! Yes, other people, and the entire world, all in one: Francesca. His first blow struck her on the cheek and ear. She raised herself partway up in bed, then slumped back, dazed. The second blow echoed with a dry, bony thwack on her legs. She cried out weakly, as though she were trying to wake up. Cristòfol kept on thrashing her, panting and sweating furiously, his purple face strangely contorted. . . .

Cristòfol Mardà, breathing heavily, stood there in the doorway, waiting in the tense darkness outside Taltavull Hall. The wind slowly died down. A taxi rumbled low at the entrance gate.

"Good evening, Cristòfol, what's new?" Bernat greeted him aseptically. Paula added, harshly, "This is no time to be coming around."

She then fell silent before Mardà could utter a word. A strange atmosphere surrounded the man, as if he had turned to stone.

"I wanted to ask you if you would have me as your guest for dinner. I used to spend Christmas Eves here as a child."

The brother and sister stood there, dumbstruck. Paula stammered, "Dinner? Here, with us?"

Mardà paid no attention to her, "I'm not alone. My wife is over there in the taxi. She's in a cast. She's been in the hospital for the last two weeks. I used to come here to Taltavull Hall when I was a child. Your grandparents were my grandparents. The fireplace was always smoky."

Bernat the Wise tried to use his wits, "Well, of course. . . . We hadn't counted on any more guests. We'd have to see if. . . ."

Paula hastily added, "And it's not just us! The others should have a say in this as well, Bernat. And that's not good manners, Cristòfol, showing up uninvited like this."

Once again Mardà interrupted her, his voice deep and husky, "I'm alone; Francesca and I are all alone."

The night had settled into a balsamic stillness, giving the feeling it would never end. Bernat Taltavull raised his head, allowing a serenity to filter through his words, a serenity born in another place long before their time. Three persons gathered there, attempting to make some sense out of the fleeting nature of their lives.

"Well, isn't one man just like another? Come on in, and we'll celebrate Christmas together!"

17

The smoke had been slowly clearing the room . . . only a fine haze remained. They had turned on all the lights in the great hall. Furniture, people and walls all appeared new, sharply defined, shimmering. The assembled Taltavulls numbered about forty in all, some of whom were tripping through the springtimes of their lives with great eagerness; others were living their autumn years in high spirits. They were all seated around the long table, chatting with each other, eating with gusto, insisting that everyone try a bit of every dish and take part in all the joy surrounding them. The grandfather clock from La Paret, which Bernat the Wise had been tinkering with, gonged forth the midnight hour in triumph.

Everyone applauded.

They broke the milky crust on the salt-covered grouper served on large platters. They peeled back its tough, scaly skin. The fish gave off a light aroma, tinged with a perfume from the sea; its flesh was tender and opaque. Someone rose and poured a thin trickle of olive oil over it. The wine was white, lightly fruity, and cooled to perfection.

"There's enough grouper for seconds!" trumpeted Marianna Mas.

"Another round of wine, that's what I want!" crowed Joan Pere Tudurí.

"Children, it's orange juice for you," recommended Marieta Verònica.

"At the bottom of the sea, everything is finely textured: the fish, the algae, even the water in its many colors and movements. It doesn't seem possible, as huge and powerful as the sea is," mused Dioclecià of Pula. Tudurí started to laugh, his mouth full of fish, but only managed to mumble instead: "I have seen some fish you wouldn't believe; they ate grass, just like a cow or a rabbit!"

"Joan Pere, don't overdo it," warned Albert the Younger.

Alexandre Tudurí looked at his brother in admiration: "What you haven't seen, you rascal!"

"Do you mean they also had fur like rabbits?" Càndida Moro asked in bewilderment as she scolded the twins for fussing with their food.

"And where was that?" asked one of the guests from Pula.

"In Burma," Tudurí declared emphatically.

"Burma? So, if . . . ," commented Bernat in surprise.

"Tell us the story, Joan Pere, tell us!" demanded Egèria excitedly.

Pollònia wiped a tear from her eye, "That son of mine will come to a bad end someday in one of those godless places."

Joan Pere Tudurí half-drained his glass of wine, ran his tongue over his lips and began his story:

"I remember that day well; it was an afternoon in Rangoon, the streets devilishly dusty, the sun exuberant, obscene in its intensity. There wasn't a soul on the long, deserted streets that seemed to stretch on into infinity. The few shops were closed. The Burmese were drowsily huddled in the shade of the temples, the air heavy with the enchantment of incense, swarms of torpid flies suspended in the hot and heavy air.

"I was just wandering around. It was a Buddhist or socialist holiday, something like that. Over there, politics and religion go hand in hand. I had already met with and given dinner parties for the bureaucrats in the Department of Commerce, and my patience was near its end. I was waiting for an order that finally came, though ridiculously small, in spite of all the haggling they did before signing it. It seems they preferred to buy their alarm clocks from Australia. And that's fine with me. They made their bed and they can lie in it.

"The capital city was made up of endless rows of fragile bamboo shanties, little cubicles always about to be engulfed by the lush, ever-encroaching vegetation. The suburb of apartment houses where British bureaucrats had lived when Burma was their colony had become a dirty, sordid sector of the city. Once I ate in a restaurant—very expensive, by the way—where the floor was made of bamboo canes.

"That was the afternoon I had gone into the Botatong pagoda, attracted I suppose by the faint illusion of coolness its miserable little garden offered. That's where the thing with the fish happened. As I was crossing a small bridge over a pond, I thought I was seeing things. The first vision struck me when I looked down into the shallow, mossy pond and saw an enormous number of goldfish tightly packed together, swimming over and under each other. There was barely any room between them. I couldn't believe my eyes: it seemed incredible that so many fish could fit in one place. They were all sizes, large, small, and middle-sized, all of them fat and gleaming. You could have harvested bushels of them with just a hand net. And little groups of turtles were swimming around them."

"Those little people must not have much of a craving for fish," commented Damià.

"Not for the ones in the pagoda, at least, because they are considered sacred," Tudurí clarified before continuing his story. "And here is where the second vision captured my eye: the faithful and other visitors to the pagoda were throwing handfuls of grass to the fish. And those sleek fish slid and splashed and jumped right out of the water, fighting for the grass, devouring it! They were gobbling it up like rabbits do here, yessir! I was so surprised by what I saw that I didn't react at once when somebody in the crowd touched my hand, and—but that's another story."

"No! Joan Pere, tell us now!" insisted Beautiful Egèria with her radiant eyes.

"Was it a Burmese girl—or whatever they call them—who had fallen in love with you and was groping you?" inquired Sebastiana insolently.

"You're always thinking the worst! Well, at that moment I didn't know who it was . . . there were so many Burmese surrounding me. But I noticed someone had tucked a small piece of rolled-up paper in my hand with a message written on it in pidgin English, something like 'Seek in the temples Môn de Pagan, where C. S. was often seen these last months.'

"I was of course perplexed, all the more so because my attention was still fixed on those grass-eating fish, until I was suddenly dragged into the sanctuary by two timid but agitated English-looking youths.

"They pulled me into the starry labyrinth of the sanctuary, a space of deceptive walls, mosaics made of little mirror-like bits of tin, located right below the golden high altar where they keep I-don't-know-what, a tooth or a hair from the Buddha's head. And right there they were, among the mass of shattered images reflected from the glittering tin—Ruth and Charles were their names. He was stammering and she was blushing from the uneasiness and confusion weighing upon them as they explained to me the woeful story of their father, Colonel Horace Marcus Singleton, the C. S. in the note.

"He had been a colonel in Her Gracious Britannic Majesty's Army, in its intelligence service. He had served in the Second World War against the Japanese there in Burma. Those were hard times. A Japanese who is given the order to do something is frightening because he does it. Anyway, the English had to abandon Burma on the fourth of January 1948, the date set for Burmese independence, chosen with enigmatic care by the local astrologers. But before leaving, Horace Marcus Singleton had carefully woven an espionage network that survived in its own methodically fruitful way until the leftist coup d'état by Ne Win in 1962."

"Spies! Danger! Assassinations . . . I'm all atremble!" simpered Adelina, as she wriggled in her seat.

"Well you're wrong, little cousin. Back then I knew quite a bit about those things; and, contrary to what the ignorant public thinks, that kind of activity requires self-assurance and calm because if problems arise, the agents have to discreetly disappear and hide out. That's why Colonel Singleton decided to return in person to reorganize his network.

"But not without first having gone through a rigorous training period in India, his supposed destination as an expert in butterflies. And that itself was a risky business, strange as it may seem, requiring technical skill because you have to be prepared to leap around on dangerous terrain in order to catch the iridescent little creatures, guessing their type and characteristics while they're still fluttering around before your nose. According to his children, Singleton caught them in abundance, and he could expound on their characteristics, as for example the *Teinopalpus imperialis,* its wings resembling the shadow of a bat; the *Thaumantis diores,* decked in almost transparent opaline spots; the *Brahmaea wallichi,* with its ostentatious design, resembling the most fantastic of saris; the *Papilio arcturus,* black and pretentious. . . ."

"Ah, Joan Pere, how nice it is that you know the scientific names of all the butterflies!" praised the engineer Albornoz.

"Just by accident, really. Singleton's two children stuffed me with all sorts of data about butterflies. And the colonel, armed with a net, cork boxes, and black-headed pins to capture and mount the creatures, crossed the border into Burma disguised as a butterfly hunter, wandering hither and yon, recruiting agents as he went . . . until he disappeared. There was no news of him for so long that he was officially declared missing.

"And that's when his desperate children decided to set out in search of him on their own. And that little note given to them by a bewildered and frightened confidant and erroneously passed to me was the only indication they had of his whereabouts. I realized Ruth and Charles were noble but helpless children, and so I helped them as much as I could by accompanying them to Pagan, which lies to the northeast.

"In those backward countries, often governed by dictators, if you don't find some distraction to keep your mind off your work while you're waiting for the details of a contract to be settled, you could go mad. Isolated and alone, thinking only of your work, you fall prey to depression and irritation, and you wind up fighting the people you're negotiating with, and that can ruin the deal. That's why, as a sort of therapy, I was trying to collect data on the Portuguese adventurer De Brito who had dreamed of founding an empire that would dominate the whole Gulf of Bengal. In 1613 he was impaled upon the wall of his own factory in Syriam, south of Rangoon, where he died after three days of wrenching agony."

"Interesting," noted Dioclecià of Pula.

"Yes, but I abandoned that project because the colonel's children seemed more promising," continued Joan Pere as he downed another glass of wine.

"And so we took off in an old, rattletrap twin-engined Fokker. It roared and bellowed as we cruised for miles and miles at tree-top level over the evergreen jungle, the hunting ground of the great Bengal tiger. The pilot covered the windscreen of the cockpit with newspaper so that the sun wouldn't blind him and force us to lose our way—one that was hard enough to follow in any case.

"We finally landed in an open field near Pagan, between scraggly fig trees and a flock of goats. It was getting dark ... the sun had become a huge, orange-colored ball. The effect was hypnotic, as if all the stars in the galaxy were coming at us. It seemed to hang there over that vast plain of livid, transparent phosphorescence, while in the distance a pale, diaphanous veil of vapors rose above the Irawaddy River.

"I knew Pagan had a population of about four thousand people, but I never would have imagined that it also contained about five thousand temples. I shivered as I gazed upon their decaying, eccentrically etched profiles against the setting sun, their peaked roofs jutting up into the deserted, dusky landscape. Have any of you ever read the work of an esoteric, sleep-walking writer from Providence, Rhode Island, by the name of Howard Phillips Lovecraft? Mysteries and thrillers are the most intriguing reading on airplane flights. Well, just as in Lovecraft's stories, those temples in Pagan rose up into the evening sky like luxurious, ruinous monuments to the long-forgotten, blasphemous beliefs of the natives.

"The breeze whispered through pagodas resembling monumental bells, rising in pyramidal steps, a series of terraced roofs, all of them terribly tall, ghost-like constructions of sienna-colored brick. And they all stood there in decay, walls crumbling, doors off their hinges, always open, as if those holy places had been suddenly abandoned long ago, or some invisible spirits lingered there, awaiting the return of their abominable gods ... cobwebs, dust, and ruin.

"The temples belonged to the Môn, the people who had originally conquered the country; they were later defeated by the Burmese, whose temples were always well-kept and freshly repainted, overflowing with devoted and faithful parishioners. But there was not a single follower to be found in those bizarre Môn monuments with their narrow windows and darkly arched chambers connected by damp, shadowy corridors. Their steep, vertiginous stairways rose toward the apex, where the light breeze became a cutting wind."

Tudurí looked off into the distance as if possessed and declared, "I know their names, those from the world of the Môn: Patothamya, Nagayon, Shwégugyi, Ananda. . . . They appeared over a thousand years ago, a delirious manifestation of Theravada Buddhism, or that of the Small Vehicle. And within their secret central chambers, they still guard a molar of the Master, a sandal, a nail clipping. Each temple had its own slaves who could never be set free and were forced to cultivate the earth and beg on the streets to support their cult. Statues and paintings of the great Buddha continued to glow from within the walls, some of them depicting him in disquieting, majestically flowing robes.

"But they all lie there now, decapitated, scarred, and abandoned. The Mongol hordes ravaged them, time has chiseled away at them, the unscrupulous have robbed them. And in the temples' darkest corners on the cool irregular flagstones a cobra suddenly coils, hisses and probes with its piercing eyes. And the silence of it all devours you."

"Pardon me, but what happened to the colonel and his two children? Why do you keep digressing so much?" interrupted Damià, the surly sociologist.

Joan Pere seemed to come down from a cloud as he continued, "Singleton and his two beautiful children? Yes, well. . . . Actually, I don't know what happened to them. It got to be a boring adventure. So I continued on, from temple to temple, seduced by that remote and indecipherable message. Later, in India, I was able to interview the Dalai Lama, a very intelligent gentleman with glasses and a shaved head, the god and king of Tibet. He was the reincarnation of Buddha himself. 'And what is Buddhism?' I asked him. And he answered, 'It is something so immense that each believer may choose from it what he likes best.'"

18

"So, is it time for the groupers now?" asked the distracted widow Magdalena.

"In Pula, it's Pula time," declared Dioclecià as the other Pulans laughed mockingly.

Albert the Younger was perplexed and asked Arcadi Frau the priest, sitting at his side, chomping away noisily, "Do you think Joan Pere has become a Buddhist, according to what he just said?"

The priest grumbled something about "spirituality" and continued munching his food. Among the chattering group of children, Niní was carefully constructing a tower of toothpicks as she whispered to Pere and nodded in the direction of the pathetic Francesca and the droopy-headed Cristòfol Mardà, who was sullenly staring around the crowded table with his bovine eyes: "First we had to take in that repugnant old deaf guy, Dídac, and now it's these two, who just got out of the hospital or something. What a drag! It feels like an asylum in here! We'll see if we get to dance after supper."

Suddenly Marianna Mas scraped her chair back and covered her mouth with her napkin. Her alarmed husband said, "What's the matter?" She replied worriedly, "Nothing, just that I—pardon me—felt like I was going to throw up. After so much time in that stuffy kitchen I feel a little faint."

"Go out and get some fresh air," suggested her daughter, Marieta Verònica. "Between the smoke and the crowd, it's pretty stuffy in here, too."

"You're right. I guess I'll go out on the porch."

Marianna left the hall, wearing a tight black-and-white print dress, ostentatious earrings, heavy bracelets, and a double string of pearls around her neck. Her dark hair accented her appetizing body, her medium height, her admirable hips and breasts.

She paced back and forth on the porch for a while. The lamp gave off a tenuous glow, menaced by the encroaching dark. Marianna became alarmed; as her physical discomfort quickly receded, she felt the night isolating her, devouring her, as if she were being carried away from the house in the tail of a comet. She leaned against the moist railing. The cold, invisible valley before her was swallowed up in the murk and damp. The moan of the wind rose in tone then subsided into deep surges.

She felt her soul being drawn out of her, inexorably, tenderly, like a huge suction cup was upon her breast: Marianna was being drawn away from Taltavull Hall to the ship, the ships. As a little girl she had heard the story of the Phantom Ship many times. Before she was born, it had sailed invisibly back and forth at the mouth of Orlandis harbor. Marianna had used her imagination to reconstruct the ship in all its gloomy dereliction as it rose and fell on the swells, manned only by the pitiful spirits of its dead sailors, composed of the dreams of the men whose lives the shipwreck had cut short, of the irreparable mistakes made by that condemned and vanished crew. And when as a young lady she used to long for something she could not have, and the desire for it languished bitterly within her, she would imagine as she stared out the window that her body was floating on the waves toward the Phantom Ship.

And she had really found the ship, that night she sailed on the steamer to Menorca, its sluggish hull humming to the rhythm of the motor and the waves. Marianna leaned alone against the ship's rail as she felt her senses drawn back to her troubled adolescence. The wind and the night closed in on her, leaving only the faint yellow glimmer of the lights on the bridge. Then she remembered: "I'm on the Phantom Ship!" She sighed to herself in astonishment.

And now on Christmas Eve at Taltavull Hall, immersed in that noisy night of doleful solitude, as Marianna brushed up against the damp railing she could have quietly wept, for it gave her the feeling she was embarking again on that ship, but in reverse, heading toward the devastating certainty of what we can never be. Marianna was a lively person who thrived on optimism and action. But a moment's fatigue depressed her to the point where all her life's decisions, her struggle for self-affirmation, seemed to amount to nothing. The impassive Phantom Ship, the wet railing. Marianna started to sob.

Marianna and Bernat had never left the island of Majorca except on that steamer trip to Menorca when he had to get a contract signed for the manufacture of plastic sandals for the tourist trade.

"Since the hard times after the Civil War kept us from having a real honeymoon, why don't we try to make up for it with a week in Menorca?" he proposed.

There were not many passengers on the modest steamer, with its small dining room of polished wood and brass and the brisk waiters with their baroque Sevillian soup tureens. Scenes from oriental films Marianna had seen in the Orlandis cinema danced through her head: a sharply dressed adventurer in a white dinner jacket, ceiling fans, Malayan servants. The pitch and roll of the ship made Bernat seasick, and he retired early to his cabin and soon fell asleep.

However, Marianna's head was still charged with a dream-like vision, both familiar and fearful: she was floating on the sea, drawn inexorably to the unsatisfied spirits of the Phantom Ship. She had barely paid attention to the tale of the woman and the boat Honorat Moro had recounted in the smoke-filled hall. It was quite different from the one she had heard and reinvented as a child. But the boat and the Phantom Ship derived from the same mystery and were getting under way again.

Marianna, on her way to Menorca, opened her porthole and peered out at the deserted deck, splashed by the black waves. From the leeward, the breeze caressed her face with a disconcerting delicacy.

A woman's figure appeared on deck and leaned against the railing. Marianna Mas recognized her in the faint light: a foreigner whom she had observed dining alone that evening. She must have been about Mariana's age, thirty-five or so. Perhaps she was German, short, with a coarse face. She must have spoken only her own language because she had made herself understood to the waiter with signs. She was wearing a pair of wrinkled pants and a sloppy sweater. Marianna continued to watch her and the dark sea. The woman seemed hypnotized by the murk, by the glitter of the cresting waves giving the impression the ship was being followed by a school of whales. Time passed.

A ship's officer, a young lad with an immaculate uniform, appeared on deck for his routine tour of inspection. He barely noticed the foreign woman. But as he passed behind her, she turned toward him and said something to him with an inviting smile.

"Pardon me?" the officer responded.

She pointed toward the sea and the ship and spoke and smiled. He expressed his confusion with gestures. The woman drew near him and laid her hand on his chest. The officer stiffened as she lowered her hand to his abdomen, his waist, his fly. She stopped there but continued moving her hand as if she were kneading bread dough. The lad doubled up as if he had been hit in the gut. Then he straightened up, held her buttocks with one hand, drew her closer with the other, and kissed her. They went into an intense embrace.

The officer pointed to his watch and indicated that she should wait for him there. He left. She leaned back indolently, with a sleepy, wanton smile. Marianna's heart was pounding as she stared wide-eyed at the couple. A flush of desire invaded her, her sex about to explode. She envied the foreign woman. How she longed to be embraced by that young man. He returned shortly, gripped the German girl by the shoulders and steered her down the stairs.

Marianna Mas felt exhausted and more lonely than ever, breathing with difficulty, sweating. Bernat was sound asleep. Marianna had never been with any other man. Was that what she really wanted now? She had no answer. She loved her husband and felt no real need to be unfaithful to him. But he was so familiar by now. . . . And it seemed to her a deep, humiliating slavery to have to spend the rest of her life deprived of an experience she darkly imagined might not only be essential to her survival, but also exalting. At that moment, she wanted to be penetrated, electrified.   ·

"The hell with husbands and all that shit!" she grumbled under her breath.

She went into the tiny bathroom in their stateroom, took off all her clothes and washed her crotch and armpits. She felt driven toward a dubious, sticky rebellion. She felt as if she were suffocating. She splashed some cologne on her pubis. The aroma made her feel drunk.

She climbed up into her bunk and touched her sex, began to rub it with increasing vigor: a boiling heat rose in her entrails, and a cry of pleasure inundated her. The hoarse blast of the ship's fog horn filled the cabin night.

She relived those lost hours there on the porch at Taltavull Hall. A quarter of a century had gone by, but the gnawing spark of passion that had swept over her that night on the open sea and had blossomed into a sterile act of self-gratification, still sent an anxious shiver through her body . . . the aftertaste of defeat in all its deep and unexplorable ramifications: "I cannot, nor do I want to, nor am I able to strike out on my own," she said to herself dully.

Marianna seemed to awaken from her reverie. She looked around her through the curtain of darkness. She smiled, distressed but at peace, knowing she could still imagine as she had as a child that the Phantom Ship sailed darkly through the windy valley with her standing on deck, without anything to do or say. But she was no longer a little girl, and she knew the ship was in truth herself.

Almost unawares, she began to softly caress her belly, then lowered her hand to her thigh. She felt her breathing increase. Her sex was crying out to her. She hoisted her dress and put her hand in her panties. She felt a muggy heat where her thighs joined; her crotch hairs were soaked. With her middle finger and index she felt out her clitoris, hard and demanding. A flush of joy invaded her as she began to move her fingers with energy . . . she was soon flying, groaning, "Oh . . . Oh . . . Oh!"

19

The Taltavull boys, Pere, Alexandre, Carles, and Andreu were absorbed in their eating. After playing with the little computer in the coach house between the big mule cart, the cabriolet, and the cobwebbed harnesses, Pere had brought out a tape recorder and a tape. And what they had heard on that tape was still resounding in their heads. Were those voices real, or were they just noises they had imagined to be voices? They were not sure what they believed, or what they should believe, but they were in any case deeply impressed.

Pere had heard of the existence of psychophonics on a TV program. And then one calm and very dark night blown free of clouds by a cutting north wind, the boy had ridden out to Taltavull Hall on his motorbike with the key to the house in his pocket. He had made up some excuse or other to get the key from his father, Bernat the Wise.

The valley lay there, black and still. No movement, everything a cosmic peace. A sheep's bell tinkled in the distance. The house loomed darker than the shadows themselves, as if it were guarding something enormously solid, as if instead of being empty it were filled with an all-encompassing power that packed its every corner.

Pere turned on the lights in the great hall—the same one where they were now eating—and had the disquieting impression that someone had just left it. Not even a sigh disturbed the silence. With a knot in his throat, the boy went up to the stairway landing and closed the little window that had been left open. That seemed to him the ideal spot. He carefully placed the tape recorder on the floor and loaded it with a two-hour tape. Then he turned it on and left.

It was eleven thirty. His motorbike thundered down the gravel road. The boy felt as if the ghostly mass of the building were zigzagging after him, silently, persistently. He slept an uneasy sleep that night. Very early next morning, he returned to Taltavull Hall. It was a crisp autumn morning, sunless but pregnant with the coming light of dawn, as if the world had never known a day's fatigue. The trees appeared new and fresh to him, and the mountain trail inviting. The sea extended beyond the pines, flat and gray.

He went in and picked up the tape recorder then locked the house. No way did he want to listen to it there. He stopped between the two crude cement entrance pillars, parked, and sat down on a pomegranate log with the recorder on his knees. The open country gave him a sense of warmth, of security. He pushed the play button.

The tape had run for two full hours, past one thirty. The psychophonics expert on TV had clearly stated that if the spirits of those who had previously lived in a house were still there, it would be possible to record them on tape.

The tape played on in the calm morning air. Nothing. Except, from time to time, some faint echoes of what sounded like a barely audible breeze. Twenty, forty minutes went by. Pere was beginning to get discouraged when he was devastated in the forty-third minute: a shrill, deafening racket and a chilling child's voice was pleading in a reedy, rising tone, "I want to live. . . . I want to live!"

Pere jumped up in a fright and looked around as if something were closing in on him. He turned off the recorder, jumped on his bike, and rode off in a spray of gravel. Once home in Orlandis, he felt calmer and turned on the recorder again. It was the same thin child's voice, weak and racked with infinite pain, begging for life. He let the tape run on. There were some hard-to-define noises, a sort of explosion, and that same weak, windy sound. And then three more human voices, three echoes that gave him goose pimples, then periods of silence, sounds of things being dragged about, confusing moans.

Some of the recorded sounds were a kind of dialog: "Pull hard!" or something like that, followed by a different voice that exclaimed, "Goddammit!"

Another sounded like an ill-tempered, effeminate vocalization of the scales do-re-mi-fa-sol, ending in a soft humming. The last one appeared toward the end of the tape and burst forth with astonishing clarity: "I know what I shall be, I know what I shall be, and so to sleep!"

Pere inquired of Grandmother Brígida and Uncle Taltavull Oliva, trying to clear up some of the mystery. But he didn't dare tell them of his recording experiment and how it had come to obsess him. He began to think there was something demoniacal, something of a desecration in it all. Until he confided his secret to his father. Bernat listened to the tape with a worried look on his face and ordered his son not to play it under any circumstance to Tomàs Moro, because he would think they were all crazy.

All the family dead whom Bernat Taltavull had known during their lifetimes, and all those he had heard of indirectly, formed the threads of stories and characters who were only vague shadows, echoes from the distant past.

He made some discreet inquiries among family members, the sum of which he used to begin to sketch out a disjointed and hair-raising gallery of horrors from beyond the grave, which both father and son studied and tried to make sense out of with fearsome care, with timorous daring.

It seems there had been a fire at Taltavull Hall when Bernat was just an infant, and his blond and chubby little brother, Ximet, had been swallowed up by the flames spiraling up the stairway. Bernat asked Brígida, "And what about little Ximetito, Mother? I don't know . . . didn't he scream or something?"

The old woman shook her head in grief, "He was a very beautiful child, and he kept saying he wanted to live."

Bernat opened, then closed his mouth as if he had wanted to ask her something else, but no words came out. And when Grandmother Brígida said the words "wanted to live," Pere noticed how his father's neck hairs bristled.

They weren't able to figure out the "I know what I shall be, I know what I shall be and so to sleep." There was an old broken-down piano in the attic at Taltavull Hall. Bernat remembered his father's sister-in-law, a gallant woman with a big mouth and an easy laugh, used to like to play it and sing. Vague, faint piano notes still echoed in the back of Bernat's mind.

As for the dialog, he remembered *La Bella de Orlandis,* the ship that belonged to his great-great-grandfather Porfirio Taltavull, its sails full to the wind, its bow slicing the waters to the south of Cabrera.

The old sea dog was missing a leg and used to set sail from Orlandis in his dirty, stinking wreck of a ship with a crew of equally dirty, crippled, hunch-backed, and toothless old men. Life and the sea had beaten them down. The only thing they had salvaged was their miserable physical existence, their hunger, their last hopes—and the lumbering, decrepit ship of that poisonous old Taltavull who had returned from the Antilles maimed and poor.

The old men used to fish the Rincón del Corneta at the mouth of Orlandis harbor. It was the only work they could do to earn a few cents and a basket of fish for their meager tables. One of them would stand watch out to sea from atop a cliff while the others either snored or argued with each other under the shade of a fig tree. Suddenly schools of sardines, sea perch, and sailfish would appear, and the lookout would bellow out his sighting. Then the gang doddered and stumbled to their nets, cursing and clumsily tossing the vast jumbles of string over the sea, and the fish got tangled in them.

Porfirio Taltavull had worked out a system. And for a couple of years it yielded meager, insignificant results for them. They would slowly set off to sea in *La Bella de Orlandis,* looking like a flock of plucked and mangy buzzards. They would navigate between Majorca and the Moorish Coast. When they spotted a Berber boat, or a little vessel flying a foreign flag, they would creep up on it slowly and board it by surprise with a frenetic, jolly ferocity. What that damned Porfirio most enjoyed, a bottle of rum in hand, was to cut out the tongues of his captives and watch them drown in their own blood as they bellowed like dumb beasts.

"Pull hard!" was probably what the sailors of the Spanish fleet shouted as they yanked the rope that hanged Porfirio, who probably grumbled "Goddammit," as he urinated on the mainmast of the frigate *Don Miguel de Cervantes Saavedra.*

20

A screaming Mother Moro had sent the twins to the kitchen to eat because they had been blowing into their soup with all their might and had spattered it all over the table. The two girls prattled on endlessly: "Mama is a stupid asshole."

"Yeah."

"I like the cat better than Mama."

"Me too."

"It's not right for cats not to have any money."

"Or guardian angels."

"We girls have guardian angels."

"Do you think Sinbad the Sailor has one?"

"Stupid asshole! Men don't have guardian angels."

"I didn't mean that! He's just in a story, and so he can have one. You're the stupid asshole."

"But I love Mama."

"And so do I!"

"I know a song you don't."

"Which one?"

"This one:

There were three little drums
came back from the war,
the tiniest of all
with a bunch of carnations!
Bunch, bunch, bumpity bunch!"

"I've got the hiccups."

"Jump up and down without breathing, and you'll get over it."

The twin jumped, swinging her arms wildly until she hit a pile of dirty plates. The clattering crash of the plates infuriated the women, and the twins were sent back into the hall.

21

"We should all get up and make a bow of appreciation: such a princely show deserves all the honors," announced commander Taltavull Oliva as he observed the arrival of the platters of chicken.

Adelina, Joana Maria, Niní, Aunt Paula, and Grandmother Brígida entered triumphantly, each bearing a platter with a gleaming, toasty-brown, well-basted fowl on it garnished with prunes, slices of lemon, and a succulent sauce. The rich aroma spread throughout the hall like a fog.

Bernat, brandishing the carving tools, spoke as he cut: "We have been able to raise these phenomenal birds in spite of the sad loss of Francesc de Borja, who left the estate in a mess as many of you know because he was the one running it. Since then we've had all kinds of problems here. The one with the seagulls, for example."

"Oh, how beautiful they are! They perch on the rocks by the sea, white as pigeons!" exclaimed Carloteta.

"More like devils!" admonished Bernat.

Skinny Gorio raised his serious little head and added, "That girl can't get anything right! Pigeons, ugh!"

"The fish in the sea are getting increasingly scarce," continued Bernat, "and the seagulls—I suppose you have noticed—have to fly further and further inland. You see whole flocks of them circling and screeching high in the sky, and when they spot something edible, they insolently fasten on it with their ravenous eyes and dive. They clean the olives off the olive trees; they peck about in the garbage dumps; rabbits with myxomatosis fall prey to their claws. When the rabbits drag themselves across the fields, blinded by green pus, the seagulls dive down and peck them to pieces.

"Then they started to appear in our barnyards, looking for the grain and chaff we feed to the pigs and chickens. But they soon acquired a taste for the baby chicks, and before we noticed, they had scattered the brood or gobbled up half of them. The chickens you are eating today are the ones we managed to save . . . and we had to do it with shotguns. We shot down a dozen seagulls and hung them out in the carob trees and prickly pear bushes with their wings spread. When the rest of them saw their companions hung out to dry, they flew off and never returned.

"Wasn't there any other way to get rid of them?" Albert asked.

"Yes, how horrible!" exclaimed Marieta Verònica.

"Don't nag me, daughter," answered Bernat the Wise. "And you, Albert, can criticize once I see you doing your share of the work around here. We had to stand guard against them for a whole week! They circled the house and raised an ungodly racket, as if they were threatening us."

"There's a Hitchcock film, *The Birds* or something like that, which shows cruel, treacherous gulls attacking human beings," added Damià.

"I believe you," said Bernat.

"You're all a bunch of beasts!" murmured Marieta Verònica.

"Do you know what else we put in the sauce? Honey!" announced Moro's wife Paula.

"Mmm, I can taste it," said Arcadi the priest appreciatively, as he sopped up more sauce from his plate with a piece of bread.

"The honey's also from Taltavull Hall! And I helped harvest it! I bought a book on bee culture," commented young Alexandre Tudurí.

"My God! Bees have no master and can kill you with their stingers!" lamented his mother, Pollònia.

"Are your hives healthy?" inquired the engineer Fèlix Albornoz, the Burgalese son-in-law of Bernat the Wise.

"Yes, in spite of the muddle left by Francesc de Borja, we have managed to get the farm back under control. It's hard to believe the amount of honey those thousands of bees make in each hive," answered his father-in-law.

"More than a few thousand!" the scandalized engineer replied. "Each hive contains from forty to sixty thousand bees. And the queen bee, who never sees the light of day, can lay as many as two thousand eggs daily, none of which are females unless a male bee fertilizes her eggs, and he only has to do it once in his lifetime. An army of worker bees surrounds the queen and feeds her royal jelly. They ventilate her chamber and harvest the nectar from the flowers. The queen lives for about four years, while the female workers barely last forty days. The queen stings to death the larvae capable of producing competing queens, forcing the worker bees to help her, much against their will."

The whole table sat open-mouthed, staring in astonishment at Fèlix Albornoz.

"Wow! That was like turning the light on in a dark room," exclaimed Honorat Moro.

"He's so vain! He thinks he's the professor and we're the school children," retorted Tomàs.

"Incredible!" Marianna Mas said admiringly, emerging from her detachment. "How they do work, those little creatures!"

"And hell, we didn't even know it," Bernat said, scratching his neck.

Grandmother Brígida raised her small white head and commented, "Honey. In Pula and here at Taltavull Hall we extract it for All Saints' Day. That's when we used to make huge batches of fine doughnuts that we soaked in bowls of honey. That sweet golden mess dripped all over. The doughnuts were golden brown. I liked them a lot. The church bells would ring all night in memory of the dead. Early in the morning you would wake up with that sweet honey taste in your mouth. There are little mice that are golden brown, too, and they live in the fields."

"What have the mice got to do with anything? The old lady is losing it. That's what we can all look forward to," muttered the widow Magdalena without a hint of bitterness.

Old Brígida had cocked her head at a quizzical angle and appeared to have heard, though nobody could be sure: "I don't know, but I don't seem to remember any of the really important things in my life. If you told me I never married Benigne, I would believe you. On the other hand, those little details like the flavor of honey in my warm morning bed, and the bells. I don't know why I thought they were coming from the mountains, ringing out between the peaks and the ravines where no man has ever gone, but I remember them! Just as if my whole life were a rosary of trivia like that.

"The mice used to run through the stubble, three or four at a time. How many years ago was it, that afternoon? The sun was about to set and had become an intense ball of light, of blazing colors that I don't think I've ever seen since. The brown rocks on Puig Gros near Pula seemed to be made of greased leather, they shone so brightly. And the wheat stubble was intensely yellow, like paint. Cattle were grazing, and there seemed to be a lot of sheep meandering up the valley as if that moment were when the world was about to begin again in a different way, and the fresh aroma of manure drifted through the air. There was a white cloud in the sky that looked like a dog's face . . . the mice ran in front of me, frolicking around and looking at me as if they were trying to tell me something."

Everyone was appalled. It had been a long time since Brígida had talked so much, and never that way. None of her children or her grandchildren had imagined she lived with those fine, subtle, and marvelous sensibilities in her, affecting her in the same way a gentle breeze makes the leaves of an elm tree tremble. Beautiful Egèria was about to break into tears, thinking, "And look at me: I don't love anything I have, and my only consolation is my world of fantasies."

"Imagine, that same afternoon," the old lady continued, "a little niece of mine named Jerònia and my daughter, Pollònia—two little girls—both saw the dog-faced cloud at Taltavull Hall. I had left them alone, and they were scared out of their wits."

"Yes! That's right!" confirmed Pollònia, "And even though we were scared by that apparition, we were just about to get on Jerònia's bike near the bridge when we saw a pale man with no eyes or teeth on another bike, a shotgun slung across his chest. What a shock!"

"Virgin Mary!" sighed Honorat Moro contemptuously.

Brígida, with a saintly look about her, her head tilted to one side, cut their comments short and returned to her fanciful stories with their capricious twists and turns: "The last time Jerònia came to see me, she sat in that same chair where Tomàs is sitting now, the one with one spindle a different color from the others. It's as if she were sitting there now, telling me about her poor wounded soul. There were a lot of flies in the hall buzzing around in that little square of light cast by the window in the corner. A strange man was sitting in that very same chair. He had an enormous beard and had come from America to announce that fiery souls would rain from the sky."

Tomàs Moro had grown visibly pale and was squirming uneasily in the chair with the replaced spindle as if it were oppressing him and he wanted to escape. Brígida continued, "Of course Jerònia had a bicycle. The first ones we ever saw in Orlandis had a huge wheel up front and a tiny one in back. Afterwards they made them with both wheels the same size. Jerònia's was one of those. I remember her pedaling and humming along the Passeig de les Palmeres, wearing a broad-brimmed hat and a yellow ribbon in her hair. I have never ridden a bicycle. Jerònia, who always wanted to go with me, told me once that riding a bicycle was just like riding in a boat with a sail, where all you notice is the breeze caressing your face in the silence.

"Jerònia always loved Carnival. During the last days before Lent, my girl-friends and cousins would always put on different costumes. We would dress as peasants, great ladies, men, soldiers, or Moors. The oldest of our group would talk like a drunk and stick a carrot between her legs to imitate a man, and she carried a thick cudgel of wild olive she threatened to use on any of the boys who tried to take our masks off. I was already married, but I still used to dress up in a costume. Benigne never really noticed. How I enjoyed running around Orlandis hiding behind a mask and observing all the people!"

"Some of my brothers and I would follow Mother's costumed group from a distance, remember?" recalled Albert the Younger. "Well, if we had gotten any closer, we would have pulled the girls' masks off. The men would buy them candy, and we counted the bags as they accumulated. We all had a sweet tooth and were spoiled rotten. The candies seemed like some treasure from *The Arabian Nights* as they lay in little piles of every color and flavor on the table."

The old lady had drifted back into dazed introspection. Paula made a gesture of objection and added, "Well, after Mardi Gras came Lent. Arcadi, now don't you get mad, but that was really too much. The sermons in that gloomy church, with tales of sin gushing and tumbling out of the mouth of the priest as if he were braiding a rope of horrors. Suddenly the preacher would halt and then let loose a terrible, unintelligible phrase in Latin, as if he were condemning us all to hell."

"All we were allowed to eat was cod and herring, all of it terribly salty," added Pollònia ruefully. "My lips burned from the salt for days. Mother didn't practice any of that, but she respected those who did."

"Who, me?" remarked Brígida, getting back into the conversation. "I was also afraid during Shrovetide. Everyone knew the stories about what had happened to others, in spite of the fact that nobody could pinpoint exactly where or when any of it had happened. One of my girlfriends told how a group of masked people went into a house in high spirits, just to have some fun, and they surrounded the owners, turned the lights on and off, moved their things around. Everybody was laughing. Then the masked people left in the dark. Finally the lady of the house turned the lights back on and saw her husband lying on the floor with a knife in his back.

"Then there is the story of the young lad full of desire who dances with a girl wearing a silver face mask, and she throws herself into his arms. Streamers line the streets and hollowed-out pumpkins serve as lanterns in the town square at night. And when the town hall clock starts to strike midnight, the girl throws him off and runs away. The desperate lad runs after her. Everything is black as pitch. The only light is that shimmering reflection off the silver mask, which has hypnotized him to such a point he doesn't realize they've arrived at the cemetery. As the girl walks up the steps to the iron gate, he calls out to her. She turns and as she removes her mask her whole lush body suddenly crumbles to dust because she was just a skeleton returning to her tomb."

"Grandma, how frightful!" protested Sebastiana.

"Jerònia had a gramophone, too," Brígida continued, buried again in the adventures of her little niece. "And the voice came out of a horn that looked like a huge lily. She was a very modern girl. On the Thursday before Shrovetide she would organize a public dance. She was a master at the fox trot and waltz. One of her records had a song I still remember:

> Little darling the boys called her,
> Little darling I called her as well. . . .

"The Italian knew a lot of songs. Oh, the Italian, how many songs he knew! He would often sing for us, standing right here. He would rest one hand on the fireplace mantle, puff out his chest, and squint his eyes, with a little lock of hair hanging over his forehead. When you listened to him your heart would burst with joy. But I can't remember his name."

"Giancarlo, Giancarlo Castagno!" added Bernat the Wise.

The old lady really didn't need to know the name as she continued, " . . . because all those Italians the war brought over here were all alike. And how Jerònia loved him! The night before the Italian had to leave, we sat around here drinking cider, and he promised as he embraced her that he would come back and marry her. Jerònia's eyes when she looked at him were as beautiful as the morning star. But he never came back.

"And Jerònia waited and waited for him, and she didn't get married, and she got thinner and thinner until one winter she got pneumonia and started spitting up blood, and the doctor discovered that it was tuberculosis and that was that. I know I'll find her sitting up there, just as she was sitting in this chair, when I go where she went.

"The last conversation we had was during Carnival. She was in bed, consumed by her tuberculosis. That year I didn't put on any costume. Jerònia told me, 'Aunt Brígida, in the end my life has been like one of those accidents they tell about on Lard Thursday, just a bitter irony: the joy disappears and all that remains is death lurking beneath the mask. And I still love him, even though he abandoned me and forgot me, because I can't help but love him if I don't want to wind up without a heart even before the worms devour me.'"

Bernat's face went pale and he rose half out of his chair, his face transfigured, "Mother! You've gone too far!"

The old woman gazed at him for a moment, not sure if she had seen him or not, although she seemed to be answering him when she said, "And Bernat asked his uncle for Jerònia's bicycle after she was buried, and he used it for a long time, even though his friends made fun of him because it was a girl's bicycle. Jerònia's parents didn't want it around because when she could no longer get out of bed, her mind would wander, and she would scream deliriously that when she was able to walk again she would grab her bicycle and pedal across the Exèquies field and speed straight off the cliff into the sea."

Bernat was about to warn his mother again, but he thought better of it. He continued eating the pieces of fowl on his plate with a frown on his face, as if he were having a very difficult time of it. But Marianna exclaimed, obviously amused, "Oh, yes! You loved to ride around on that bike! Oh, Bernat, with your hat pushed over your brow and singing. And as always, you were out of tune, and I and my girlfriends had a good laugh when you rode by because you and I weren't engaged yet."

"And where is that bicycle now, my boy?" asked Brígida, staring directly into Bernat's eyes.

"I don't know . . . what a thing to worry about! Mother, you have nattered on and on with all this nonsense from way back when. The bicycle! It must be somewhere," replied her son, his eyes on his plate and his mouth stuffed with chicken.

"You don't even remember, what with so many things on your mind," responded his wife. "It was stolen. I'll never forget, because you came to propose to me one night right after you had returned from a trip to Italy to get some kind of raw material for the alarm clock factory that you never did find after all. I didn't know what to answer you; I wanted to say 'yes' but I was afraid you'd think I was giving in too easily. And like a silly twit, I asked you why you were walking and not riding your bike, and you told me, 'While I was away, somebody stole it off the porch at Taltavull Hall.'"

"Stolen from here? I would never have believed it. Ay, my memory is failing me. Who stole it, Bernat, who?" urged the old lady.

"How should I know! Let's forget it!" Bernat the Wise interjected, suddenly irritated.

Old Brígida clasped her head in her hands, left the table and sat down in a rocker, saying, "I'm very tired, awfully tired. I want to rest a while." And she closed her eyes and fell asleep.

22

Cristòfol Mardà spoke for the first time, perhaps to relieve the tension that had inexplicably arisen in the conversation, or perhaps driven to speak by the fond memories his taste buds were reawakening: "God knows how long it's been since I've tasted a chicken like this! And this minced pork stuffing with boiled eggs and sweet marjoram, sprinkled with pepper. There's even parsley in the sauce!"

Bernat the Wise took a deep breath to calm himself. Oh yes, order in the universe; but disorder was always just around the corner, just about to erupt on the scene. He, the kingpin of the family, and suddenly someone comes out with the story of Jerònia. Neither he nor Marianna would ever know that this very evening, within a few minutes of each other, they had both been so close to what so deeply separated them and they never spoke about: their unsatisfied desires of the flesh.

Jerònia. . . . The demands of his work, his faith in and ability to make practically anything a success had for Bernat Taltavull—beyond the obvious result of respectability and wealth—created a second nature. His first nature was one of enthusiasm; his second, a tenacity capable of fighting off all challenges to his survival. But only he knew that. And on this Christmas Eve, he had discovered much to his surprise that his mother, in her foggy mental state, had intuitively guessed his secret.

Why had he become alarmed? No, it wasn't alarm. Not at all. Nothing from the past, dead and buried by now, could affect him. The problem was that his intimate inner self—the only thing that was really his—did not in any way square with the stereotyped image of the efficient automaton he had become in the eyes of others. And he wanted desperately to be able to continue being one person to himself and another in the eyes of his friends. His sense of balance resided in this duality. In order to win the battle—even for the brave and agile—one had to have a secret weapon.

Young Bernat had observed men functioning in their separate environments and quickly had come to understand the forces that drove them. But he did not understand men. Or rather, he was incapable of reducing to a theorem the only man and the only woman that interested him at the time—he and Jerònia—and thus come to control their impulses.

One idea had finally stuck in Bernat's mind when that disturbing and yet fruitful secret part of his life (the duality again) had come to an end: "Orlandis, the world we live in, is so small and narrow-minded! Like the small two hundred-page textbooks at school, the town is a limited space. We either control it ourselves, or it has us by the throat. The heavier pan on the scales goes down first. They can give me all the wise man awards they want, but nothing exceptional will ever happen in this town, buried as people are in their trivial routine. Mother doesn't remember anything but insignificant drivel. That's why the only things we really get obsessed with are sex and death, the only two extremes in life that we shall never really know or be able to control, but which drive us hungrily on, in the name of some mysterious force."

Two extremes and only one person, Jerònia. His cousin was two years older than he. She was tall, with smooth, dark skin, her smile an implicit promise of something more, a promise of giving herself completely. Lanky, well-built, always smiling, romping naked from room to room in Taltavull Hall one whole day, the day Grandfather died and the rest of the family had to hurry to Orlandis. Except the two of them, who were left to feed and water the animals. But none of the animals saw their troughs filled that day, and the hungry hogs grunted, the thirsty chickens cackled, the ass brayed, and the dogs yipped and whined.

Jerònia, standing on the stair landing, had taken both his hands in hers and challenged him, "Touch my tits," she invited, ordered, him, with her moist smile and opaque eyes.

Her breasts were small and firm, skin like velvet. And then the crinkly fluff, her thighs and vulva. He sucked in her saliva frenetically, feeling a suffocating void in his temples. They ate fruit now and then, closed all the doors and shutters as they chased each other through the house in the dark. They frolicked in every bed. Jerònia clamped her fist around his penis, riding it until he shrieked with pleasure . . . and then they grew still because they knew their interlude had to end.

But an anguish welling up from somewhere within him told Bernat that when he left it would be his flame—now burning wildly—that would have to be extinguished or it would consume him, while Jerònia's life would go on, graceful and reserved, her existence attentive to change. Bernat felt he had given himself over completely to the girl, but she had only toyed with him in their delicious rompings. Was Bernat exalted by the discovery of sex, or by the flame of love? No, in truth it was neither one nor the other that Jerònia had revealed to him, in spite of the fact that he was deeply moved by both and had never been with a woman before. What his cousin had given him was the gift of his own body.

Before that day Bernat had considered his body only as some sort of organism, a vehicle for his thoughts, his intimate self, his plans. Jerònia, with her languid, warm and elastic body, had demonstrated to him that the most intense pleasures came only if you let your body completely go, that the flesh was an indissoluble part of the glory of night and day, sun and storm, the crashing waves and life itself. He concluded that feelings and ideas, in spite of their pretentiousness, were the direct consequence of the body that bore them.

His body then, was like the body of others, which for him meant the body of Jerònia. Bernat had not known until that day with her at Taltavull Hall that the ties between two people could be truly eternal, that flesh demanded and enjoyed other flesh, that human beings were their bodies, not their daily routines, which were only substitutes or mistakes. The tenderness and the demands of the body. Nobody had ever explained to him, nor had he been able to imagine that a body could dissolve within another, that two bodies could open themselves unto each other like the splendor of the dawn. Jerònia was already his destiny.

"Now you keep this to yourself. Don't tell anyone what we've done," she ordered when they set out for Orlandis that afternoon.

He had agreed. Jerònia, already a young woman, and Bernat, still an adolescent. It was ridiculous to think she would ever have him as her lover. And he understood that.

"How could we marry if you're still in school and won't be making any money until who-knows-when?" she had objected later, laughing without malice at the boy's urgent suggestions.

But then it would happen all over again: one time at a birthday party, again under the almond trees, another day alone together at Taltavull Hall, and that hike to the labyrinthine caves at Covas de la Monge. Jerònia would come on to him, her mouth invitingly open, her body vibrant. And always the secret between them.

"But you're still just a child," she would coo as she caressed him.

And when he saw her together with young men Sunday afternoons on the promenade at the port, the only thing he could do was to repeat the promise he had made to himself: "I'll wait, and I'll be the first." That was when he was dreaming of making piles of money. His second nature, that stolid, persistent exterior of his, had just been created. His powerlessness made him realize that if you didn't have something you had to buy it. The difference in their ages wouldn't be noticeable three or four years later. Jerònia had had a good laugh the couple of times Bernat had shared his thoughts with her. But he had never let her indifference bother him because he had to keep his convictions alive.

On the other hand, how Jerònia used to laugh at the arrogance of Giancarlo Castagno! She laughed as if her body were no more than a thirsty and submissive appendage to his masculinity. Bernat noticed it immediately. Jerònia had discovered in that Italian sergeant the all-absorbing pleasure that Bernat had discovered in her. He feared Jerònia would never be his again. But he also noticed during frequent family get-togethers that the Italian displayed the same passive, condescending indulgence toward his cousin that she had displayed toward Bernat. The indirect proof of it was that Giancarlo would accept everything she proposed concerning their future together, no matter how fantasy-laden it was, without once asking anything of her in return.

Bernat had calculated he could win out over Giancarlo, one way or another. Only one set standard ruled society: what you don't have you have to buy. What did the Italian want, if he only considered Jerònia an object to be used, even though he could marry her? Bernat the Wise could now offer her what would make the Italian envious, for he was beginning to make money. Hope and hard work, a hard outer shell and constant attention to what was going on, that was Bernat Taltavull.

But there was no need to do anything. Bernat could barely contain his joy once Giancarlo had returned to Italy, and it became apparent he had shaken off all thoughts of Jerònia, even the memory of her. He had not even sent her a postcard. Now Bernat the Wise was sure of his prize: he would get his cousin back immediately. Since she never left the house, he invented some pretext to go and see her. He was shocked at what he saw: she had become as thin as a stick. Sharp bones and long tendons stuck out beneath her flaccid, yellowed skin. And anger flashed in her eyes. Jerònia wanted only to accuse, to spit out her venom: "A fine thing, you coming after me! You're an idiot! And he's a swine! Do I love him? I suppose so. But do you know where I need him now? Right here!" And, looking somewhat defiant and lost, she cupped her hand to her crotch. "Come here, touch it! Feel how it burns!" Jerònia hounded Bernat, pulling him by the arm, trying to force him to put his hand under her shabby dress.

"And when he used to throw me on the bed, he spoke to me in that strange language of his, and he was like a barbarian conqueror from afar, from the world of fairy tales! You think I'm crazy, don't you? I could tell you a whole lot more. Listen to this: one day I went up to his room at the hotel, and he had a friend with him. Giancarlo started laughing and feeling my butt and talking dirty to me. He made me get undressed, and I was afraid and excited. I noticed how intently both of them were looking at me, so I deliberately slowed down taking off my bra, my shoes. I would love to have done it to music! Then he handed me over to his friend as if I were some kind of animal, and I knew I had to obey. As his friend penetrated me, Giancarlo watched breathlessly, his bloodshot eyes about to pop. That's when I had such a violent orgasm they had to slap me to stop my screaming."

"Shut up, Jerònia," Bernat blurted out. "What I wanted to. . . ."

She screamed back at him, "The only thing you can give me is what I already have! And when I think of him I feel like I'm going to explode! I know I'll explode!"

It was a cold and brisk night, and once on the street Bernat threw up. The Jerònia he had just seen was not his Jerònia. As for her body, it had been deprived of the man who had given it life and so was being consumed by fever. She in her obsession was not yet aware of what was going on inside her, but her parents had confided to Bernat that her moral and physical deterioration was due to the tuberculosis that was ravaging her.

Bernat recalled that phrase of hers, "the barbarian conqueror from afar." It was from a play entitled *Atilla in Rome* that he, Jerònia and other students their age had put on in the Orlandis parish church. She might be teetering on the edge of death, but even the most lifeless detail from her past acquired vital, heartrending dimensions at the thought of Giancarlo Castagno.

Bernat's desire for Jerònia, his sharp memories of the drunken fullness of their bodies together, turned to disgust at the thought of this ruined and obscene woman. But the world had to be an orderly place, and Bernat the Wise its most orderly defender. And if the world were indeed a duality, then apart from the crazed abomination she had become, there would always remain in Bernat's memory the sublime image of the cousin he loved. And since that image did not require the least bit of pragmatic proof, it would remain unaltered within young Bernat Taltavull's spirit.

"Balls," he was forced to admit to himself soon after. The duality wasn't formed by two parallel realities, but by a gross and shameless mixture of god and the devil. That licentious and tattered Jerònia of her last days remained unexpunged in his imagination, infiltrating his idealized vision of first love, sullying it. At night Bernat dreamed of macabre dances between the two women who finally melted together, forming one and the same marionette. Once she had died, the phantasmagoria into which Jerònia had turned her life had become a part of Bernat's. He could no longer control his thoughts or feelings. He would relive those first experiences with Jerònia in his mind under the perspective of her last days, and thus his admiration cheapened into hate. And he was stubbornly determined to demolish what had been the sublime moment of his life.

He tried going out with other girls. That Marianna Mas, with her generous flesh, firm and exciting. But the only girl he was somewhat attracted to was Antonieta de La Paret. Or was it that rarefied, haunting atmosphere at La Paret that really excited him? Furthermore, what racial mandate was it that induced him to move from one cousin to another, from Jerònia to Antonieta, as if he were only able to feed off his own sickly entrails? He let the spineless Antonieta go. The butterflies who lived only for a day fluttered indecisively over the sleeping fields.

He had asked his uncle for Jerònia's bicycle because she used to look so beautiful pedaling along and singing to herself so contentedly, a smile on her face, her broad-brimmed hat about to fly off into the playful breeze. Bernat's brain had become a jumbled nightmare. He thought he was about to lose his mind. The bicycle was for him a physical fact, as Jerònia's body had been, something he could hold in his hands and struggle with physically. Bernat the Wise would put on a wide-brimmed hat like hers and hum bits of songs as he furiously pedaled the bike. Was he exorcising the memories of the rotten part of Jerònia? He didn't know. But his ability to make so many daydreams come true, even if through such a ridiculous means, placated his raging spirits and showed him the road to redemption.

And Giancarlo Castagno became that road. The whole phantasmagorical nightmare had its origins in him. He who lives by the sword shall die by the sword. He would find the solution to his mental meltdown through the Italian himself. Bernat would seek out Giancarlo and he would. . . . Yes, what exactly would he do? What could he do to him? That was the least of his problems. The duality appeared only through the turbid river of contradictions. Instinct or chance would dictate whatever he had to do when the moment came. The search for Giancarlo took patience, and that helped calm him; it was a search for something concrete. The trail started to get warmer. One day he received a letter containing Giancarlo Castagno's address in Venice from the Italian consulate in Palma. He invented an excuse to travel on factory business. A couple of days on the train, then the Grand Canal shrouded in fog, the warm colors of the building facades, like fine embroideries. He could see Saint Mark's Square from his hotel window. The pedestrians seemed to be strolling through another century, through the raw enchantment of winter.

When he arrived at the address on a small side street bordered by a tiny canal behind the Schiavoni Wharf, he read the sign: Castagno's Dry Cleaners. He entered through the plate glass door, his heart gripped by fear, euphoria, and confusion. A withered woman and a dark-featured young lady stood behind the counter. He asked for Giancarlo. There wasn't much to say.

"He died a couple of years ago . . . drowned in the lagoon," answered the woman, and added, "I'm his widow." Bernat's jaw dropped.

But what stunned him even more was the girl.

"And I am his daughter, Andrea."

Which meant she had already been born when Giancarlo Castagno, Fascist sergeant, had made love to Jerònia in Orlandis. Bernat quickly shifted gears and put a new strategy into action: "We were friends in Majorca, yes, ma'am. Traveling through Italy, I remembered him and thought I would look him up. . . ."

They invited him to stay for supper. The dining room was humble, the walls stained with mold. The widow, obviously bitter, often drifted, lost in thought. Andrea offered to show Venice to Bernat in the morning. He accepted gracefully, rented elegant gondolas, invited her to dine in brilliant baroque restaurants, the most expensive of everything. Andrea's body was as noble and attractive as an ancient statue. He bought her gifts, a dress, a necklace, several pairs of shoes.

"Your father had lent me money and fed me in those difficult times during the war, and it would give me great pleasure to return the favor to you now."

Andrea paused, doubting whether to accept his gifts or not. But she had fallen in love with Bernat. His unexpected generosity lifted her out of her wretched existence. And he was happy, a relaxed happiness he had never known before; he embraced Andrea, admired her beauty in the glitter of the moon on the dark surface of the canals. The unique landscape, so different from what he was used to, renewed and invigorated him. Andrea couldn't take her eyes off him, eyes that became disconsolate and burst into tears when Bernat told her he had to leave the next morning and that their love was impossible because he was married and had a little baby girl. He had to make believe he, too, was weeping to keep from laughing: his exercise in impious cruelty had been just as successful and satisfying as his business deals, which he had learned to structure the same way in his mind.

He was not avenging Jerònia, because he had practically forgotten her in the course of his trip. Nor was he punishing himself. By abandoning Andrea—whom he rather liked—by punishing her with the same kind of farce the dead Giancarlo had used in Majorca, by enjoying the magnificence of Venice with impunity, Bernat was freeing himself from the tentacles of that dark nightmare that had held him prisoner in the oppressive atmosphere of Orlandis. Man was also a landscape, a reflection of his environment.

"Even the nature of animals changes as their environment changes," it comforted him to think. Andrea disappeared from his life forever as she slowly walked away down the divine curve of the Rialto Bridge.

23

The women cleared the greasy plates of roast chicken from the table while the men slowly sipped their wine. Then the cakes were brought out, with their tiny many-colored sweets placed in the meringue frosting, the lightly toasted bitter almonds, the delicate, cottony "nun-farts," the hard and soft nougat, the crunchy caramel-almond cookies, the thick and snowy cottage cheese, the flat cakes sprinkled with anise, the toasted, sweet almond kernels. A fine aroma of cinnamon and warm pudding spread an air of optimism over Taltavull Hall. The crackling hearth no longer gave off smoke. Nobody had stuck his head out to check, but the wind had died down and the valley seemed to have vanished, leaving the ecstatic old manor house like a lonely ghost floating atop the hill.

"Everything is homemade here!" Paula reminded everybody, her arms proudly spread wide in triumph as she showed off the desserts.

The retired judge and commander bit into one of the subtle cakes and commented circumspectly to his table mate, Dioclecià of Pula, "Since we're here together, now would be a good time to talk."

The patriarch of Pula didn't think the judge's words were exactly meant as an attempt to communicate, nor as an expression of his friendly nature, but as a way of feeling out his colleague, or perhaps setting a trap. Anyone attempting to make Dioclecià or any other Pulan believe that a person's word and the truth were one and the same would have failed. The old *número uno* from Pula had guessed correctly that Taltavull Oliva had begun his attack. Sucking on an almond, Dioclecià broke into a jovial smile that turned his broad face and well-larded carcass into the epitome of amiability, "My dear relative and friend, you must have read my thoughts! I, too, wanted to talk with you."

"What about?" inquired Ignasi condescendingly, well aware of Dioclecià's shrewdness.

But Dioclecià scorned his adversary's sly tactics. He was trying to tie the judge in knots, to trip him up. So he took an unexpected tack: "Well, I just wanted to invite you to Pula, and should you deign to accept," and he lowered his voice, "we have a special treat for you."

The judge hadn't expected that. "A special treat?"

"I'm sorry, I meant 'very special,'" corrected Dioclecià with a belly laugh he muffled with his hand over his mouth, leaving only an echo of it in his girth, which shook as if he were about to come unglued. At the same time he winked at Taltavull Oliva.

The commander lowered his head and took a sip of malvasia wine. He was now gauging the import of Dioclecià's maneuver: "I suspect I can corner him . . . he has baited the hook, but hasn't yet revealed the lure. . . . That special treat probably has something to do with women. Hmm. . . ."

The judge was irritated that his weakness was so apparent. But an itch began to grow in him. The visit might prove promising.

He was pretty sure that if Dioclecià realized he had not completely hooked him, the Pulan would convert his "very special" into something completely innocuous. He decided to ignore what the Pulan had alluded to and stress the official nature of his inquiry. If necessary, he could always add water to the wine: "Thank you for your kindness, but at the moment I'm too busy to . . . well, to go partying. The real question is that some of your neighbors, Ramon Roig among them, are accusing you and others in Pula of moving boundary markers and—pardon my frankness—of several robberies of fruit, wheat, a well pump. . . ."

Dioclecià's joviality became exuberant. He had guessed Ignasi's thoughts exactly. And now he had an advantage over the judge, who believed that by avoiding Dioclecià's invitation he had won the first round and thus lowered the other's guard. But the invitation, in spite of its initial rejection, remained temptingly planted in the judge's subconscious. Dioclecià therefore decided to attack on another front. His jolly bulk vibrated like a boneless slab of meat as he emphatically replied, "Friend, relative, military officer and judge: you are everything to me!"

"Wait a minute," the judge cut him off, at the same time swelling with self-importance.

Dioclecià studied him carefully: "He thinks I have overdone it, that I wanted to lick up to him like a sniveling dog, and he made the mistake of cutting me off. Perfect, perfect!" Then he continued: "Ignasi, I can tell you from my heart: we Pulans are nothing if not faithful! And because of that you shouldn't believe all that silly stuff you hear."

"Silly stuff? Let's define our words here. Are you saying that the accusations against you are insignificant?"

"Of course!" replied the Pulan, tossing back two almonds at once. He could only suck on them, for he had no teeth.

"Well then, Dioclecià, you have confirmed the facts; you don't deny them:

ergo Roig was right," argued the judge, pleased with his astuteness. "I've got him! He must be getting old," the judge mused.

The Pulan chieftain remained lost in thought for a few seconds, or at least appeared to be, then said modestly, "Thank you for clarifying these cases at hand . . . poor me, I must be kind of slow on the uptake. As you very well have shown, the facts aren't based on what we might have done, for in that case there would have been an investigation. Quite the contrary, it's apparently just a question of an accusation by our neighbor Roig . . . or however many they were."

"Eh? What's that?" was Taltavull Oliva's annoyed response.

"Of course, what a dolt like me and a wise man like you should really be talking about is not the non-existent evil in Pula but the reason why Ramon Roig is breaking the law with his false accusations."

Offended, the judge snapped back, "He said . . ."

The judge suddenly grew quiet, his eyebrows knit in a frown. Ignasi had unexpectedly gotten himself into a corner where he felt obliged to defend himself. He was now no longer the prosecutor but had become the accused. Dioclecià observed him out of the corner of his eye, overflowing with his hypocritical joviality, as he tasted one of the tiny toasty nun-fart candies.

With a gesture of exasperation, the judge reached out with his glass and asked, "Pass me that Malaga wine, will you, you tiresome old bastard?"

Ignasi had known the Pulan all his life. It would be better for him to lay off. You had to pounce on them by surprise without being finicky about it. If they got a chance to recover, they would slither off like seven-headed snakes. During the war, young Dioclecià and the Hunchback of Pula, among other members of the same gang, had been the authors of that incredible escapade of the radio station and the espionage, which in the end had really wound up hurting the innocent more than the guilty.

At the time, Ambròs of the Mad Animal was the Pulan chieftain. The clan seemed to be eternally linked to animals. Ambròs was a wiry runt of a man with a fastidious look on his tiny face, wrinkled as a dried fig. He could always be found somewhere in Orlandis in the company of some kind of animal— often a Great Dane or a mule. But then he was also known to appear with a falcon or a litter of kittens, and when somebody approached him on the street, he would warn them off, saying, "Hey, this animal has a bad temper: it gets angry at nothing at all. It's crazy and might attack." Of course, nobody dared come near him.

"That's the best way to study people because up close they could be dangerous," reasoned Ambròs with a twisted smile.

The men from the Republican troop ships of the Generalitat of Catalunya had disembarked at Porto Cristo on the Majorcan east coast. But they were unable to defeat the defending Fascist forces of the island. That was when the natives began to fear another Catalan attack. It was supposed to come on the west coast near Orlandis so as to catch the island insurrectionists in a pincer movement between the two armies. The island supporters of the Republic were submissive on the surface but were actively and secretly agitating for a Republican victory. And they had detected ships, or so the rumor ran, that could only belong to the enemy and were sailing off-shore near Orlandis in the early pre-dawn hours.

Lieutenant Taltavull Oliva had been ordered to move prudently because the National Army didn't have enough troops to drive the Catalans from Porto Cristo. Furthermore, they didn't want to raise the alarm and stir up the people, thereby causing a possible uprising from the left.

Count Rossi, the black-uniformed Italian officer with imperious voice and pointed goatee, pranced through town on his arrogant white stallion, waving his cross and his sword and proclaiming the new Fascist civilization in the name of Benito Mussolini and hailing the pleasure of executing the enemy by firing squad. One night, at one of the parties given by the Duchess of Orlandis, the count had told Taltavull Oliva, "They are a miserable lot, and we have all the intelligence, like Julius Caesar in Gaul. That is, what we need to do is to set up a diversion, militarily speaking. Comrade, we need a radio station!"

They had brought an antenna tower and an old worn-out low-powered transmitter from Palma that could be heard in Orlandis and occasionally at the western end of the island and at sea. They made two kinds of broadcasts: one as Fatherland Radio, to heat up the Nationalist Movement supporters, and the other as Radio Liberty, designed to confuse the Republicans by appearing to be one of them, either the invaders or the fifth column already on the island. Since the operation demanded absolute secrecy and technically qualified personnel, they had to have recourse to the slippery and ever-watchful Pulans, who closed off their devastating mountain passes to any out-siders venturing near them and who were handy with mechanical things.

Ambròs of the Mad Animal, who at the time was followed around by a Peruvian llama, had had to cooperate in exchange for a miserable salary and some outrageous threats from the Fascists. When he told the assembled Pulans of the deal, he had warned them, "Furthermore, we favor respect for law and order, which is what this Falange thing is all about, while the Republicans are an outrageous, revolutionary lot."

A murmur of agreement from the townspeople was his answer. Ambròs, scratching the neck of the Mad Animal at his side nibbling away at some poppies, added, "Because, you see, if we don't keep them happy and avoid trouble, how are we going to be able to move around as we like, where we like, and at our own convenience? When the world's on fire, everybody becomes a cook. And under the Republic, everybody wants to be like Pula, and that means we have to scrap with people like ourselves instead of hoodwinking the yokels."

The assembly also agreed with that. The runty patriarch picked his nose and reflected out loud, "And if we're in business with Ignasi Taltavull and those scoundrels from Palma, at least we'll know what's going on, and if we have to we can make the ship yaw in our direction because we shouldn't let the wind blow all day long from astern in favor of that mob of priests and officers. If we let them get too ambitious, they are liable to come down heavy on us. And on the other hand, the anarchists are on the Republican side. A good measure of salt makes the meal taste better."

The opinion of the Pulans was unanimous. It was very clear to them they had to do what Ambròs had recommended, that is, tie the situation up in knots. They all clapped Ambròs on the back, while the nervous little runt brought a bucket of water over to the Mad Animal and watched it drink.

The transmitter was installed in an abandoned lighthouse located on one of the cliffs near Pula which fell straight to the sea. The operations group was composed of a staff sergeant, a couple of soldiers, a technician, and a journalist. All the rest of those milling around the transmitter were people from Pula who—nobody knew quite how—had in one way or another all become indispensable. Those who weren't simply roamed around the installation, sticking their noses into everything they could.

Staff Sergeant Montalbán and the two confused soldiers soon half-way delegated guard duty and supply services to the Pulans, who were led by the skinny Belisari of Pula, in spite of his sleepy appearance. The only language he used was the movements of his eyebrows. The technician, a man with flat feet, had no idea why he had been sent to that godforsaken place. Dioclecià of Pula never left him alone for a minute, encouraging his complaints and playing with the transmitter all day.

The journalist, a vain youth from Palma named Llompart, who wore a toothbrush mustache and the dark blue shirt of the Spanish Falange, was quickly absorbed by Lavínia of Pula, a sharp beauty with a large mouth and firm breasts, who with her deep voice served as the announcer on Radio Liberty. The Hunchback of Pula, a versatile and resourceful fellow with a squeaky voice, was the announcer for Fatherland Radio. He was also an unsuspected graphologist about to enter a period of dark and ambitious growth.

Lavínia would look at Llompart intensely out of the corner of her eye and slowly lick her lips. The journalist's heart would skip a beat; then he would slip his hand under the table and start to knead Lavínia's thigh, burrow under her skirt and. . . . Every time he came close to his goal, a Pulan would invariably wander by the table and interrupt the operation. The frustrated Llompart would then try to figure out how he could get back into her pants as he irritatedly handed over the pile of papers to the Hunchback of Pula—full of signals, countersigns, speeches, and news, all of it tiresome propaganda sent from Orlandis that was distracting him from his unsatisfied sexual ardor. It was from these papers that he was supposed to write the brief and exalted scripts for both broadcasts.

The Hunchback of Pula was short and rotund with a face and nose like a funnel, the hump on his back slightly twisted to the left. Since he was useless to the risky raiding parties run by the men of Pula, he had gone to school and had become pretentious as a result. Ambròs liked him because he was educated and shorter than he was. Amid the piles of news sheets, the hunchback laughed like a lunatic, waving his pencil and writing away, snipping and pasting with theatrical gestures.

At a certain time each day, Ambròs would discreetly saunter by the lighthouse. Belisari, Dioclecià, Lavínia, and the rest of the Pulans, either ambling about or in the bushes, would cautiously come up to him for a moment, tell him the latest news and disappear again. He had the most fun with the hunchback, who bounced around him like a ping pong ball as he talked. Everybody would ask Ambròs, "What shall we do now?"

"The same damn thing! And keep your eyes peeled!" ordered Ambròs.

Not even he would have known how to explain what those maneuvers were all about, as they took on ever stranger proportions day by day. The whole clan at Pula turned up at the lighthouse and devoted all their energy to the accumulation of enormous quantities of information, whether useful or not. When one of them asked Ambròs about it, he said, "The more nets we set, the more fish we'll catch. And if a rumpus starts here, better we see it coming."

The folks in Pula had heard that there was a sacred place in Greece called Delphos, where in the old days a buried serpent had spoken with the voice of a woman and among other truths had declared that nothing is ever excessive.

And since it was evident the general situation had taken on exciting and complex dimensions, Ambròs the patriarch had exchanged his Mad Animal of the moment—that stupid llama—for a billy goat. He was a gigantic beast with long, curly hair that reached to the ground. He gave off an odor of semen so offensive it made you want to vomit. His thick horns were long and curved. Two errand boys from Pula had to hold him with a rope tied to each horn, otherwise he would furiously butt anyone near him.

"You never know who you'll have to depend on," confessed Ambròs, sniffing the air so as to stand up-wind from the genital stench of the goat.

During the three months the transmitter lasted, Lieutenant Taltavull Oliva found it impossible to clarify the things that had gone on up there on the cliff when the captain general's office demanded a report. When the situation finally became unmanageable, Ignasi himself turned up at the lighthouse leading a platoon of soldiers after a half-day's strenuous march through the mountains in the broiling sun. When he got to the radio station, he took inventory of the only obvious facts. Ignasi Taltavull still had the list of things he had written down that day:

> First. The place is overrun by rats. It looks as if they had been thrown in there by the sackful.
>
> Second. Staff Sergeant Montalbán and the two soldiers take their siesta in their tee-shirts and without boots, their weapons abandoned elsewhere.
>
> Third. The mechanic has disappeared.
>
> Fourth. The journalist Llompart looks like he has been drunk for days.
>
> Fifth. The transmitter is working perfectly, thanks to civilians known as Lavínia of Pula and the Hunchback of Pula, both of them exemplary servants of the cause.

In spite of noting down the facts as he saw them, Ignasi doubted whether they really represented the truth of the matter. It was a question of being in Pulan territory. And things had changed drastically from the time of his first report. Now things bordered on chaos. So his new list specified:

> First. Until now, nobody had ever seen a rat, except Lavínia of Pula and the Hunchback of Pula, who both declare that the lighthouse has become a dung heap.
>
> Second. The staff sergeant and the two soldiers now explain that there are so few of them they stand watch at night while volunteer neighbors help them out during the day, especially a man named Belisari, whom we haven't been able to find anywhere.
>
> Third. The mechanic turned up at his home in Palma with false discharge papers about which he claims to know nothing except they were given to

him by a man named Dioclecià, whom he barely knew and who is also missing at present.

Fourth. With reference to the existence and functioning of the transmitter, Llompart claims to know very little about it apart from the fact that he is in a very dangerous political situation. In spite of the fact that he won't admit it and claims loyalty to the National Movement, he reeks of Republicanism.

Fifth. Lavínia of Pula has made a complaint against the journalist for repeated rape with moral coercion, offering as proof several articles of ripped clothing and underwear, together with the testimony of the Hunchback of Pula who, due to his physical deformity, was unable to prevent the rapes or flee for help. He and Lavínia had finally decided to overlook such personal matters and carry out the mission the Fatherland had charged them with.

The sentence handed down by the military tribunal also contained five points, which Ignasi had also kept notes on:

First. These conclusions have been arrived at based on the report filed by the lieutenant commander of Orlandis, Ignasi Taltavull Oliva, on the deplorable state of the lighthouse and its occupants.

Second. A large quantity of food, fuel, and every other type of material supplies had been consumed at the lighthouse, enough to supply troops for a mission twenty times larger than this one. The accused obtained these supplies through fraudulent manipulation of quartermaster requisitions.

Third. The radio broadcasts had been converted into subversive propaganda for the Republic, and they broadcast countersigns to the fifth column.

Fourth. The prisoners steadfastly maintain that they not only had nothing to do with the acts imputed to them, but they also claim to know nothing about them.

Fifth. The family relative and business representative of the civilians Lavínia of Pula and the Hunchback of Pula, by name Ambròs of Pula, has risen from the sickbed where he has lain gravely ill for the past four months in order to intercede before the court in favor of the accused, pleading for Christian clemency, in spite of the fact that he does not know them personally. Moved by such sentiments, said Ambròs of Pula withdraws the accusations in the name of Lavínia of Pula and the Hunchback of Pula, which the latter two persons felt obliged to present to this court.

The court condemned Staff Sergeant Montalbán and Llompart the journalist—who by then was in a frenzy of rage—to death by firing squad for acts of high treason. The two soldiers and the mechanic were each sentenced to ten years and a day of forced labor for criminal negligence. The sentences were carried out in every detail.

Lavínia of Pula and the Hunchback of Pula were both awarded the Cross for Military Merit, with which they were decorated at the port park in Orlandis by Count Rossi in person while the national anthem was played and a multitude of people applauded fervently. Ambròs, dressed in his Sunday best, kept a serious face as he sat among the guests of honor, all the time keeping watch over his fierce goat out of the corner of his eye. The beast was creating a an uproar as he reared up and snorted behind the fish market where he was being held by Belisari and Dioclecià of Pula.

In spite of what he suspected, Ignasi was unable to begin to understand what really had happened at the lighthouse until two years later when a group of men from Pula rushed the hunchback to the hospital. They claimed he had fallen off a cliff and appeared to be all broken up inside. Later they had to transfer him to a hospital in Palma. Between moans and groans they loaded him on a military jeep driven by Ignasi himself. Halfway to Palma he pulled off the road and drove down a dry riverbed and there in the shade of a canebrake he lit a cigarette and sat back to relax.

The hunchback, when he noticed they had stopped the jeep, opened his eyes thinking they had already arrived at the hospital and in an imploring voice said, "Ay, doctor, if you only knew . . . ," but the canebrake and the lieutenant sitting there smoking alarmed him, and he shouted, "Hey! Hey, what's going on here? Where am I?"

Ignasi answered him as he toyed with a snail he had just pulled off a tree, "Calm down, dear boy, calm down. We're waiting for the journalist Llompart and Staff Sergeant Montalbán."

"What?" squeaked the hunchback.

"You had better tell me the story of the lighthouse, or you're never going to reach Palma."

That rumpled and bloodied ball of fat looked at Ignasi with terror in his eyes. He suddenly broke out in uncontrollable nervous laughter and, twisting his tortured and rotund body, his pain increased as he said, "Lavínia. Ha! Ha! Lavínia . . . the journalist went crazy whenever he was able to get his hands in her bra. Ha! Ha! Ha! And she fed him brandy by the bottleful. Ha! Ha! Ha! Ambròs had told her how she had to work on him."

"So you were the one who pulled the wool over Llompart's eyes!" Taltavull Oliva said accusingly.

The hunchback stared at him, stupefied, "No!"

"No? Well, who was it then?"

The Pulan gasped hoarsely, "Nobody did! Ha! Your side sent a pile of papers to the lighthouse every day, just like the Republicans did. And all the information Ambròs broadcast was either false or altered, so it would serve as propaganda for the other side and throw you off! Ha! Ha! Ha!"

"He? Who was he?" insisted the judge.

"Ambròs, who else? He brought the news and other Republican things in a bundle tied up in wrapping paper."

"But who gave the papers to him, and why?"

The only thing the hunchback seemed to be listening to by now was his inner voice. His face had turned green, and he had broken out in a sweat.

"I was supposed to mix everything up and change it—Ha! Ha!—once we got the journalist out of the way. With those papers in hand, I couldn't tell the difference between what was true and what was false in the end, and after I had mixed them all up, I understood the whole mess even less. Ha! Ha! Ha! And then, so as not to go stark raving mad up there in the lighthouse, and fearful that I might get caught, I wound up believing what I had put together. Which is what I later explained to Llompart. And he—Ha! Ha! Ha!—chased after the brandy bottle and Lavínia and didn't worry a bit about the war and accepted everything I told him as fact. Llompart! Llompart was my friend. I became more self-confident when I was able to talk about what I believed in with someone else who believed the same things—Ha! Ha! Ha!"

That long dissertation left him swollen to the point of bursting and his eyes suddenly glazed over. The lieutenant continued to insist on answers to his questions even after the little tub of lard was dead: "And what about Lavínia, did he screw her, eh? Did he screw her?"

Lavínia was the one who appeared the next morning in the office of Ignasi Taltavull Oliva instead of Ambròs of Pula, whom the lieutenant had originally called in for interrogation.

"This is intolerable! I'll send a squad of soldiers to bring me Ambròs in chains!" Ignasi had shouted.

The girl sat down in a chair without saying a word and slowly hitched up her skirt, revealing her lack of panties. The officer, swallowing hard and feeling a great heat in his entrails, got up and bolted the door.

24

Beautiful Egèria got up and raised her arm to request silence. She seemed to vacillate, but it was clear she meant to keep going. Her cousin Niní clinked her glass with a spoon. Everyone turned toward Egèria and grew quiet. Egèria began to speak, hesitantly, with emotion.

"You all know, well, that one of the family is no longer among us. He would have been here with us today, if. . . . Last Christmas we were all here. All of us who were around then, of course. How many of the Taltavulls have died through the course of the generations and centuries! How many of them spent their last Christmas Eve here? Francesc de Borja Taltavull, my father, is the one who isn't here tonight."

Her terrified mother, Magdalena, tugged on Egèria's skirt to make her sit down. Her brother mumbled in irritation, "Well! That stupid girl. . . ."

"No, Mama, let me go on," continued Egèria. "I want to talk about Father. And not because you didn't all know him. Many of you, logically, were much closer to him during his lifetime than I was, like Aunt Brígida and my uncles. And of course you, Mama. But I have read that the ancients pronounced solemn funeral rites over their dead . . . a man dressed in a tunic with a background of cypresses. I think Father needs something like that, don't you? Words are, in spite of being carried off by the wind, well, they are. . . . Well, what I mean is that we humans are also words. My father has died, and I still feel all choked up about it, and I imagine if I talk to you about him here, where evidence of his presence abounds, I will come to know the instinctive birth of hope, which is perhaps the most noble thing in our lives and which disappeared in me when he died.

"I'm also inclined to imagine his spirit will in some way become. . . . Because I ask myself, What's happening to his spirit now? If any of you know, please tell me, because I don't know."

Arcadi the priest, who was chomping on a chunk of cake, offered his services: "I could. . . ."

"No!" she cut him off fearlessly, and for the first time, confidently. "Not you, Arcadi. Whatever you might say I already know by heart and it's of no use to me. We buried Father clothed in the rites of your church. But I know a firm conviction is growing in me that our religion is a consequence of ourselves and our acts and offers no key to the great beyond or to oblivion. We believe that this old house—this estate—belongs to us, the Taltavull family. But none of the dead Taltavulls from past generations has ever returned to ask for his share, or to tell us he still belongs to this piece of earth. Until that happens, nobody will have penetrated the wall of death."

Tomàs Moro whispered so that nobody could hear him, "She's awfully daring, claiming the dead don't watch over us from the dark."

"On the other hand, what I do suppose," continued Egèria, "is that my words would please my father even more—if he could hear them—than the words you said at the funeral, Arcadi. At least he might discover a tiny bit of joy in what I'm saying and plan to say, while in the church service there was only an endless sadness. And I'm speaking tentatively because I don't know whether even the tiniest identifiable echo of us remains beyond the wall of death.

"If we speak of Father, however, we might get closer to who we ourselves really are. We would be making a statement in favor of our own everfading essence."

Egèria took a sip of water. A feeling of deep serenity ennobled her, drove her on.

"Father worked these lands; he was born in this house, and he loved the earth surrounding it; he loved each one of you, his people. Only after you could he love justice, goodness, or the nation . . . only after you. That is, if he ever believed in all that. He used to think, without being aware of it, that man was an inheritance, not a project, that man is blood and clay, that a house is not built for pleasure but for defense. The world—his world—was an endless family chain, with its own interests and its own people. Under his secret code of conduct, laws were never written but always obeyed anyway because they were born of the womb of the people and conditioned by the earth.

"He hated anyone who wanted to change all that, not because he doubted other realities or solutions, but because if things were to change, the Taltavulls would also be changed or even destroyed since they would become something else. And what would that something else be? Without the protection of the Taltavulls all that remained were clans, hostile unknown people, wars, distant lands, strange characters, doubts, and conflicts, while here at home the knowledge and collective laws came down to us through the centuries, and everybody knew who his ancestors were. To my father that meant everything in his life. He loved us because his wholeness came from the fact that we were everything to each other. We were everything to him, too. 'I love you very much, my little girl, very much,' he used to tell me. I remember how he used to say it, almost as if to himself, when I was a little girl and he would tuck me in before I fell asleep."

She sobbed, raised her head and a few heavy tears ran slowly down her radiantly flushed cheeks.

"What is Egèria up to? What a spectacle!" exclaimed her brother again as he downed another whiskey.

She didn't hear him, or preferred to ignore him, as she picked up where she had left off, filled with a sense of devotion and eloquence.

"I thought of him when we went by the cemetery on the way home from Orlandis. He's there in the cemetery, and a couple of—how shall I say— anecdotes occurred to me. Nothing very important, if you will, but. . . . One of them is from the day of the funeral. We were all gathered in the cemetery. The mason was bricking up the niche. Uncle Bernat asked him when he would place the marble plaque, and the mason answered, "When they bring it from the stonecutter with the name engraved on it, but I suppose that won't be until next year, more or less. I wouldn't be able to cement it in until later anyway, because to do that I have to open part of the niche, and for the next few months it'll smell too bad to open." What he meant, of course, was that his body was being eaten up by rot, at the peak of putrefaction, decompos- ing, violently so!

"The flesh. . . . When Mama found him dead, I was in Palma. When I returned, they had already laid him out on the bed. He looked so peaceful. I kissed him on the forehead. It was ice-cold and hard. And when they took him from the house to the church the next afternoon, I kissed him again before they closed the casket, and his flesh had already started to get soft and spongy, as if he had been soaked in water overnight. And tonight, when I drove by the cemetery on my way here, my father continued to rot in his niche. Was that putrefying flesh still my father?

"The answer is no—it isn't him. It's only flesh and bone, matter in the process of transformation. But I can assure you that's a big lie: that flesh is my father, my dead father. For me he is still my father, but he is not his own self in his own eyes. Because our flesh belongs to us only as long as we are alive. And only in life can we wander the paths of the spirits.

"Father didn't want to die, but during the past few years, he had the look of death in his eyes, and he knew he was going to die soon. That's why he was always so silent. He had almost stopped talking all together: if his flesh was already melting away, of what importance were words to him? Words are life, but they cannot defeat death. It would be a consolation for me, for all of us, to know he would appreciate what I'm saying now. Not because he imagined he would get anything out of our remembering him as he was while still alive. We are the ones who live on through him by evoking his memory now . . . we are his heirs.

"When we buried our cousin from Volta del Carro, we were all gathered at the cemetery as well, standing before the niche, the mason sealing it up. I looked at Father out of the corner of my eye: he was so thin he seemed about to collapse, and you could see consternation in his eyes, as humble as it was horrible because he was thinking he was the oldest one there, that soon it would be his turn to follow in the footsteps of his cousin from Volta del Carro . . . and he was right. Death is always right."

The fireplace crackled loudly. Nobody had noticed it until then, when the voracious roar of the newly awakened flames seemed to grow and advance like an army of insects through the expectant hall and the silence of the night.

After a pause, Beautiful Egèria continued: "Don't worry if I seem to get lost sometimes. I don't know whether I ought to repeat—no, clarify—that I only want to talk about a matter that still torments me, and it's this: that Father lives on in your minds just as he was during his last few years of life. I myself am struggling with that thought. His vertigo, his arteriosclerosis, his terrible colds, you know. . . . He was bedridden for weeks at a time, moaning darkly, obsessed with his illness. He would look at us hostilely, angry with us if we didn't feel his pain, and then he would become even more depressed if we lamented along with him. And like a child with a sweet tooth, he would ask for his medications and refuse to eat. I knew that wasn't really him, because now he believed in the magic powers of the medicine bottles and the pills. He wasn't being the realist he normally was.

"But the afternoon before he died, he was marvelously lucid. He got up from bed, and the skin on his face seemed taut and clear. His eyes were vibrant and shone brightly. He pushed his medicines aside and ate some fresh fava beans from the garden, boiled and dressed with olive oil and vinegar. We talked together a long time. I told him what was going on in my life, what I wished would happen, what my dreams were, and I could see he was excited and wanted my dreams to come true for me.

"That was what he liked the most, to dream, to imagine himself respected in the eyes of others, to be happy, to have everything work out right. That was the real father I knew, a man who could look at the sky and see himself reflected in it. And that's the father I want to remember. What a mystery it is, to become in one's last hours of life the person one had been in the best moments of one's whole life!"

Damià raised a skeptical eyebrow. Old Brígida listened with rapt attention and murmured, "Francesc de Borja Taltavull, he was my son. What's the girl saying? I hadn't ever thought of anything like that. I always had him around, and I taught him to eat, and he was my son."

"He was never ambitious," Egèria reflected, her gaze lost over the chaotic table brimming with food, "I mean ambitious for worldly goods. On the other hand, he was proud of everything that was his, of his little Taltavull universe: his little hatchet was the best-honed there was; his chair-caning was the best; there was no better landscape than at Taltavull Hall; if somebody had to graft a cherry tree or train a dog, he was the best teacher. He didn't talk, I suppose, in order to define a problem and later find its solution, but instead to demonstrate his and the Taltavulls' perfection.

"What a feeling of pleasure and satisfaction I had in my childhood when I could be at his side! He surrounded me with a high flower-filled wall of security, quite the opposite of the black wall of death. For him, the world was made to his and the Taltavulls' measure, as I said before. The heroes of the past were not the heroes of history and the great *chansons de gestes,* but the heroes from Taltavull Hall, like that great-great-grandfather who owned the largest flock of sheep ever known, or that uncle who had fought the Barbary pirates aboard a galley in the waters around the island of Molta Murtra.

And in Cuba, when a tropical storm roared over his schooner, he was at the wheel riding out those gigantic waves. The sugar plantation, the wailing songs of the blacks. . . . That Caribbean island was what he had constructed and engraved in his mind. When someone would explain a tale he didn't know, he would look at them incredulously. Could anything have happened without his knowledge? With Father it was as if you not only had the best there was here, but the best there was anywhere."

Egèria felt very happy as she spoke. She felt like a Greek goddess astride a sweet mythological beast. She had sought to express in words the life that death had stolen from her father, and she had found it.

"I have heard the stories of the sacrifices he made, too. When food was scarce after the war and my brother was just a baby, when what we lacked at the farm could only be had in Palma on the black market—such as sugar, chocolate, rice, and gasoline—Father would ride his bicycle to the city over rough old roads so as to avoid the Guàrdia Civil. Then he would slowly and painfully make his way home, loaded down with packages of the things we lacked. He pedaled for five hours with the weight of the bike and the bundles through the cutting winter winds. It touches a tender spot in my heart when I think of that caring man on those lonely roads, the provisions for his loved ones on his back.

"When Mama told me about those trips, she said he would arrive with a beautiful smile on his face, wash his feet and tell of his trip as if it were an epic. Then, satisfied, he would fall asleep.

"He used to take me by the hand and whether to contract a worker or to visit a retired sea captain, we would traipse over all the trails around Orlandis, over rough mountain paths to distant farms, and he would tell me the name of every place, stories about their families, the phases of the growth of the trees. A big white stone on top of a hill reminded him of his grandfather telling him a roan horse had once fallen off the cliff there, in front of an abandoned house with a bush of rue by its door. He recalled that a beautiful young blonde had planted it there to ward off witches. The sight of a jujube tree would make him improvise an elegy full of sentiment and details about the fruit trees that were disappearing: the haw tree, the hackberry, the strawberry tree, the service tree."

Egèria paused there. The silence was explosive. Then she spoke her last words: "You might think all this is not very much. But it's what we are."

And before Dioclecià of Pula could move, everyone had turned toward him, because in that atmosphere a vibration from far back in time had drawn the people's attention to the Pulan; they knew he was to be the next to speak. The large man's countenance was grave. He filled his glass with champagne and drank it, his eyes fixed on the liquid. He poured himself another and, mesmerized by the flames, teetered toward the fireplace. Tomàs Moro, his face transfigured, understood how far they had come, how very far. He downed another glass of champagne and then, refilled his glass and with a hypnotic look in his eyes, followed his relative to the halo of fire.

And the fire was roaring. Dioclecià of Pula threw his champagne onto the burning logs. The liquid splashed with a hissing pop over the flames. Dioclecià didn't know why he said what he was about to say. He had never known anyone from Pula ever to speak from his heart so well, though he was sure all the men of Pula felt the same every night—absorbed as they were in their own mortality—when the subject of death came up.

"If Francesc de Borja Taltavull is anywhere now, he is here with us. We are fire; we have to make fire."

Tomàs Moro emptied his glass. The jolly crackling of the flames was energetic and warm. And with their glasses filled, everybody moved over to the fireplace, led by Beautiful Egèria.

25

"Father used to get back from Palma just as it was getting dark. When I—just a little boy then—heard the tinkle of his bicycle bell as he rolled through the almond grove at Taltavull Hall, I would come running to meet him. There he stood, my father, balancing the bike loaded with packages. There would be a tired smile on his face. First he would bend over and give me a kiss; then he would produce a little package in which there were some slightly squashed pastries and some comic books," thought Damià while he listened to his sister, Egèria, engrossed in the commemoration of her father.

"I would wolf down a pastry and that sticky, dreamy sweetness was pure ecstasy out there in the middle of those abandoned fields; to me it was a kind of communion with the fabulous and unknown delights that existed in the cities and palaces of the rest of the world. Then I used to read the comic books, and my imagination anxiously devoured the stories that rose and disappeared like rockets from their pages. Yes, good old smiling Dad, exhausted at the handlebars because he had also gone whoring. Egèria, that imbecile. Just as much an imbecile as her father, as if for both of them the world was limited to the size of their mosquito brains.

"Certainly he found things in Palma that were lacking in Orlandis, and he brought some of them home. What my dumb sister didn't realize was he really went there for the women."

The first time Damià went to the city and dared go to the rowdy barrio around Porta de San Antoni, he went into one of the bars, attracted by the solid thighs and deep décolletage of the provocative tarts standing around, and a voice greeted him, "Hi there, Damianet! Come to turn in your bottle nipple for a real one?"

It was the voice of Pau Pujol from Orlandis, a cripple with a large goiter on his neck who worked there as a waiter and who had often accompanied him and Francesc de Borja Taltavull when they went fishing for squid on winter evenings, the humid night air biting into them, the lantern shining brightly over the smooth surface of the harbor, both men casting their weighted nets and hauling up those pale and viscous little beasts from the oppressive, murky enigma of the deep. The boy would inevitably fall asleep, and when they woke him and told him it was time to step ashore by lantern light, he could never make out the shoreline and would break into tears, thinking they wanted him to jump into the deep dark sea. Both men would crack up laughing.

"That kid is a chicken-shit," sputtered his father in his nasal voice, cutting off whole syllables, like a barking dog.

In the end, Damià always jumped, twice humiliated because he had misjudged the distance to the shoreline, and because his father had insulted him. And he trembled from the damp cold encrusted in the marrow of his bones.

"Pujol, don't tell my father I've been here, for God's sake!" exclaimed Damià at the bar.

Pau Pujol raised his arms in a gesture of helplessness, enjoying the moment, "But I haven't seen him for a hundred years! You would have run into him here, and quite content he was, some time back."

"What do you mean by that?" asked the boy quizzically.

"Oh, now that the boy has become a man, he needs to know where the devil sleeps!"

Damià listened to the story in confusion: his father used to arrive in Orlandis every week or two, park his bicycle in the storeroom behind the bar and when he came in—a short little man with his hair all slicked back, his shoes shined—the first thing he did in his stentorian voice was to offer drinks all around.

"Just like the conceited little ass," mumbled Damià Taltavull aloud that Christmas Eve as he recalled the incident.

"What did you say, son?" asked Magdalena.

"Nothing, Mother. Do you really think I have anything to say to you?"

"Ay! What do you mean, talking that way to your mother?"

"Just what I said, nothing."

"Well, all right."

But Damià was still listening to Pau Pujol in his imagination, in that bar in Palma that stank of urinals, stale beer, and cigarette butts: "Oh, and after the round of drinks, he would take one of the girls up to bed, and I can assure you he got his money's worth! Look over there: that's the one he screwed the most, Susi. Susi! Come over here a minute and meet the son of Francesc, my countryman. I assure you, Damiàcete, your father left quite a wad of bills in her box."

A plump older woman with dyed blond hair, her thick lips painted a glaring cardinal red, came over to Damià, took his hand and rubbed it against one of her enormous soft breasts, as she told him, "You have the face of a corrupt youth, just like him. Come over here and I'll show you some tricks."

Damià had instinctively drawn back . . . not from disgust, but from the suffocating avalanche of vulgarity pouring from the woman. The blonde's swollen features hardened "You dress like little Lord Fauntleroy. Ain't I good enough for you? Well, your father, that pesky bastard, used to talk my ear off, praising himself as if he were the Pope of Rome! And he had to cry and beg for this crack that I've just decided not to rent to you, not for all the gold in the world, you fussy little snot! Imagine him, giving me syphilis, the swine! He had to pay me for every last injection of penicillin, too!"

Pujol the waiter grew uneasy and started tugging at Damià, who was trembling with anger and shame: "Your father just had some rotten luck. A skinny girl fresh in from Casablanca gave it to him, and by the time we found out, she had given the damn syph to a whole bunch of guys. I took your father to a doctor friend of mine. After that episode, though, he's hardly ever come back here . . . it left him sort of shattered."

Damià recalled how a few years before, his father had developed some sores in his mouth, his hair had started to fall out, and they had had to give him injections of penicillin, which cost a lot because they had to be smuggled in as contraband. He became emaciated and had to spend many hours a day in bed.

"He's got the weakness," his wife said, as she prepared rich, frothy cups of chicken broth for him at home.

"The simpleton! She has always taken it on the chin for him," grumbled Damià. It didn't matter whether his father had or had not gone to screw in those hovels. What did bother him was the childish vulgarity in which he had wallowed there in that bar, smiling like a little ruffian while that tart, that monstrous caricature of a woman, pawed him over.

So that was his father: the ridiculous vanity of the insignificant. Francesc de Borja Taltavull, sitting there caning a chair, building another. The end results were enormous and junky-looking, crudely made pieces he spent weeks on, and which he proudly showed off as he explained the most minute and obvious details of their construction. And Damià had seen in his friends' houses stylish wicker chairs, lathe-turned legs, varnished until they shone like crystal goblets. The whole town had been buying them in Palma for years.

Egèria continued with her funeral oration, while Damià recalled how his father had refused to cooperate in the family effort to rebuild the alarm clock factory. Instead, he had spent entire weeks seated there under the shade of the grape arbor, sipping the new wine from the Taltavull harvest, all the while mumbling very sound reasons why the effort would ruin them all. And in that fashion, his family had finally ground to a halt at the edge of the slowly increasing prosperity of the rest of the Taltavulls.

"Perhaps he didn't want to admit even to himself the real reason for his attitude: the fact that he always turned his back on any job that was the least bit demanding," Damià repeated to himself for the nth time, and irritated to the nth degree at the thought of it. "Father ridiculed and feared what he did not know. And he wanted to stay here, a recluse on his farm, so that nobody could pry into his business or question it, so that his circumscribed, repetitive, inert world could not oblige him to do anything. I feel sure he married Mother because he knew she was simple-minded."

"And if he used to hang out in that whore's bar it was, no doubt, because he wanted to go there, just like everybody else around here, just like all the Taltavulls. The only thing we do—believing we are escaping our own monotony—is jump into bed with women. But I'm also convinced he hung out there because, among those miserable unfortunates, he felt like a god . . . until that girl from Casablanca or whoever it was really rubbed his nose in the shit, that same shit he used to dish out to me when I was a kid."

At home there had never been enough money to buy new chairs, new clothes or anything else that might shine like new, all of which Damià observed others had as the face of Orlandis changed. The overcoat he had worn as a child was an old tabard from his grandfather that had been cut down, resewn, and was still clumsily mended, the buttons sewn on backwards. His classmates used to pinch him and kid him about it: "You look like the boogie man in that thing!" As a child he never had a piece of folding money in his pocket to show off, as the other kids did.

Damià, Egèria, and their mother were forced to live off what remained of Taltavull Hall, tied as if in a nightmare to the heritage of the place, the valley, the dead weight of the past.

"Did Father love his family, his ancestors? Hell no! All those words he babbled only served to protect his obtuse mediocrity, his laziness . . . the raving pride of the midget! The cult adoration of the ears of a jackass." Damià trembled every time he started to think about the old man again.

"And all of it in exchange for a labyrinth of futile fantasies," he continued thinking bitterly. His father used to sit beside the fire, slicing bread for the typical, scalded Majorcan soups. And he would sit there, talking for hours on end, a cheap vainglory it was: he would brag that he knew how to do any kind of job; Taltavull Hall was the best estate in all Orlandis; he had said such-and-such to so-and-so and had left him with his mouth agape; he had just honed his pruning hook and it became a tool like no other in the whole world.

"Ah, yes, Francesc de Borja," his mother would chorus, her eyes as big as dinner plates—Damià didn't know whether from somnolence or admiration—while little Egèria gazed into the dancing flames of the hearth and dreamed of princes.

The father scalded the soup every day, and everybody had to eat it, along with a piece of bacon fat broiled over the coals.

"We're eating the same stuff all the dead Taltavulls did five hundred years ago!" roared Damià in his raging inner dialogs, as he jammed his spoon into another bowl of soup and soggy bread, just as if he were sticking it into hog slop, his eyes cast down in anger.

And his father continued arrogantly about how the graft on the cherry tree needed to be cut in a special way, in the shape of a shield in the bark, a technique nobody knew anymore, but which he would do when the season came around because once as a youth he had seen a peasant do it at Coll de les Santes, though he had done it wrong, because what should have been done was. . . . The light would grow dim at the hearth late after supper, heads would nod off as sleep overtook everyone in the family except his father, just reaching the peak of his proud, rambling soliloquy of trivia.

A graft was maybe a half-hour's work . . . but his father would talk about it for weeks on end. And in the end, he would leave it for next year, and when that moment came, it would be drizzling rain, and he. . . . Damià had been studying his father with an ever more critical, embittered eye. If a job became too long or complicated for his father, he would abandon it halfway through. He was only able to submit to a discipline as long as his initial emotional impulse lasted.

He had no desire to seek and make comparisons. All he wanted was to repeat what had been done. When his brother Bernat found water, Francesc de Borja had to take to his bed from the fright. And it was a double fright because it was someone else, not he himself, who had succeeded and because the water well created a new situation for him: that imperious, magnificent abundance of water demanded a response from him. An air of musty age and decay floated over Taltavull Hall, of old things half-done then abandoned.

"Everything turns to dust," mused Damià as a youth, overwhelmed by a destiny that each day weighed on him more and more and became more repugnant to him, and which he identified with his father.

As he had done with Egèria, Francesc de Borja had also taken Damià by the hand and hauled him all over the countryside near and around Orlandis. In the morning when he got up, his father would drink a bowl of *café con leche* sweetened with honey, along with some Inca cookies. Then he would look at his son and begin to mutter, a sure sign of his smugness, "We have to go to Cantàrida, because they've got a bedeviled mule there they can't tame, and I'm sure I can do it."

Damià imagined the picture in his mind: "Walk for three or four hours over those godforsaken trails, only to wind up jabbering on forever with another hallucinating, lazyboned peasant." But he didn't protest, and so they set out . . . what his father could not tolerate was disobedience or back talk from anybody. If he was not surrounded by submission, he would get so angry that he seemed to go crazy.

And if anybody dared challenge him he would collapse and shrivel up, his nostrils flaring, his skin turning blue, until he burst forth in a strange hoarse voice laughably out of all proportion to his tiny body.

On one occasion when his father blew up like that, Damià couldn't hold back his laughter, and Francesc de Borja screamed at him and knocked him around until he broke his nose.

Damià hated those walks through rugged, long-forgotten mountainous terrain, through the parts of Orlandis where the boy found only loneliness and hostility. Houses built into the hillsides like caves, with tiny windows, little light, and an air of larval filth. The people were rustic, physically worn-out, deformed, and they endlessly repeated the old legends, invariably the same every time. As they walked, his father would invoke the events and players at each place.

And when they came upon a certain stone or a certain bush of rue, Damià would think with such exultant sarcasm he couldn't understand why he didn't say it outloud, "Now I'll have to put up with the story of the roan horse for the hundredth time. Man alive! And here's where he'll tell the story of that miserable girl who planted the rue and then wet her panties all in a fright!" In the meantime, his father the vociferous protagonist babbled on in his heavy, nasal voice, " . . . And the roan horse fell right over here and I. . . ." The fall of his father, his final illness. . . . He was no longer himself, Egèria said. But he was, more so than ever. His physical debility had been eating away at him ever since he got syphilis. Maybe he never recovered from it. As his weakness grew, he lost his ceremonious tone, the pretentiousness that he had previously dressed his insignificant ego in and that until then had been his whole existence. He was now reduced to his primal functions: skin and bone, walking with difficulty, every movement anxious, self-absorbed, his lips dry from lack of saliva. All he thought about were his medications . . . his skin stank of medicine. With all his little boxes, tubes and vials lined up, he felt in control, and this reassured him at the same time it satisfied him, for it took less energy to swallow the pills than it took to talk or eat. His pills were the last act in his comedy of self-sufficiency.

Damià had been unable to avoid this thought: "My father had become repugnant to me in his later years, as if whatever had afflicted him—his sordid decrepitude—was contagious. And it could be, as Egèria said, that he experienced a moment of peace before he died because that happens to a lot of people. But I think he died because, inspired by his slight improvement, he wanted to regain what he again thought was his, from the fresh fava beans—which might even have killed him, hard as they are to digest—to the esteem of his daughter, deceiving her with his verbal drivel as he had always done."

At that point Damià broke out in laughter and started choking from it; he drank some water, and it went down the wrong way. He coughed half-to-death as tears rolled down his cheeks and everybody turned to stare at him.

"Ay, my son! What's the matter?"

"He must have been overcome with emotion by Egèria's speech," said Càndida, Tomàs Moro's wife.

"Skin and bones impregnated with medicine! How the hell is he ever going to rot in his tomb? He's probably embalmed from all that stuff he took, just like the monkey from Pula," Damià imagined as he choked again on his own laughter.

26

It was time for the ice cream, with the sensuous flavors of fresh and toasted almonds added to the creamy white frothiness of the ice cream itself. It, too, was homemade. Joana Maria, wearing her seventeen years like a garden of ripe fruit ready to be plucked, wolfed it down so fast the cold made her temples ache. She decided to leave it alone. Why go for something that hurts? In her own eyes, Joana Maria lacked the patience to commit to what she liked. She often said to herself enthusiastically: "Ah! If only a whole lifetime could be squeezed into just one day!"

Unobtrusively she caught Niní and Sebastiana's eyes. They had brought a record player. When they first mentioned it, their parents and aunts and uncles had objected, somewhere between doubtful and condescending: "Nobody has ever danced anything modern here in Taltavull Hall."

"We're not saying they danced with Michael Jackson a thousand years ago, but we would like to do it today," they replied, stitched in giggles.

But Joana Maria pouted with displeasure: Egèria, with all that boring stuff about her father, had raised the question of his recent death at the table. And Cousin Damià—no doubt impressed by his sister's tale—was twisting around in his chair with a strange look on his face . . . he must be sobbing.

"All we needed here was a funeral!" thought Joana Maria in her petulant mood. "Because now Grandmother Brígida or any number of the aunts would probably protest, with the stupid argument that organizing a dance now would be a lack of respect for the dead."

The girl went back to spooning up her ice cream after the icy ache in her temples had subsided. And then she remembered Uncle Francesc de Borja: an obsequious, runty little man. Some images of him crossed her mind, isolated silent images in her memory: her uncle walking down a street in Orlandis carrying a basket of eggs; her uncle at Taltavull Hall, holding out his hand to see if it was raining; her uncle with one cheek badly swollen from an abscessed tooth. Joana Maria shrugged her shoulders.

"Shall we bring on the music?" Tina asked, pointing to the portable record player they had parked in a corner.

Joana Maria desperately wanted to dance. When the music grew louder, when the music floated through the air, she felt as if she were entering a sublime region of luminous clouds. She didn't know anything about music, nor did she pay much attention to the singers, but when she heard a melody, she vibrated with its rhythm as if her whole body were being shaped by the sounds themselves.

So Joana Maria submerged herself in the dancing, especially when they put on something exciting; and it was as if the flight of the rhythm were an authentic physical translation of happiness. And she noticed the unmistakable beginnings of love transfiguring her: during a dance she would have given her by-then misty self to any boy, she would smoothly absorb him within her—a boy who of course also knew and interpreted dancing as life, both so beautiful.

27

" . . . Yes, exotic, sweet-smelling chocolate. In Budapest, of course. One afternoon, I was absent-mindedly thumbing through Delacroix's journal on the table, slowly sipping a cup of chocolate. When you have to travel around the world for a living as I do, you can get devilishly bored. I have come to appreciate two things in order to survive: the museums and the history of each place I've visited. Both paintings and historical events are holy, a mass of people and battles, all in all quite entertaining—he lowered his voice and winked—as well as women, whom I have come to appreciate as well . . . and they often turn out to be quite succulent! Ha! Ha! Ha!"

The others chuckled along with Joan Pere Tudurí. Old Honorat wise-cracked, "Yeah, this guy with the excuse of his goddamned alarm clocks has won the lottery!"

"That afternoon I was reading Eugène Delacroix's notes dated the third of April, 1847, where he was describing with admiration the mansion of the Duke of Morny, which he had visited: 'I saw luxury the likes of which I had never seen before.' As I say, I was reading his description when an old lady, seated at the table next to me stared at me fiercely and commented in French, 'You'll never know, dear Julia, from which direction to expect misfortune or well-being. How perplexing it is for human beings to receive and hold on to the gift of life, as complex and fragile as it is. Life starts with one's own body chemistry, which on the other hand lacks any reliable hint of what fate awaits it!'

"In my surprise, I abruptly raised my hand and accidentally brushed against the pitcher of chocolate so hard I sent it flying into an elaborately embellished marble bust of Mihály Vörösmarty, the famous romantic poet whose verses the Hungarians will recite to you at the drop of a hat . . . and which I frankly don't like a bit. Have you ever heard of him?"

"Of whom?" asked Cristòfol Mardà as he moved his chair closer.

"Vörösmarty," replied Joan Pere.

"And who was this martyr, some Christian persecuted by the Hungarian communists?" ventured Bernat the Wise.

"Don't kid around, Uncle, he was a poet!" Tudurí retorted impatiently. "I was sitting in the Vörösmarty Café, which is the old Gerbaud salon in Budapest—I mean in the part called Pest, the flat, new part. The old part, Buda, is perched on a cliff. And in the café there was a bust of the poet Mihály Vörösmarty."

"The one you slopped the chocolate all over," nodded Mardà knowingly.

"That's right. And I was saying that I didn't like his poetry a bit. His strings of exalted pro-nationalist clichés make me sick. Listen to this choice example:

I know of your unbreakable
Fatherland, Hungarian, faithful servant;
It cares for and protects you,
It is your cradle and your tomb.

"Above all a tomb, what with all the invasions and revolutions those poor people have suffered. Ha! Ha! Don't you agree?"

"Well, I wouldn't go so far as to agree. I've never heard of such things from anybody," Moro interjected, looking at Tudurí as if he had just gone crazy.

"Poetry . . . we're not exactly in the habit of using it here, Nephew," added Bernat the Wise sarcastically.

Joan Pere Tudurí paused long enough to dip his cake in his ice cream. As he raised it to his mouth it broke into soggy pieces. People began getting restless around the table. A few got up; the men gravitated into a group and began to chat, some of them lighting up cigars, while others continued chewing on bitter almonds. Joan Pere had just recalled the anecdote about the chocolate when Carloteta upset her bowl of ice cream, splashing it all over her cheeks and down her dress, and then burst into tears of desolation.

"Ha! Ha! Ha!" continued Tudurí, enjoying himself immensely, "I was also just about to burst out laughing that afternoon when I saw the silly chocolate running over the bust of that haughty, hair-splitting poet. But I stopped short when I noticed the old lady watching me. She pointed to the journal I was reading and said, 'Oh, what a terrible mistake! I saw you with that book in French, and since you don't look the least like a Magyar, I decided to consult you about some language doubts I have in a letter I'm writing to my granddaughter, who lives in Orleans and only speaks French. I was thinking out the sentence I wanted to ask you about, and I must have been so obsessed with it, or the years have caught up with me and made me so absent-minded, or because I'm always alone and can't distinguish between what's going on outside and inside my head . . . and that's why I said what I did. Oh, pardon me! The chocolate . . . oh, oh, oh, and the poet, oh! Waiter! Waiter!'"

"We don't have old ladies like that here either," commented Albert the Younger, glancing slyly out of the corner of his eye at the little group that had formed around his mother, his sisters, and his sisters-in-law, who were chatting up a storm.

Tudurí continued, "However, the whole episode would have been reduced to an insignificant traveler's anecdote had not the old lady later become almost my only partner in conversation during the rest of my stay in Hungary. For you see, we ran into each other every afternoon in the Vörösmarty, which was located in a sad little square near the great and silent Danube. Its high ceilings were decked with elaborately carved reliefs, the walls hung with silk tapestries framed in plaster moldings. The Bohemian porcelain, the marble-topped tables with their brass legs, the windows hung with embroidered lace curtains, all an enchanting, tangible tribute to an exhausted bourgeois past, the pathetic elegance of a final fiction, a desperate effort not to sink into the sordid present without at least caressing an echo of those dreams.

"The clientele of the Vörösmarty, still sporting gold stick pins and Astrakhan coats, came there to politely take their tea or chocolate along with a pastry before they had to return to their drab homes, which before the war had been superb villas and were now converted into narrow, warren-like apartments with dingy staircases. The same kind of lodgings were to be found in the newer buildings too, prefabricated cement cubes divided into tiny cells. Those people could only find a vestige of a past that had been theirs and their parents' before the butchery of the wars and ideologies. And only there could they practice a sort of childlike, high society theater where the young, rosy-cheeked girls even managed to sport the odd Italian foulard or a crocodile-skin purse.

"The old lady gazed in satisfaction around the lively café and told me proudly, 'We are all reactionaries in Hungary!' And she used to repeat it to me in the street when I accompanied her on occasion, as she pointed out the groups of people gathered in front of the modest jewelry shop windows. They were spending their small savings on the only substantial things they could carry off or hide during the alternate periods of unrest and submission they suffered.

"Winter was setting in. Suddenly snow buried the dull cityscape in mystery. I began to frequent the café, no doubt attracted by its peculiar characteristics in that precarious Budapest, but also because I had nothing better to do all day. The vice-minister of foreign trade hadn't gotten around to examining our alarm clock bids. At the same time Eva incongruously refused to see me, claiming complicated reasons over the phone as to why her husband was becoming suspicious."

"Who was this Eva? Some day you're going to get an unwelcome surprise!" pontificated the engineer Albornoz, equally concerned with the health of the forest and family morality.

"Let's not get ahead of the story . . . everything will become clear in due time. Do you know what I did then, apart from hanging around in the Vörösmarty? Well, to avoid becoming neurotic I tried to research the correspondence between King Matias Corvino and Lady Beatrice of Aragon, as well as her indignant correspondence with His Holiness the Pope. But the Ministry of Culture would not authorize my research. The project had occurred to me one damp afternoon as I was wandering through the ruins of Matias's palace, located on the green Visegrád hills where some Gothic capitals and Renaissance fountains still remained, high above the quiet curve of the Danube, stretching out divinely, implacably, below me.

"I used to ceremoniously greet Madame Rákos, the old lady, by kissing her wrinkled hand. She would then launch into her froth of chatter, 'Patience, my dear friend, patience. Your problems will find solutions even if nothing happens, for after you have been waiting and hoping for so long, your tension will finally dissipate. The only feeling that will remain will be a sense of what you lack, but it will be stripped of its urgency. You will feel as if you were floating, as if your spirit had shed all its chains.

"'I suppose the same thing must happen in the course of a long voyage: the makeshift becomes reality. In that way the traveler achieves a new and youthful sense of liberation. And please understand that I don't speak from experience, because few of us have traveled, and even fewer have done so with any pleasure in this unfortunate country of ours.

"'But perhaps I have been able to experience this sense of tentativeness in another way. You see, I have lived through the wars we have suffered here. Measured in time, they may appear to have been short. But you cannot imagine unless you have experienced them the absolutely definitive character war imposes on one's life. And afterward came the endless repressions, the unseen presence of terror reigning over all our thoughts and actions.

"'All my family was either killed or imprisoned. Not a single one has survived. All I have is my granddaughter in Orleans, whom I haven't seen since she was four months old when my daughter was able to escape with her . . . a trail of infinite sadness. I hope, my dear sir, that you understand me: if the provisional aspects of this life had not replaced the essentials, tragedy would have devoured me as well.

"'I once read the story of a long expedition through deep jungles, which at a given moment lost sight of its objective, advancing out of the sheer will to continue, to struggle forward, banal daily incidents taking on the aspect of the transcendental, the infinite.'

"Well, that's how the cultivated Madame Rákos spoke. And that's why I answered her with another verse quoted from the poet Vörösmarty:

Let your heart overflow with the pleasures of wine,
Play the violin and forget the world of pain.

"I mean, if the adventure of life has no goal, if it is only an expedition on the march, then we should take part in it happily, enjoying every day that goes by.

"But just thinking of those verses left a bitter taste in my mouth, because Eva had taught them to me, turning them into a symbol of our relationship. I learned them one day when I had thrown her face-down on the bed and was boring her from the rear while she recited those verses exultantly and half-drunk. . . ."

"Holy Christ! I'd give a year of my life for a tart like that!" Tomàs Moro exclaimed with envy.

"Let's not exaggerate. . . . But if you didn't see her in Budapest, how did you ever get that tight with her?" commented Fèlix Albornoz disdainfully.

"The whole affair started on the cruise ship *Ludovico Ariosto.* I was sick of traveling for business alone, tied up for days and weeks at a time in city hotels. I was tired of reading the same old books on the same old subjects until I was bored out of my skull, and so three or four summers ago, I took my vacation on a Mediterranean cruise, as you will recall. Brief visits from one place to another, a carefree sense of leisure allowed me to pick and choose from the activities on board ship. What bores me is exhausting, demanding activity.

"When I boarded the cruise ship in Genoa, I immediately spotted Eva standing alone. I offered to buy her a Coca-Cola, and she accepted. While we were going up the steep ship's stairs to the bar, she waggled her succulent buns—as rotund as her voluptuous breasts and lips—in such a way that I kept bumping into them—shall we say—with my stomach. I noticed—and she noticed—the erection that overcame me. 'The essence of life,' said the waiter with a wink, as he served us our drinks. Ha! Ha! Ha!

"Eva was taking the cruise with a girlfriend, Margit, both of them married to respectable Hungarian bureaucrats, members of the Communist Party. Ever since she had come on board, Margit wasn't exactly vomiting, but instead seemed to be leaking a sort of stringy drool, always covering her mouth with a hanky to hide it. She spent most of the trip curled up on her bunk in the cabin she shared with Eva. This situation miraculously facilitated the wild union of Eva and me in my cabin.

"At the same time, Eva had begun telling me the story of Matias Corvino and the intriguing Neapolitan princess, Beatrice of Aragon. The ship docked in Naples on a scorching hot afternoon, and we had passed from a torrid, exhausting session of screwing to the suffocating heat of the ruins of Pompeii and then paused to recoup our energies with a cool glass of Chianti under the welcome shade of a grape arbor. She loved to bend her elbow and managed to down a number of glasses of Chianti while at the same time jabbering on endlessly about the king and queen."

"I wonder if it isn't Joan Pere who is drunk . . . what the devil will he come up with next?" said Ignasi Taltavull Oliva in a prudent voice.

But Tudurí didn't hear him as he slowly stirred the sugar into his coffee and continued his narration: "Beatrice of Aragon, a rare beauty adorned with all the art of the Renaissance, daughter of Ferdinand I of Naples and granddaughter—obviously—of our Alfonso the Magnanimous, was for that reason called the Virgin Maiden of Aragon. Alfonso, as you know, had become a migratory bird and had flown off to better climes, to sun-drenched and spicy Naples, leaving his wife and subjects at home on the Iberian Peninsula. Ha! Beatrice had married the Hungarian, Corvino, at eighteen.

"Encouraged by the young queen, Hungary was soon filled with books, music, and sculptures, all of it inflated with Italic gentility, until the cloak of death covered the king. And his illustrious widow diligently conspired to remove the crown from the head of the dead king's natural son and have it placed on the brow of one Ladislao VII, whom she then married in a hurry.

"The new monarch imitated her ruthlessness once he felt securely seated upon his throne, for he then began annulment proceedings against her. Pope Alexander VI—that fat Borgia plagued with piety and lechery and originally from a town near Valencia in Spain—granted Ludovico his annulment with great pleasure. So Beatrice, by then forty-three, vexed and bitter, was forced to return to Naples, where the Sad Queens, as they were called, lived: Joana of Aragon, widow of Ferdinand the First, and her daughter, also known as Joana of Aragon, widow in turn of another Ferdinand, but this one the Second.

"By the way, I saw a painting of an Italian Joana of Aragon in the Louvre, painted by a Jules Roman, in which the subject was wearing a red dress and a huge red hat over long blond hair, her face very lively and beautiful. I don't know which of the Joanas it was. Meanwhile, when Beatrice arrived in Naples, they became known as the Three Sad Queens."

"Ah, but what about the Hungarian?" asked Albert the Younger in confusion.

"Yes, back to her. We had still not broken into the Eastern European market with our alarm clocks, which would have been an advantageous thing to do, what with their depressed economies. So Eva and her bureaucrat husband seemed the perfect avenue of approach. She offered to help in any way she could. And the fact is that after I set up the operation here with Uncle Bernat, all I had to do was request an interview to make the offer, and a visa and official approval were immediately forthcoming. She surely must have had something to do with it. The strange part of it was the cool attitude with which they received me afterward in Budapest. Perhaps her husband had smelled a rat. The sales contract, however, turned out to be very profitable."

"What a mess! Life is surely strange," meditated Albert the Younger with a shrug of incomprehension.

"Ah! Life!" echoed Tudurí the salesman, as he took off again on his verbal adventure. "The old lady from the Vörösmarty when she heard a sweetened version of my encounter with Eva aboard the *Ludovico Ariosto,* and after quoting the waiter's comment about 'the essence of life' to her, interrupted me, arching her brow and exclaiming: 'The essence of life? The truth? Uf! Let me tell you my story of the Russian violinist. It happened right here on that platform where they sometimes give recitals. A small but delightful orchestra had come from Minsk. Our bureaucrats called this obligatory traffic of humble functionaries 'cultural exchange,' which goes on between those eastern countries that declare such great and suspicious friendship to each other. Mozart, Chopin, and Liszt, obviously. . . . '

"I remember interrupting the venerable old lady, driven by my by now-maniacal obsession, quite possibly an exteriorization of the irritation I felt toward Eva, 'Pardon me, Madame Rákos, but didn't Vörösmarty dedicate a poem to Liszt in which he proclaimed him the "Grand apostle of the tempestuous Fatherland?"'

"The old lady shrugged her shoulders and continued: 'Perhaps. . . . The orchestra from Minsk performed some very select pieces, and the public listened attentively. And a sort of heaviness, as if nothing in the world could ever change, seemed to settle over the salon, over us all. A discreet and courteous Rumanian here on a business trip used to come by every afternoon, delighted by the music . . . the same way an ancient opulent lady with finger-waved hair used to sit over there by that column, bewitched by the violinist.

"'Because he was the star of the group, the soloist played with electrifying drive, a lock of hair dangling from his brow. How she trapped him with her submissive gaze! The Rumanian soon became aware of her. And he also noticed the musician had begun to regale her with subtle, though reserved, attention: a sign, a gesture, a look. And since the Rumanian also felt lonely in Budapest, he focused his yearning eyes more and more on the lady as his attraction for her grew and grew.

"'And she, as the Rumanian discovered one afternoon, had also begun to trade glances with him! His heart throbbed with emotion. A few days later the situation became more heated and more complicated: she showed equal attention to both men. The Rumanian became tormented by his paralyzing timidity; at the same time his love for her grew. He both sought and avoided the lady, who brashly seemed about to devour him with her huge eyes.

"'The violinist finally noticed the Rumanian as he stood upon the stage, drawing his bow and searching the audience, and his expression of irritation grew apace. 'He hates me,' the terrified Rumanian thought. And then one day the Russian violinist charged out into the audience, no doubt at the lady and the Rumanian. But his colleagues managed to restrain him.

"'The next afternoon our Rumanian arrived prepared for anything, from beseeching the lady to challenging the violinist. But both she and the orchestra had disappeared. Astonished, he questioned the waiters, who explained that the Russian had shot himself to death, and the concerts had been postponed while the police investigated.

"'The Rumanian went into hiding. The police! In our country those are frightening words. He became desperate when he realized the complications the affair might cause him and so sought asylum in his embassy, which acted as an intermediary with the police, explaining the following to them: the violinist was suffering from cancer; his exaggerated ogling was in effect a gesture of pain he could no longer bear, and after he had almost collapsed on stage—saved from falling flat on his face by his colleagues—he dispatched himself that very night.

"'The police had also tracked down the aging lady, and it turned out she was terribly near-sighted and had to constantly blink her huge, myopic eyes in an attempt to focus on the stage, which to her was just a jumble of fuzzy moving shadows. She attended the performances at the Vörösmarty Café because she was enchanted by the music and always followed its rhythms with corresponding movements of her body. And she stopped going when they told her there would be no more performances. She wasn't in the least aware of the existence of the Rumanian. As for the Russian, she had only heard him playing the violin since she could not focus well enough to see him. She couldn't understand why the police were interrogating her. My God, the aberrant passions of a Rumanian!'

"And that's how the story of the old lady of Vörösmarty ended. I left the café late every evening and took long walks afterwards. The sky was low, a dull gray. There were few pedestrians and fewer automobiles on the streets, and at times, as I mentioned, it would snow. The marble monuments throughout the city had been shrouded in heavy canvas tarpaulins so they wouldn't crack from the freezing weather. They looked like enormous, forgotten ghosts carved in tufa. There was no word from Eva at the hotel.

"'The essence of life. . . . ' My life had been reduced to my trips to the Vörösmarty, to my pitcher of chocolate, to my conversations with Madame Rákos, who was always so well disposed: 'I met the Rumanian out of pure coincidence, just as I did you. I can get by with my French quite well when it's a question of speaking to someone from another country whose language has Latin roots. Didn't you find it strange that everything the Rumanian had observed and analyzed had turned out to be false? In the end he was only able to communicate with the likes of me because we both shared the roots of a dead language, Latin.

"'It's similar to the poetry of Mihály Vörösmarty: you hate those poems, you find them boring. Well, that's all fine and good. But I can assure you— because I have seen it myself—that numerous excited youths, their hair to the wind, their courage bristling, have thrown themselves against the Nazis and the Communists driven by a love for Hungary and for freedom that they had learned in great part from the fervent verses of Vörösmarty. . . . My God! My son was one of them. My God! Reality is hardly important, for we are in essence our dreams and our beliefs.'

"I would leave the Vörösmarty, as I said, alone, and walk alone beside the broad, smooth, steely waters of the Danube. Although it lay there at my feet, reflecting the spectral and elegant parliament building with its legion of towers, balconies, and galleries, all of it an emptiness in the night, it seemed that the river was distant, far away. And on the opposite cliff-like shore, in Buda, the gigantic Monument to the Liberation rose sorrowfully against the horizon like the shredded shadows of a huge dead bird. The Danube flowed silently on through the night. I returned to my hotel late and very tired. I read a few pages from Delacroix's journal as I sipped a chilled pear-flavored aquavit.

"'Don't think I can't recall my past just because it's been terrible,' the old lady would begin every time she saw me in the Vörösmarty. 'Quite the contrary: I can think of its horror and still somehow feel content. I have overcome my memories of misfortune, forcing myself to keep and hold dear those happy memories that remain, like the time someone lovingly offered me a bouquet of violets. I no longer have passions or ambitions. I can still enjoy and feel ecstasy when I recall that scene of the gentleman with the violets, which I accepted with a slight bow and an inward smile of pleasure. Perhaps, in order to achieve peace and a stable happiness, dreams and anxieties first have to be rooted out. I challenge you to find such happiness. I dare you.'

"They signed the alarm clock contract at eleven o'clock one morning, and by twelve-thirty I was on a plane out of there, sick to death of Budapest. I didn't even say farewell to Madame Rákos. I was up to my eyeballs in her sermonizing, which always led absolutely nowhere, a thousand leering faces from the past. And I was fed up with Eva's neurotic slipperiness, with the mummified intrigues of Beatrice de Aragon, with the rotten luxuries exposed by Delacroix, and finally fed up with the Danube—so vast it didn't seem real—along with the overly well-groomed phoniness of the Café Vörösmarty and that poet's damned poetry as the pathway to death."

Joan Pere Tudurí had turned sullen and aloof as he wound down his tale, a tale he had begun in high spirits. Those memories from his past had slowly joined, forming a screen with premonition written all over it and which smelled of condemnation. He poured himself a glass of whiskey and without realizing it, downed it in a single swallow.

Arcadi the priest, who had joined the group, observed, "It seems that trip to Budapest left you in pretty rough shape. . . ."

Tudurí whirled about as if he had been slapped, "And why the hell did I have to set out on an expedition with no purpose? Shit!"

"Well, old man, in the end, happiness is. . . ." Fèlix Albornoz had begun to philosophize, when Joan Pere interrupted him, "Happiness and pleasure are like the hunt: you have to take risks to bag your game."

"However, and to continue with the example of an expedition, I believe. . . ." began Ignasi Taltavull Oliva, the judge.

"Every expedition has a goal . . . or you have to invent one! What would be the reason for setting out if not toward a goal?" Tudurí continued obstinately, without allowing room for argument.

"And what happened to that Hungarian tart, eh?" Tomàs Moro interposed.

"Eva had only existed on board the *Ludovico Ariosto,*" the alarm clock salesman answered categorically.

"But you, there with her. . . ." wagged the priest. Joan Pere Tudurí slammed his fist down on the table: "That's enough! I have never been, nor do I ever want to be a Rumanian in Budapest!"

28

"I want to gather a bouquet and take it to Father's grave," said Egèria as she stood up to leave.

"Out there in the dark?" said her mother, alarmed.

"What kind of flowers are you going to find out there in December?" queried Albert the Younger.

"Probably none. But they don't have to be flowers . . . just a bouquet of twigs, of foliage, something from Taltavull Hall. I'm going to get a flashlight." As she resolutely headed for the kitchen to get it, Tudurí joined her.

"I'll go with you."

"Oh, thank you, Joan Pere. Yes, please come with me," Beautiful Egèria smiled.

The night languished like a long, tremulous breath, vague and harmonious. In the beam of the flashlight, the trees and the fields seemed to come alive and move toward each other. There was something supernatural in the way the silence seemed to move as well. The two young people searched for bouquet material in the flower pots, in the cactus bed, in the small vegetable garden. All they could find were barren twigs and stubs of winter-sleeping plants.

"Carob, pine, cypress, whatever we can find," said Egèria as she cut a branch here and there with her pruning shears.

"It will be a very earthy bouquet, something truly from Taltavull Hall," agreed Tudurí as he held the flashlight.

"Joan Pere, you fascinate me when I listen to your travel stories. Oh! How I envy and admire you, a thousand times over!" she enthused.

Flattered, Joan Pere took refuge in his modesty: "Well, there's nothing special about them, they're just normal business trips."

"Normal! Joan Pere, my God, but you've been everywhere and experienced everything!"

"No, Egèria, not at all. The thing is, when I explain things that way, tailored to suit my listeners, it can sound . . . how can I say? But seen in their real context, ugh! How boring they are! And as for the work itself, don't forget, Egèria, I'm just an alarm clock salesman."

Beautiful Egèria listened to him without paying much attention. The branches and twigs she was cutting were still laden with droplets from the recent rain. She laughed as Joan Pere ducked to avoid getting wet.

"And the girls, dear cousin, what a collection of girls! Love. . . . You can tell me all about it now that we're alone. You are an attractive wretch, you know," and she patted him playfully on the cheek. "What you must know about us girls nobody in Orlandis could possibly know! Come on, how many have you made love to, really? Don't you panic when you move on and have to leave them?"

Joan Pere Tudurí drew closer to Egèria. Depending on how she moved, she brushed up against him. Every time she turned to say something, her splendid shock of hair grazed his face like a caress. His voice grew deeper: "There's always too much of what you don't need, while you never dare to ask for what you really want."

"Oh! What an intriguing enigma!"

"Not really." Joan Pere let his hand glide over the girl's smooth, exquisite hair. "For a long time now, I've been wanting to. . . ."

"Look over there! An almond tree already in flower! Let's go! Come on, let's go!"

Egèria grabbed Tudurí's arm and excitedly dragged him along the terraced field to where an early-blooming almond tree had already burst into flower. The flashlight caught it in its beam. The white and fluffy petals seemed to have sublimely drifted in from some distant region.

Egèria slipped in the mud. As Joan Pere grabbed her, the flashlight slipped from his hand and went out when it hit the ground. He felt the girl's warm and fragrant body in his arms. She returned his embrace, deliciously.

"Oh, hug me, Joan Pere, hug me!"

Joan Pere Tudurí drew her even closer to him and kissed her ardently.

"Egèria! How I've longed for this moment! I love you. Oh, how I love you, you sweet creature!"

She carefully disentangled herself from his embrace and said, "Well, well, my man. . . . Let's get on over to the almond tree." He felt around for the flashlight and turned it on again. "I'm going to have to throw these shoes away. I've ruined them in the mud. How disgusting! So you like me, eh?"

Joan Pere held her from behind, resting his hands on the soft, hidden firmness of her breasts. Egèria distractedly chose one of the almond twigs and cut it.

"Yes, I like you, and I suppose I love you."

"Of course, we're cousins."

"Don't be silly! I mean as a woman . . . you know what I mean."

"So why have you waited until now to tell me?"

"Well, I don't know. What you just told me tonight, out here, and the way you were looking at me during the conversation in the hall. Everything together has driven me to say it. You ask me about my experiences with women: only in a woman's eyes can you discover whether she loves you or not, because when she looks at you her eyes appear to grow larger and reflect an enormous inner light."

Egèria broke off a twig laden with bloom. A few petals fell and drifted lazily to the ground. She spoke, pensively, "You mean I was looking at you like that?"

"Egèria, I don't mean to appear presumptuous! I'm serious about what I said."

"And I as well, I assure you."

"Well, yes, you seemed to be. And I'm deeply impressed."

The girl had returned to the terrace and scraped the mud off the soles of her shoes on the edge of one of the flagstones. She was carrying the flowered almond twig. Joan Pere turned the flashlight off and embraced Egèria again. She sighed and abandoned herself to his warmth. The kiss was intense, wet and deep.

"Ay! Let me catch my breath!" she said as she drew back from him and smiled.

"I'm so happy!" exclaimed Tudurí as he pressed the solid curve of her buttocks closer to him.

"Would you go to bed with me right now, Joan Pere?" Egèria whispered into his ear.

Joan Pere almost jumped out of his skin, "Yes, of course! Where can we go? What about right here? Later there'll be. . . ."

Beautiful Egèria laughed uproariously as she lightly brushed his face and chest with the flowering almond twig. A few stray petals stuck to his forehead and his shirt. Then her smile turned grave, "But we're not going to do it, Joan Pere. And you don't love me, either. And if you do, so what? There's nothing strange about your liking me."

"What? What did you say?"

"My eyes no doubt reflected love while you were telling your stories. But not for you, for the one I'm still waiting for, Joan Pere."

Tudurí turned the flashlight back on. Shaken by her disclosure, he stammered "But . . . we've just kissed, and I thought. . . . It was your idea to jump into bed!"

"Yes, you're right. Sorry about that. It was a sort of game I was playing. I knew what I was doing."

"But you say you're waiting for somebody . . . are you in love?"

"Well, yes, I am."

"Ah! So that's why you don't want to sleep with me?"

"Yes, I'm saving myself for him."

Joan Pere Tudurí didn't know what line to use to convince her. He felt an immense desire, a visceral urge to possess her. He had admired and liked Egèria for years, but he hadn't dared insinuate himself upon her. She had always seemed so distant, so indifferent. And her beauty, her elegance had inhibited him. But tonight he found her attention so fixed on him, so stunning. . . . He pricked up his enthusiasm as he took a new tack with an old line he had used successfully with other girls, and which could easily make her waver, "But if you like me, and I am deliriously infatuated with you, Egèria, we can make love, because. . . . I understand that you love another, but fidelity is only a concept, not a truth that reigns to the exclusion of all else. What on earth should make your ideas on fidelity—respectable as they are—force you to reject what you truly desire? You and I. . . ."

"How funny you are, Joan Pere!" She cut him short. "You're very convincing, you know? Your technique for hunting your prey is perfect."

"Ah, now I get it!" exclaimed Joan Pere. "You heard me when I was talking about Budapest. You're offended when you think you're but one of many . . . but I can assure you that. . . ."

"Hold on! Stop! I was listening from the kitchen. But that doesn't worry me at all. In my eyes, you stand well above those little adventures from your past."

"Well, then?" smiled Joan Pere Tudurí, desire in his eye.

Egèria finally took a firmer stance. "Listen to me, Joan Pere. The person I told you I was in love with doesn't exist for me yet. He's still out there somewhere. I suppose you'll think I'm old-fashioned, or foolish, but I'm so sure the man I will fall in love with, the one who will love me infinitely, exists somewhere. And part of my dream is for a more attractive world, with a touch of grace. Without that, I would be nothing! And I don't want to lose any of what I am, because then I wouldn't have it to offer him! I don't want to become bored, sullied, or disillusioned. None of that. I want to wait, to dream, and I'm sure my desires will come true. Don't you believe that by thinking very hard you can erase reality to the point where only the thought remains, that you can achieve anything you want because that's the way new things are created? They say we are the dreams of the gods."

Tudurí hesitated, overcome by her speech.

"I. . . .You kissed me willingly, Egèria, you looked at me as if. . . ."

"Right. But, as I've already told you, I wasn't looking at you—even though you're a handsome guy.You are only the prophet of the world I yearn for. Through you I was looking into the future."

A spark of irritation overcame Joan Pere: "A lot of women before you have had their heads full of birds, Egèria. And it always came to nothing. Ramon Consolat came by before supper. He was thinking about the dream of the gods of his relatives at La Paret."

"You're right. But am I supposed to be limited only to what I already know and have? If I lose, so be it. I don't know why, but right now with this rare flowering almond twig in my hand, I feel there is an open door awaiting me, that Orlandis is the port of departure and not the port of arrival."

"Egèria. . . ."

"Give me the flashlight and leave me alone, please. And don't get mad, Joan Pere. Let's forget what we just said, as if nothing had happened. I still love you deeply as a person."

"What I mean is. . . . Well, forget it . . . see you later then. Are you staying?"

"Yes, I want to pick some more flowers. I want Father to have them."

Framed in the beam of the flashlight, Beautiful Egèria set off toward the silent white almond tree, which seemed to be waiting for her.

29

The boys and girls were all dancing to the light, graceful rhythm of the music from the record player in the corner under the stairs, booming out its magnetic euphoria. Of all the ancestral rites, this was the last that remained, and they devoted themselves to it with the same energy their forebears would have used centuries ago as they offered up their hearts to the gods or the devils of their time. The early morning light reflected dauntlessly and diaphanously off the walls. The music resounded as if it were a commandment.

The rest of the Taltavulls had taken seats at the other end of the hall near the fireplace, sipping coffee and liqueurs. Then suddenly a couple of grown-ups laughingly joined the group of dancers, breathlessly trying to keep step. The night had entered a phase where neither time nor spirits seemed to have a beginning or an end. It was a vague but comforting sensation that seemed to seize everyone.

"It's as if we had always been like this," Egèria thought admiringly. And Bernat scratched his wife's back, repeating affectionately, "Well, well now, Marianna, well now. . . ."

There was only one of the guests who remained at the margin of the general high spirits, and that was the priest, Arcadi Frau Taltavull. He watched the dancers apprehensively, and with even more annoyance he berated himself: "Why do I have to be against all this, against everything they ever do or want to do in order to have some fun, as if mine were a ministry of darkness?"

He moved back away from the crowd and stood at the bottom of the staircase. With firm resolve, he started up the stairs, the effort contorting his wan face. It had been years, many years, since he had seen the desk. And now he was going to look at it for a singularly petty reason: it had just crossed his mind for a few seconds, as inconsequential but pleasant scenes from his childhood often did. It was one of the few memories that remained from his distant infancy, but which formed a sort of cornerstone to his existence.

It was a scene in which the boy Arcadi, dressed in baggy shorts that came well below his knees, was standing beside his Grandfather Benigne, who was wearing a fur-collared jacket and boots. He was going over some papers under the light of a three-armed copper candelabra; a tall inkwell in the shape of a duck sat on a wide writing desk with drawers on either side. A picture of a sailing vessel with a broken mainmast, dashed by mountainous waves on a stormy sea, hung on the wall above the desk.

Grandfather Benigne Taltavull had died when Arcadi was only five. Arcadi's mother, Josefa Taltavull, followed him in death shortly thereafter from appendicitis. And his father, a taciturn man, had embarked for America, never to return. Nothing was ever heard from him again. The child Arcadi was put in a seminary at an early age on the initiative of his grandparents on the Frau side, church-going people. Arcadi the priest thought it prodigious to have been able to recall the exact, insignificant scene at the desk from so long ago.

But at the same time he knew very well that the scene had been absorbing the rest of his memories of Grandfather Taltavull, polarizing the images that still endured: Benigne Taltavull, wearing boots and a fur-collared jacket, his little grandson warmly at his side, a lifetime of adventure awaiting him. Once again as he thought those same thoughts, Arcadi was overcome by a wave of tenderness.

He found the desk tucked in a tight corner under the arch of the staircase. That was where the estate's accounts were kept, along with all the old deeds and other records. The priest had let an incredible number of years go by without going up to see the old desk for many reasons, not the least of which was the staircase itself, and the fact that the estate had fallen more and more into the hands of the family in Orlandis and the fact that he was attending seminary and later sent to serve in many distant small towns. Last of all, his uncle Francesc de Borja Taltavull had been living there. Often when the scene with his grandfather crossed his mind, he promised himself he would return and revisit it. He didn't know whether it was out of gratitude for the moral warmth the memory had created in him with the passing of time or whether he was attracted by the slight hope of still finding in that scene an echo of the security of his lost youth.

Arcadi found the little three-by-six cubbyhole, lit indirectly by light from the stairs. In it there was a crude, thin-legged table, its veneer top peeling off in strips, with only a pencil-drawer in the middle. Piles of dusty file folders lay on top, along with a square glass inkwell black with dried ink, a rough, wobbly little wooden candlestick with vestiges of green paint and a blackened stub of a candle. An old calendar hung on the wall.

Arcadi was stunned: nothing coincided with the memory of the place he had so carefully and affectionately conserved. He sat down, disconcerted, in a tattered reed-bottomed chair. A stab of pain made him murmur, "Everything I touch seems to escape me." He didn't understand what had happened. They no doubt must have changed things around, he said to himself. One of the children must have taken the old double-drawered desk, the elegant candelabra, and the unique inkwell, leaving this ratty old table in its place. And with it they had carted off part of his childhood as well.

Arcadi Frau Taltavull got up slowly. As he turned to leave, his eyes fell on the wall calendar. What year was it from? The priest couldn't make out the date too well, so he lit the candle stub and held it up closer to the calendar. Later, at home in bed at the rectory, he couldn't get to sleep in spite of his exhaustion and splitting headache, his stomach upset from all the alcohol. That's when he realized he hadn't noticed the date.

What had riveted his attention, however, was the picture on the upper part of the calendar. He was left speechless when he saw it: it showed a well-groomed man examining some papers, seated with his back to the viewer, wearing a fur-collared coat and boots, with an apparently happy boy wearing baggy shorts that came well below his knees standing at his side, a three-candled copper candelabra shining brightly, together with a modernist inkwell in the shape of a duck, all of it laid out on a wide desk with drawers on either side. On the wall behind the desk there was a framed picture; Arcadi Frau had to come even closer with the candle to make it out: it showed a sailing vessel being tossed about in a storm, its mainmast riven in two, its sails ripped to shreds.

"Who am I, then?" the priest asked himself in anguish. "That Rumanian Joan Pere mentioned had only mistaken his impressions, but the violinist, the fat lady and the baroque café all existed. What was I as a child? What was my grandfather like? Who were we? All that has evaporated. I have substituted my life and memories for a calendar picture! That stupid clichéd scene drawn by a commercial artist on commission!"

Arcadi Frau Taltavull went back downstairs to the hall. Everything was the same as when he had left it. He poured himself a stout snifter of brandy and tossed it back. People were still dancing; others were standing around chatting. They were happy.

"Happy? Things are only what they appear to be, façades," mumbled the priest with his brows knit. He drank another snifter of brandy. He knew people . . . he knew them from the days when the confession was still a sacrament people believed in and practiced.

"Young boys who came to the confessional knelt and recounted their innocent sins. And I trembled when I imagined the incalculable and inevitable vileness that would take possession of their souls. One of them would become bitter through envy; another would wallow in lechery; another would feel the bestial pleasures of sadism; some would become thieves; and there was always a blasphemer or two. The laborious intimacy of each one of them revealing themselves to me through the years. They were shams! Degraded, egotistical wretches! And I had to try to understand them. No, man is not free in spite of what the Holy Mother Church preaches. Man is destined to collapse irremissibly under the crushing weight of omnipotent sin!

"Is man made up only of sin? Or does sin reside in me and the Church? Do we only want men who suffer, crushed by their awareness of sin? And if so, do we use sin to dominate them or because we are the product of a monstrous error that has confused divine grace with the dehumanization of man?"

The priest poured himself another brandy.

"But who's interested in all that now? Very few people. But it has perverted me, made me see only the wickedness in man, converting me into an inspector of evil. Perhaps because I didn't want to admit who I was as a child, that initial nucleus of degradation. I subconsciously renounced my real self, seeking refuge in the stupid image of that calendar picture! Perhaps religion has been nothing more than another dead picture in which I have sought refuge out of fear of a life I only saw as a source of sin. And so I have become a reprobate, without passion or ambition." Arcadi Frau drained his glass.

He filled it again. Aunt Paula saw him and chided him, "Arcadi, aren't you overdoing it?"

He grunted. Overdo it? Underdo it? He? But he had stayed put in one spot all his life, like a scarecrow!

The priest felt the thick taste of the brandy, its concentrated heat as it coursed through his veins. In the old days when people were forced to live off the land, they used to stick scarecrows in the middle of their wheat and barley fields to scare off the birds. Arcadi used to take frequent walks, and between spring and summer he would notice the scarecrows: they stood out there stiffly, an old pair of pants and a shirt stuffed with straw, a ball of rags for a head, topped with a shaggy straw hat.

What made shivers run up his spine, however, was the sensation they produced. In spite of the crude and ridiculous human rags that hung from them, their silhouettes appeared to be really human! Shadows of disturbing, sarcastic beings. The rags supplanted the essence and became the reality. Arcadi shivered again. "Weren't the scarecrows the same as I? Wasn't I just like them?"

The priest had broken out in a sweat. He decided to get some air. He set down the snifter and picked up a water glass, filled it to the brim with brandy. He walked outside. The night was calm. A few stars were shining, but all he saw was the darkness of the night.

"The darkness of man's soul," he murmured, his lips to the liquor. "I have to baptize, to give extreme unction to the biological magma and rot of humanity. I have to baptize the newborn, still-shapeless lumps, their mothers all torn up by birth. The umbilical cord. The soft skull of the little creature, the mother's sagging belly, her womb an open wound. The baby screams, defecates, sucks, and swallows—all of it an obscene mass of viscera. The instinctive, immodest animality of it all. And I bless it! Like an idiot I pursue the Prince of Darkness through that fistful of heartbeats and tripe!"

Arcadi was sweating fiercely now. An indomitable sense of fury was overpowering him. He drained the glass of brandy. He was tempted to bellow with joy as he felt the alcohol saturate his body. Instead, he furiously threw the glass against the wall: it exploded in a shower of tinkling shards, a noise which the priest enjoyed enormously in the silence of the night. It seemed to him exultantly huge, like the tolling of church bells years ago on Easter Sunday morning, celebrating the resurrection of the Lord. The scene returned to memory: the church and the church square decked out in festive colors, the glory of God. . . .

"God?" The word, the concept, left Arcadi perplexed. He was breathing deeply, his mind in a swirl of confusion, like a cornered animal. He started waving his arms furiously, panicked in the dark, as if he were trying to scatter what he could not see. He strode over to his car and tumbled into the driver's seat. He started the motor, released the clutch and roared down the drive in a hail of gravel. The word God had evoked in him a tight vortex of vertiginous, compact blackness, an abstraction which wouldn't go away. The car's speed, the headlights, the din of the motor, had rebalanced the universe for him, had converted it into a space of narrow and tangible proportions.

The car raced down the hilly twisting road toward Orlandis, its lights like long clumsy fingers probing vainly into the night as the trees flashed by. Arcadi drove hunched over, gripping the wheel tensely, staring at the curving road with bulging eyes. On the straightaways he floored the gas pedal. The car trembled, but charged ahead. The priest jammed on the brakes at every curve, then floored it again.

There was a loud bang then the scraping and clatter of sheet metal: the car had grazed a stone guard rail. Arcadi paid no attention; his only concern was his speed, which wasn't fast enough. He needed to go faster. He jammed the pedal deeper into the floor. The car skidded, bounced in the air, and he bashed his head against the roof, but the vehicle came back on course. He was careening along the road like a lunatic. Arcadi noted his mouth thirsting for more brandy. His thirst was burning him up.

"Shit, I should have brought the bottle." His head felt like a huge, fuzzy polyp. The bottle. . . . And the music! Suddenly an insatiable desire to hear music filled him, possessed him. He wanted to become a mass of delirious sound as he roared down the road.

Then the deafening crash. He was thrown brutally forward in the car, which felt as if it were twisting and crying out in pain. Everything came to a halt. Arcadi laboriously climbed out. One of the front wheels had run into a rock on the high side of the road. He tried the motor, but it refused to start. Night and darkness. He could barely make out the lights of Orlandis in the distance. He left the car and started out on foot. He felt overcome by weariness. He walked slowly, almost on tiptoe. In the faint starlight he was able to make out the white center line on the surface of the road. He slipped in the muddy ditch and fell. He wiped his hands off on his clothes and kept on walking. His fatigue increased by the minute. Orlandis was still very far away. He noticed he was talking to himself. He was indignant with himself, with the car, with everything and everybody. He would have picked a fight with the first man who came along. He wanted another drink.

For a while he moved down the road like a robot, half-asleep. All he could feel was his infinite fatigue. The sight of the first streetlight in Orlandis cleared his mind. His mind became clear, cold and choleric all at once. His whole body, his whole being had become a raw and jagged nerve. He felt clumsy, defeated. The town was deserted at that early predawn hour. He heard the exhausted sighs of the dark sea. The parked cars reflected the vague light along the street, somber and sinister.

In a fit of anger, Arcadi Frau Taltavull came up to one of the cars and ripped its windshield wiper off and twisted its rearview mirror. A dog sleeping under the car sniffed at the priest, who gave him a kick in the muzzle. The animal ran off yelping down the street.

Arcadi's anger grew, but it was different from the instinctive anger of a few minutes ago: he had now become voraciously vengeful, aggressive. He went up to another parked car and, laughing between clenched teeth, he destroyed its rearview mirror and ripped off its wipers. And he moved on to the next car. He kept on vandalizing cars, an enraged, shadowy hulking priest moving through the dim light of dawn. His head seemed to buzz and squeal at him in his frenzied outrage.

30

The fire was burning low and needed more wood, but nobody felt like bringing any as the night wore on into early morning. So every time the fire died down, someone would toss on old newspapers, pieces of kindling, and even the dregs from the wine bottles. Behind a stolid, dignified little wooden horse which, along with an elephant, a giraffe, a carriage, and a fire engine had formed part of an old carousel, Sebastiana found a large, dusty book, its covers already ripped off, its pages wrinkled and torn.

"This thing would sure burn great," she thought, without daring to tear it up herself.

She looked through it. It was a monumental biography of Antonio Maura, 'The Savior of the Country,' the sub-title said. There were some old papers stuffed in it: a tailor's bill, a good conduct report from the police, an unopened letter, a physical education diploma, an appointment as a voting member to a Marian Congress, an engraved invitation to a party given by the Duchess of Orlandis. Everything was in the name of Ignasi Taltavull Oliva, all of it dated from forty or fifty years before.

"Uncle," said Sebastiana, "look at this stuff: if you don't want any of it, we'll toss it on the fire."

Ignasi glanced over it superficially, paused a moment over the duchess's invitation and murmured indifferently, "Burn it."

"Yippee!" screeched the girl, as she set about tearing up and throwing the papers and the book pages into the fire.

The fire surged hungrily, giving off blue-green flames. A dull woman, pale and thin, emerged from the kitchen drying her hands on her apron. It was Roseta, the retired commander's wife.

"Ignasi, when are we going home?"

He answered her absent-mindedly, "In a little while."

They had arrived together by car, but now the judge realized he had neither seen nor remembered her all during the evening. He shrugged his shoulders. The parties in the castle. Taltavull Hall and the duchess's mansion on the outskirts of Orlandis. He looked around the hall: reed-bottomed walnut chairs, shiny from use; huge cracked Manis earthenware crocks hanging from the walls; heavy, worn carpets; a seaman's chest with paintings of Majorcan peasants on it; two whitened stone mortars; five candlesticks on the mantle over the fireplace. They were all signs of a persistence based on firmness, modesty, and equanimity, vestiges of a race of people whose supreme gesture toward life had been to survive it.

Taltavull Hall was the polar opposite of the Duchess's castle during those war years that had passed through his life like a luminescent rainbow, like the magnificent tail of a comet, a fiery traveler in the summer night. Ignasi, hypnotized by the late hour, relaxed by the digestion of the sumptuous meal, smiled as he thought of the times he had walked proudly through the ornate salons of the castle. He recalled a Renaissance ebony secretary inlaid with ivory that pictured Biblical scenes; sputtering lamps of Murano crystal; Turkish tapestries from Konya, their geometrical designs in warm earth tones; a green, dynamically arched horse from the Tang dynasty; a dome by José Maria Sert, bronzed titans constructing the grandeur of the earth; a coagulated drop of milk from the Virgin Mother in a Gothic reliquary encrusted with rubies and opals.

Then there were the emeralds in the duchess's diadem. She would descend the grand staircase into the main salon wearing her jeweled tiara on her forehead, extravagantly crowning of her aquiline and azure-veined countenance. The staircase had a modernist wrought-iron banister representing idealized adolescent female faces with long, flowing hair sinuously woven among the rungs of the railing. The Duchess would descend triumphantly, her body erect, the slack skin of her neck twisted slightly, her gaze fixed indifferently, vaguely distant, for she was myopic. She would offer her liver-spotted hand, and the guests would fall over each other to kiss it.

She spoke volubly to one and all: "Ah, yes, I knew your father in Warsaw. Young lady, your hair is exquisite this evening. Oh, yes, the Tang horse. But I like Chinese ceramics less than the Bavarian Rococo kind. Captain, you'll have to bring me a young stallion, but a tame one. Valentine, more champagne please. This war is boring us stiff here, while the season is just beginning in Paris. Good evening, Madame Olga. What a pleasant autumn. . . ."

Ignasi had developed a certain friendship with Monsignor Estopañán. The priest was constantly feeding on sweets, as he uneasily watched the duchess. He would grab Ignasi by the arm and point at the great lady with his finger: "Yes, she defies the ruin of time with majestic malice. She doesn't realize that nobody can restore her lost days, that not a one of her errors can be corrected. She confuses the dead past with the present; her mind recalls the past as if she were blowing on a heap of ashes in the hope of bringing forth flame; and all she gets is filthy dust. She doesn't grant clemency nor does she beg for compassion. Her obstinate, dehumanized efforts become cosmic and thus are destined to the most absolute failure."

The Duchess continued her elegant ramblings: "I was very naughty and jolly as a young girl. What a time that was! A stormy afternoon in the Sicilian garden with everyone taking a siesta under the quiet, carmine clouds. The violet lilies gave off a sickly fragrance. A cool, stimulating perspiration drenched our skin. Yes, that afternoon the First Lord of the Admiralty had arrived from Australia on his way to London. And he gave me a bird of paradise borne by two Hindu servants in a huge golden cage. Ah, what a lively bird it was, with its long, lavish yellow plumage!"

Monsignor Estopañán, his mouth stuffed with cake, chattered into Ignasi's ear, "That afternoon in the garden at Syracuse she imagined then and still imagines that every particle of her world is incorruptible. She never understood that the capricious girl she had been soon vanished, a desolate carcass forgotten by those who loved her, just like the bird of paradise they brought her from New Guinea—a beautiful, gaudy splash of color—that died one day and became a disgusting sack of feathers dumped on the terrace among the copies of Greek statues. Did you know that Archimedes was from Syracuse?"

Ignasi had to laugh when he understood that the person the domestic prelate of His Holiness was really describing was himself: the nonchalant attitude of the duchess induced the monsignor to whisper, fearing even more his own coming demise. And as a consequence, Ignasi concluded that if no truth was absolute, if each person was an island unto himself, if everything happened because it had to happen, he could adapt to Taltavull Hall in the same way he had to the castle, that is, by simply doing so. Not even time existed, but instead, only a succession of situations that motivated and satisfied one's own needs.

31

The unopened letter became a brief, radiantly rosy tongue of flame when Sebastiana tossed the papers into the fire. No one had ever read it. It was one of the many unopened letters Ingeborg von Nassau-Istrij had sent to Ignasi Taltavull Oliva almost half a century ago. Now nobody would ever read it. Ingeborg and her husband and so many of the people he had known and loved back then had been dead for years. With that letter one of the last vestiges of that time had passed, along with the now-effaced and forgotten energy of the mind, the sensitive heart, the delicate hands of that gentle woman.

The letter, dated in Paris, had said, "I need to write to you, dear Ignasi, even though you have not answered any of my previous letters. I need to talk about my memories of you, of that golden isle where I, with you at my side, was the happiest I have ever been. Are you still alive? I hope so, and in spite of the circumstances or feelings that keep you from answering me, perhaps you will read this.

"I feel so low. The war seems to be going well for us, and France is almost completely ours by now. But I don't belong to anybody, not even to myself. Yes, Rolf was assigned to Paris, and we have rented a house facing the Luxembourg Gardens. I am looking at them from my window now as I write you. They seem like a perfect and practical lesson in geometry. How different they are from the intricate exuberance of the gardens and woods in Bavaria, from your devastating, delicious mountains!

"The house we rented must have belonged to people with means. It dates from the eighteenth century and stands in elegant, neoclassical style, in spite of its derelict condition. There are some rooms, some small patios, and the entire upper floor that seem to have been uninhabited from time immemorial. They told us that during Napoleon's time it was used as an army recruiting office and has gone steadily downhill ever since. We have started to remodel it to fit our personal needs and those of Rolf's position. We both know French well, and the Reich wants to maintain a large mission here. When the war ends we will have to treat the new France we have created more cordially.

"But what parties can we give? Almost as soon as we arrived, my husband started being away from home for longer and longer periods of time, first giving the call of duty with the Wehrmacht High Command as an excuse, and then eventually giving no excuse at all. And then I learned he was dining at Maxim's or strolling down the Faubourg Saint Honoré in the company of ladies toward whom he demonstrated an intimacy that irked me deeply.

"Rolf had never done anything like that before, and I don't understand why he has started now. I haven't had a lover for months now—I have told you how I have drawn within myself. The old saying, 'one is a beauty until the grave' is a lie. Every time your experience comes full circle, you become a new person. I am sated with men, but lack love, your love, as it used to be. Now I don't know. And I thought that there might still be something with Rolf.

"Is he falling in love with other women? Has he changed and have I failed to notice? Have I been imprudent with my letters to you? Have the Gestapo or the censors caught on? It doesn't seem to matter any more.

"Undecided as to the attitude I should adopt, I buried myself in the remodeling job and spent my days with the repairmen. And then suddenly one afternoon a wall collapsed in the basement, revealing a hidden, windowless room. Its walls were chipped and peeling; everything was covered with a fine layer of dust . . . it was like discovering a bell jar lost in time.

"The walls were lined with shelves piled high with documents dealing with draft notices, discharges, and promotions from that glorious time of the Empire, I suppose very similar to our own.

"But what disturbed me most was the discovery of a skeleton sitting perfectly upright on the floor in a corner. Basing his opinion on the ragged sky-blue uniform with white stripes that still covered him, the curator of the Pantheon whom we consulted concluded that the soldier must have been a Hussar officer in Napoleon's army.

"Perhaps when the Emperor was dethroned the soldier feared some sort of reprisals that made him entomb himself alive. Or was he perhaps condemned by the royalists to the horrible death of being buried alive? We haven't been able to clear up the mystery. I was struck by the dignity of those old bones. Don't be surprised that I thrived on such ideas, because I was under the influence of a deep depression.

"It rains gently every afternoon, as if someone were tiptoeing by who didn't want to look at me. In the cozy garden behind the house I burn the autumn leaves. It's still me, Ignasi; I'm still the same Ingeborg."

A violet flame in the hearth at Taltavull Hall, an early morning moment.

32

A youngster from Pula came inside and went over to Dioclecià the master and whispered in his ear. The stocky fellow turned and announced to the rest of the guests, "The priest has taken off without so much as a by-your-leave, after smashing a glass on the porch. He's been bending his elbow."

"Ha! He probably thought he was consecrating the wine and kept on drinking it!" was Tomàs Moro's merry comment as he gluttonously sank his face into a quarter of a watermelon, his jaws dripping copiously.

"Tomàs, don't be a heretic!" admonished his wife, Càndida.

"But he's a beautiful person, our Arcadi," said Aunt Pollònia sleepily, as if she were praying.

But Moro wasn't listening to her. "He should crash his car, break a leg, the goddamned inquisitor!" Moro thought as he imagined a scene with the priest's car crumpled up like an accordion, smoke rising from it with the priest trapped inside, contorted in pain, one leg bent and bleeding, a bone splinter protruding through the flesh.

Dioclecià of Pula seemed to be reconsidering aloud, as he prudently spoke, "There's no doubt he's an honest person. Nobody has ever denied that. Although there are several kinds of honesty and the fact that they aren't all the same doesn't mean one has to impose itself over the other."

"What are you getting at?" asked the judge, cautious and distrustful for the second time that night after hearing the circumlocutions of the patriarch from Pula, wondering all the while what he could be referring to.

But Dioclecià, who was sipping a cup of coffee with unusual care, continued to lose himself in a spiral of purely formal sentences. He didn't want to get into it any further. He was only fulfilling the implicit mission of Pula, which was to throw dirt indirectly on Arcadi Frau whenever they had the chance. Because if he had to explain to an outsider the history and the enigma of the Black Stone, he would not be doing Pula any favors.

That enormous obsidian rock; its tight, abrupt blackness, from which the sun and the moon derived an intense, silvery brilliance. How had it come to be there? Who had transported that amorphous block, as tall as a person, to the tiny island of Molta Murtra? That stone and the smaller one from which they had carved the shield of the Orlandis clan, which stood over the entry arch at the castle. What symbolic relationship was there between the two strange rocks? The island of Molta Murtra was circular and practically flat, about as large as the city limits of Orlandis, and seemed to lie like a supine beast in wait on the remote horizon in a straight line from the port.

Its vegetation, low and rough, seemed to clutch at the stony soil: fennel, mastic trees, asphodels, thistles, and dwarf pines. Among all that thick brush throbbed a vigorous animal life: svelte green lizards that seemed to have emerged from some Chinese ceramic piece; small rainbow-colored snakes that everybody feared were poisonous; many cormorants and sea gulls whose clumsy and featherless young spent the spring and summer evenings squawking so loudly it seemed the island was filled with souls in great sorrow. And in the marine depths at the base of the island, the powerful, furtive, and flesh-eating moray made its nest and attacked man. The sun burned straight down on the isle. On the Majorcan side, Molta Murtra sloped gently to the water, forming a small cove. The side that faced the open sea was a rugged series of jagged cliffs, a dramatic procession of rocks against which the waves crashed in seething foam. And there in a pile of monumental stones that seemed to have been hewn by stonecutters, arose the great block of obsidian.

The bas-relief resembled an astonishingly human silhouette with thin extremities and a wide rectangular torso, capped with a sort of miter. A professor had ventured the opinion that it might be from the Sardinian megalithic period, to which he attributed certain Etruscan influences. It was clearly prior to or distinct from naturalistic Greek art forms and it lacked the ornamental accessories typical of works from the Levant. But it had been impossible to establish its provenance, complicated by the fact it was made of obsidian, unknown in the Balearic Isles, but which could have come from Asia Minor. It seemed to reflect the whole deep and seminal Mediterranean culture, emblematic and impenetrable.

For many years now the people of Pula had managed to keep abreast of what was being said about the Black Stone: they considered it theirs as part of their mythology; they felt an implicit aura of sacredness resided in it. In a way they could not specify and which did not respond to any objective data, the Pulans recognized a primitive link between them and that singular chunk of rock, that grotesque representation of a hard, authoritarian and solemn primitivism. And the very name of the tiny isle—Molta Murtra, or "much myrtle"—derived directly from that implication.

Every summer, on the night of the first full moon, the entire population of Pula would fill their boats with myrtle branches and sail out to the island. They navigated by following the magic line of the seashore glittering in the moonlight, all of them singing, drunk with the perfume of the myrtle branches, heavy and fragrant as an exotic Asian spice. Once on the island, they sang and ran about and laughed; they braided hoops and wreaths of myrtle and richly decorated the area, except for the vale where the obsidian rested; there the myrtle became a cloak, a proud bower, as if an auroral thicket had been born to protect the occult symbolism of the Black Stone and draw its sustenance from it.

The sailors of Orlandis had been mystified for centuries as to how the small isle had suddenly appeared covered with that abundance of myrtle at the beginning of every summer. In the course of time, they related it to those slight shadows they observed on the sea during the nights of the full moon. They believed it had something to do with some kind of large, unknown marine animal that once a year brought those huge bundles of myrtle to honor its king, the Black Stone, king of the storms and of the deep, king of the sea monsters. Only in modern times had they connected the event to Pula.

And that was because the fishermen from Orlandis almost never landed on the rough shore of Molta Murtra. When they tried, a heavy stone would usually come flying over them like a kestrel and drop upon their ship; a hunting dog would appear from nowhere and rabidly charge at them; a sudden and unexplained fire would burst forth from the rocks jutting out of the sea. If they stuck to fishing the small beach on the cove, however, nothing ever happened to them.

But the outboard motor boats—the eyes of a new generation with their rapid mobility—soon discovered that between the little coves and thickets there were always some Pulans lurking about and never in a friendly way. And the recently ordained priest Arcadi Frau Taltavull had spoken severely to the rector of Orlandis, demanding of him in the name of truth that the pagan festival of the strange stone dressed in myrtle be brought to an end and the idolatrous silhouette that reigned over the place be destroyed.

Then came the post-war years. Nobody dared stand in opposition to Arcadi's fever for purification as he, stiff as a poker, strode through Orlandis with his long gait, his cassock an admonishing black shadow stalking the streets. But now the rector was more cautious in his duty because during the war he had seen and even practiced too many excommunications. And all Pula had appeared before the young tonsured priest to remind him that he was related to them through Grandmother Brígida. The priest proclaimed that the faith as taught by Jesus Christ knew neither parents nor brothers. Pula was forced into silence, for in effect they were living the postwar years, and the political waters Pula had until then adroitly navigated had become murky in the extreme. Then came the first full moon of summer. The sea resembled an immense nocturnal plain, smooth and becalmed, traced with paths of light that took shape as if they were prodigious revelations from beyond and then disappeared as if they had never existed. The whole Pulan populace was dancing about on the tiny island when a cat-boat unexpectedly appeared, its motor rumbling, its lights dancing on the waves. Molta Murtra fell into a deep, tense silence. The boat circled the isle and dropped anchor near the obsidian rock.

Arcadi and the rector jumped ashore, dressed in their cassocks, aspergillum in hand, flanked by four torch-bearing altar boys. A couple of Guàrdia Civil officers discreetly brought up the rear. The Pulans stood there mutely and allowed them to pass. In the silence the baby cormorants ceased screeching, frightened by the mass of people.

The small group of recent arrivals had difficulty walking on the unstable footing of the rocky shore. Amidst that virgin, resplendent landscape, the ceremonious clerical procession gave the appearance of something between fragile and aberrant. They had come to confront an even more abstruse abstraction than that of beliefs, precisely because of its inhumanity: the mystery of the stone.

They came to a halt before the Black Stone. The breeze made the torch flames flicker. The rector produced a book and began to read out an exorcism in a trembling, stuttering voice, while at the same time he splashed holy water from his aspergillum onto the obsidian: both hell and the devil had to abandon their hold on it. Arcadi trembled all the while, sensing the howling retreat of the evil spirits. The Guàrdia Civil stood there woodenly, their rifles at the ready.

Arcadi suddenly took a step forward, produced a hammer from beneath his cassock and brandished it in the air while he made some guttural exclamations. The Pulans, to a man, began to gather angrily around their stone.

"Out! Out! In the name of God!" hissed Arcadi.

Nobody moved, but many knives glinted in the hands of the Pulans. The police took their weapons off safety with a loud click. More silence ensued.

Arcadi took another step forward and forced a wedge between the Pulans, then leapt at the obsidian, striking it with a frenzied hammer blow, then another. The Pulans became more agitated; they rose as one like an angry dinosaur about to throw itself upon Arcadi.

The guards gave warning they were about to fire into the crowd, and everything was about to happen as horrible fate would have it, when a silhouette bathed in moonlight emerged atop a rocky promontory and exclaimed in a penetrating, authoritarian voice, "Enough! I say that's enough!"

Everyone looked in surprise in the direction of the voice. It was Grandmother Brígida. She was wearing a long, white housecoat, a giant bunch of pungent, flowering myrtle cradled in her arms. The moonlight had erased the years time had etched on her face: she was just Brígida, the ephemeral daughter of the eternal. The cormorant chicks, tricked by the stillness, thought they were alone again and began their usual screeching, making it sound as if ancient monsters were emerging from the sea, cheering on the queen of the night.

Arcadi, who was not much of a Taltavull, hadn't known that Brígida still took part in events at Pula. And Brígida, in a voice laden with menace, thundered to the opaline sky and to the dark earth and to the crashing waves on shore until her words and the elements were one, and she ordered, "Get out of here, Arcadi, and never come back, dead or alive! Get out of here, everybody who doesn't belong here. Let everyone be who he is and may our paths never cross again!"

Panic gripped Arcadi. He ran, tripped, fell, and finally crawled back into the boat, not because he had been afraid of his grandmother or any evil deed from the obsidian stone, but because he understood with a start that the old lady just might be right. The rest of his group followed after him in confusion, the two guards still cautious, their rifles at the ready. They shoved off from the beach.

After that nobody ever heard of the Pulans returning to Molta Murtra on moonlit nights. But the Pulans, now that the Black Stone had been profaned, felt it was even more their own. Because they not only saw it but were left to marvel at the permanent and occult symbolism of the obsidian which lay beyond its mutilation.

The waters of Molta Murtra. . . . Yes, the Pulans claimed them, for in them lay the memories of their most noble deeds, like that of the Phantom Ship— the one that still coursed through the mental sea of Marianna Mas, the ship that had one day appeared, slowly adrift on the open sea to the west of Molta Murtra. A lookout from Pula stationed on the tiny island had spotted it: it was an iron steamer, riding high at the gunwales with a tattered flag they suspected belonged to a country from the icy north.

The lookout from Pula watched it for a day, then two days. There was no indication of life on board, not even the rudder moved obedient to a course marked by the binnacle. The sea was becalmed; the ship barely moved, adrift. Then some fishermen from Orlandis approached it, curious and fearful. The Pulan watchman on the island, hidden among the myrtle bushes, instinctively sounded his conch horn. The fishermen were frightened by its eerie sound, like the groans of a dying animal spreading over the languid waters, and they turned back to port.

At dusk the Pulans went into action. Their boats sailed silently out to that immobile iron hulk. As they neared it, they could make out the rust lines running down its hull, the beard of moss floating at the waterline. A flock of seagulls perched in a row on the edge of the gunwale. The Pulans bumped against the ship, whose plates seemed to vibrate, a sort of empty echo, a distant emptiness. Two Pulans shinnied slick as rats up a hawser hanging from the poop deck.

And the first thing they stammered when they returned was, "Rats!" Enormous rats, afraid of nothing. They had the run of the ship. They sniffed at the crew and began to nibble on them, dead men, dying men, a crew sprawled out on the decks, on the bridge, in the hold. An epidemic must have unexpectedly overcome them, weakening them, sapping their strength, their eyes, and their minds. They had been able to struggle against the disease during the first few days and help each other. Then all that was left were weak survivors scattered about the ship, living off the few remaining provisions. They tried to protect the bodies of their dead mates from the rats. Widow Mandilega, a wiry and choleric woman who was the leader of the Pulans at the time, stood up in the lead boat and demanded, "What is there of value on board?"

"Lots of things! Mahogany furniture, porcelain, bedding, carboys of oil and wine, tools, and lanterns, and the main cargo: about a hundred cartloads of salted cod."

Mandilega meditated, "Are there many sailors still alive?"

"Maybe half a dozen. . . ."

"And how long do you think they can last?"

"You can't tell how tough these birds are. Maybe a couple of days, maybe a week."

"And you say they still have some provisions?"

"Yes, and they've asked us for more. And for water. And a doctor. And they're weeping and giving us letters to send to their loved ones." The widow kept her eyes on the enormous hull, touched it with her hand as if it were a stethoscope as she stood alongside in the small boat. Then she contemptuously ordered, "Take their food away and toss it into the sea, together with all the letters, papers, and books on board. Don't kill anybody, but if any of them tries to get up, knock them back down again. We'll wait here."

And they awaited the inevitable death of each of the remaining sailors. At the same time, they spread the rumor in Orlandis that it was the Phantom Ship, the one of the evil omens, manned by unredeemed spirits who navigated darkly and with no defined course all over the globe. And they said that if anyone came near the ship and if one of those condemned souls appeared and waved them nearer, then all was lost: that person would be sucked down with the crew of the Phantom Ship until the day of Final Judgment.

The Pulans surrounded the ship with their boats and lashed heavy lines to it in order to control it when the sea got rough. . . . The people in Orlandis watched the cursed and immobile ship, and the few fishermen who dared steer near it watched with crazed eyes as unreal, yellow dancing serpents rose from the sea. They scurried back to port, rowing furiously. The Pulans had moved and were busy in their little boats hidden on the other side of the ship, raising and lowering the serpent-like paper kites they had made for the occasion.

The dying crewmen on board, barely able to make out those soft chimeras capriciously floating through the air above the ship, imagined the doors to the other world were opening to them, in which there were supposed to be unknown exotic plants and animals.

Dioclecià of Pula gave a friendly slap on the back to Ignasi Taltavull Oliva, who was also nodding off due to the late hour and said, "Judge, judge! We will have seen and learned a lot of things by the time we cross that threshold."

"What? What's that?" replied the retired commander with a start.

"No, nothing important," indicated the patriarch with a vague wave of his hand. "A fine kettle of fish, when death is the only thing you can't rebel against!"

"What the hell do you mean?"

"Nothing, judge, nothing. . . ."

33

A light coat of ash veiled the remains of the logs, the embers concealing their previous brilliance. Around the fireplace all that remained was a warm atmosphere with no apparent cause . . . the presence of an absence. The Taltavulls' evening together had begun its decline; dawn would soon break, demonstrating to everyone—including the Taltavulls and their words and dreams—that the universe was governed by one immense law. They would not dine together again until next Christmas Eve.

But meanwhile nothing came to an end, because the wheel kept on turning: the Taltavull wheel, that is. They were Christmas Eve; they were the ones who were alive. Some were napping in their chairs; others had started back to town; some had put their children to bed. The busy women were clearing the table and leaving the kitchen ready to wash the dishes in the morning. The whole family had spoken so much and about so many things that those who were still talking had wandered onto some of the most rugged subjects. Their words, like scythes through brush, had cut paths through the heaviest, most unusual thickets of life and death.

Honorat Moro raised his index finger and said, "When you finally own something, it's less yours than before you get it. The more I have struggled to succeed, the more I have feared defeat and misfortune. And when I own nothing, it seems I have everything, beginning with time and myself. I can sit and recall the past for hours and hours at a time until I can remember insignificant and beautiful details about, for example, what I did and dreamed as a child. And I have discovered that I have lived more fully and happily than I had imagined. That's why I live on the mountain, far from everything, but near myself."

"Well, the worst is what you leave behind," said Albert the Younger. "Aunt and Uncle Pixedis didn't come this evening because he is locked up in himself the whole damn day. He only moves when he wants to destroy something. They tell him about the leaks in his roof, the trees that need to be pruned, and a thousand other things that need doing, and all he does is either not answer at all, or in a rage he'll get somebody to cut down the trees completely, or he'll go out and stone his own tile roof and break dozens of tiles. Aunt Pixedis told me that Uncle passionately and darkly believes that a kind of deep and legitimate truth exists, according to which the world should always continue in the very same way he has always known it. If not, it will have to be destroyed. Every time someone suggests a change to him, he considers it an intolerable, offensive intrusion into his affairs."

Magdalena sighed as she was going by with a pile of dirty plates and commented, "Old people either seem blind or seem to see more than we do. My father was always loved by everyone, and he always treated us with uncomplaining generosity. And you all know what happened last year: he disappeared. And when we found him down there by the Valencian garden, he said that people forget the old folks and that his mind and body were falling apart. He wanted us to keep the fond memories we had of him; he said he would die better alone because he wouldn't have to see his steady decline reflected in the pained faces of the family, and so the end for him would be just one more act of life. Isn't that crazy, and at the same time a great truth?"

"Of course, Magdalena, your father didn't know anything about that while he was wandering around Latin America," interjected Cristòfol Mardà. "But I remember that sometimes in America—and I don't really know what caused it—I got irritated when I thought of the past, the time when I had been happy in Orlandis, the time when I had still loved my wife. I felt like I was falling into a deep trap about to suffocate me. On the other hand, if I made the effort and projected hate over the past, I felt better; I felt freed from that suffocation; I felt stimulated."

"You people are talking about things I don't understand. Where are you getting all this stuff, anyway?" Alexandre Tudurí queried as he got up from where he had been sitting beside Adelina Albornoz. Both of them had been listening carefully without saying a word.

"Because you're very young," Bernat the Wise answered. "There's something about old age that's a lie: that old folks know themselves better and are more sensitive than young people are. Since a young person has to respond to the demands of life and act on them, he makes plans and disciplines himself. But an old person doesn't have outside obligations any more, and he goes around a bit lost, like when he was a child, which makes him unpredictable."

His wife, Marianna Mas, who was arranging the cushions on the stone bench by the fireplace, commented, "Look at our cousins from Alaró. What more devoted couple than Micaela and Hilari? And they were happy together. Then that day they were slaughtering the hog, the cauldron got to boiling too hot, the sausages were splitting open and Micaela screamed at her husband as if she'd lost her mind. Hilari didn't answer, but his face grew more and more purple with rage, and when he picked up the butcher knife, he felt like sticking it right through Micaela. Now they're separated, each of them with one of the children, and you can't mention her to him or vice-versa: they hate each other to death. Forty years of peaceful living together doesn't mean a thing after a five-minute fracas."

"I have a neighbor living on the Porciúncula farm, an old lady," said Bernat as he shook his head with a worried look on his face, "whose name is Luisa Menescala. Now you're about to hear a story that will amaze you. First I noticed that the ripening apricots and pomegranates were disappearing pretty quickly off the trees; later, I noticed my woodpile going down pretty fast. I didn't have to watch very long to discover that the thief was that old woman who had come back to live on her little piece of land after working for many years in Palma or somewhere. When I was a youth, we always had problems with her family because they didn't respect the boundaries of our farm. So one day I caught her red-handed and stopped her thievery, or so I thought. But things kept on disappearing. She was doing it at night, of course. And when I caught her at it again, this is how she answered me: 'Since you're so concerned, let's talk about this. Didn't you know that my father and my grandfather had always had problems with your family because every once in a while they would cut down a wild olive or swipe a sack of peas?'

"'That's right,' I answered, 'do you deny it?'

"'Just the opposite!' she exclaimed happily. 'Just the opposite! If my family has always stolen from your place, why should I stop doing it now? I have a right to do it, the same right you have to your property, more or less. And if your rights are written down on deeds, mine are an inherited custom. I couldn't live at peace with myself when I got up in the morning if I didn't feel a tie to those silent fields, all of them! That's the way I've thought all my life, just like the ones before me thought! I'm not doubting your rights, but you also have to respect mine! An individual person—me—has to be worth as much as your silly paper.'

"And so now she steals my stuff openly. She'll walk right by with an armload of my firewood, looking at me defiantly out of the corner of her eye, and I...."

"But can't you do anything to stop her?" interrupted Albert the Younger.

"I ... I believe when somebody thinks a thing, that thing ought to be possible," replied Bernat the Wise slowly.

"And what about that scandal at Santa Perpetua?" asked Pollònia.

"Ah, yes!" exclaimed Marianna Mas.

"What scandal?" asked Joan Pere Tudurí with interest. "Since I'm always traveling, I never hear any of the gossip."

Marianna Mas began to tell the story: "You all know them, the family that ran the Santa Perpetua Flour Mill, the ones who made so much money with silver during and after the war, when they bought the gold and silver people had to sell out of necessity or so it wouldn't be requisitioned by the government. You and I always saw how Marta Maria of Santa Perpetua used to cry: she would sit in the little room in her house looking out on the rocks in Caleta Griega cove. She would contemplate the sea and whine because Salvador had abandoned her, and she would pray for his return."

"Yes, I remember Salvador as a child. He was her husband," nodded Tudurí.

His mother, Pollònia, continued: "Well, he left her more than twenty years ago. Marta Maria and I have always been good friends. However, I never liked to be with her in that little room. There were too many velvet drapes that made the place feel hot; too many mirrors that made me feel spied upon; and too much sea: its snorting and roaring came right in through her window. I didn't feel comfortable there. I felt as if I were about to be thrown out to sea or set upon by something.

"And all poor Marta Maria wanted was for somebody to keep her company. She used to wander around the place in those tatty housecoats of hers, her stringy hair hanging loose, always exhausted and whining, back and forth from the sofa to the window to the dressing table, where she would pause and admire herself languidly in the mirror and then dab a bit of perfume behind each ear. Her perfume had a sticky-sweet aroma. Marta Maria was healthy enough, but always looked sickly."

"She must have been very much in love with him," murmured the girl, Adelina.

"Yes," confirmed the judge, Taltavull Oliva. "I had been friends with Salvador, and she used to come and see me sometimes after he left. She spent a fortune trying to find him, but all we found out was that he had been seen once in Madrid, that he had been in Miami, always living from hand to mouth, always the cheeky type—plenty of women, dubious businesses, fraud. . . ."

"So why did he run away?" Joan Pere asked.

The judge gazed at him, surprised: "People run away. It's just one of the things people do."

"The times she told me . . ." Pollònia added, picking up the thread of her story, "how she would get through the nights, thrashing around in bed, on the floor, wanting Salvador so badly, imagining what would happen if he were to walk in through the door, a tall shadow that would slowly lie down on top of her and cover her. Then Marta Maria would have to get up and throw cold water on her face, on her whole body, to calm the heat of the dreams that tormented her even more than her desire."

Marianna Mas was more precise: "She didn't even want to hear the truth about that scatterbrained Salvador who had abandoned her because he wanted to. When he did live here, he was always running after every stick of flesh with a skirt on it. Marta Maria waited for him; she waited overwhelmed with anxiety and sadness. Yes, her perfume did have a heavy, damp sweetness to it; it seemed like another manifestation of her misery."

Ignasi Taltavull Oliva added, "Once I suggested to her that if she did some paperwork, we could—ahem—have him declared dead, or at least declared definitely disappeared. Then she could have remarried. Her reaction was to almost scratch my eyes out: 'He's mine and I'll wait for him!' she screamed hysterically."

Bernat the Wise confirmed the fact: "Yes, because even after the young man had come into her life, she was just the same. He would sit in the living room, a blank stare on his face, watching TV or nibbling on snacks, while she gazed out to sea, wailing for her Salvador who had abandoned her and never returned."

"What young man was that?" Joan Pere Tudurí asked.

Marianna Mas shrugged her shoulders: "Who knows who he was? Just a young man, dark-complexioned, thin and ragged; he spoke only Spanish. He was seen wandering around Orlandis for a couple of days; then—nobody knows how—he showed up on the doorstep at Santa Perpetua wearing a new suit. Yes, Marta Maria had taken him in."

"Taken him in? Taken him to bed, you mean," cracked Bernat ironically.

"Of course! But they put on an act in front of people. He would look off into space, and she would traipse back and forth in that old housecoat, her eyes brimming with tears," clarified his wife.

Pollònia spread her arms wide, as if receiving the Lord himself: "I was there that afternoon. The young man was clipping his nails with incredible attention, silent as usual. I noticed he was wearing a fat new gold watch. Marta Maria lay on the sofa, raving away with the word Salvador constantly on her lips. Then the rowboat drew near. What ever made him come to her by sea?

Because that's the way she had always dreamed he would come. Was he ashamed to be seen in town? Or was it his theatrical way, like the Knight of Orlandis when he came to kill the dragon? Maybe Salvador had been told what was going on at Santa Perpetua by someone from town who knew.

"As I was saying, there's Salvador, standing in the bow of the rowboat while its owner Raboa rowed to shore. Then Marta Maria got up, looked out, her eyes bulging out of her head, her jaw agape, her right arm and index finger extended so stiffly it looked like it might poke right through the window and touch the man standing there like a statue in the boat in the middle of the solitude of the sea on that chilly, sunny autumn afternoon.

"With a leap Salvador was ashore, marching up the beach. Marta Maria started breathing heavily, half-choking in her agony. And when he entered the living room, she sort of kneeled before him, took him by the hand, exhaled and stuttered her unfinished sentence: 'Salvador, Salvador. . . .'

"He looked at the young man—about whom it was now certain Salvador knew—and with a clear jerk of his head he indicated the door. Marta Maria, enraptured, continued: 'Salvador, Salvador. . . .'

"And just at the moment when the young man had his hand on the doorknob to leave, Marta Maria added more to her litany: 'Salvador! Salvador, your hair has gone white and your neck and cheeks are all wrinkled and sagging, you've grown so old! You disgust me, Salvador; you make me sick and I pity you!'

"He took a step backward, exclaiming angrily: 'What?'

"She nodded her head. He paused for a second, absorbing what she had said, then retorted in a fury, his lips tightly drawn: 'Same to you, Marta Maria, you repulsive old hag!'

"The young man stood stock-still. Without changing her tone, she sat down casually and, as if meditating, declared to the air: 'Yes, me too. That's why I like young flesh now, his energetic body. I was no longer young when you started running after the younger girls in town. I can understand why you did it, now that I have had a taste myself. I'm just doing what you did, Salvador. Ah, Salvador. . . .'

"He still tried to defend himself: 'Let's not get excited now, Marta Maria. What you felt was a strong longing for me. Think of it. I have always. . . .'

"She almost jumped out of her skin as she screeched at him like a hellcat: 'Me, long for you? That was before he came into my life! And I want you to know that for years now I have barely been able to remember anything specific about you. The only thing I remembered were the desolate words that expressed what was lacking in my life. But ever since the day he came around begging for a crust of bread and I gave him everything I had and am, it has been easier for me to keep on whining and acting like a martyr than to face people and tell them I'm just a lascivious animal howling under his body. But now that you're back, I'll have to remove my mask.'

"Salvador changed his tactics: 'Marta Maria. . . . I'm your husband. I'm poor and have no place to sleep tonight. Learn to pardon and you will learn to love. Nothing will ever be the same as it was, but in real life, every new beginning takes a different form, Marta Maria.'

"She smiled mockingly: 'No, Salvador, no more little sermons! And you make me feel neither pity nor anger. In reality you have freed me, yes, from my disconsolate, hypocritical image of myself. I'm going to buy a new wardrobe in Palma. I'm going to haul out the family jewels and travel! We'll travel, he and I! You're out!'

"The young man had positioned himself, slick as a cat, next to Salvador, to whom he now gave such a sock in the jaw that it knocked him clear through the door and down the stairs. Salvador looked like a bundle of rags and bones piled up beside the rowboat.

"I went out after him. Raboa was picking him up and managed to haul him into the rowboat. Marta Maria closed the window, and that was the last time I saw her. We know she's been seen decked out like a queen in the finest hotels in the company of that young man. You can still see Salvador in Palma, too, staring through the bars of the old folks' home, La Misericòrdia."

There was a long silence. A piece of bark popped in the fireplace.

Aunt Pollònia said something about a knight and a dragon.

"What was that all about?" asked Adelina Albornoz.

Tomàs Moro groaned, for that was his territory: "Just because you live in Burgos, Cousin Marieta Verònica, you don't have to completely isolate your daughter from her roots."

Bernat affectionately took the hand of his granddaughter and began to tell the story: "In olden times, the wetlands in the valley of Orlandis were enormous. Legend has it that a terrible green dragon lived there, spewing flaming sulfur from its mouth and carrying off all the young virgins he could sink his claws into. But then the Knight of Orlandis arrived by sea, astride a foamy steed, armor and God's benediction protecting his muscular frame. And he fought the dragon and defeated him by driving his lance through the beast's only eye. The wetlands swallowed him up, and they dried out almost immediately, becoming what you see today. And that's the story."

The girl's father, the engineer, joined the circle: "No, no. You're confusing roots with superstitions, Bernat. When you don't know anything about something, you immediately explain it away as something supernatural. And that reflects the persistence of magical thinking here, which is out of touch with our time and keeps you people crippled and enslaved. I suppose all this comes from the fact that Majorca is an island and the town of Orlandis, stuck out on the westernmost end of it, has become an island within that island."

Bernat the Wise looked at him calmly: "Well, and so what?"

"I have studied," Albornoz boiled forth, "the history of the wetlands in the archives of Orlandis; I published an article about them in the *Quarterly Review of the College of Engineers*. In the seventeenth century, the Duchy of Orlandis undertook the drainage of those swampy lands, opening them up and establishing a cart road through them. In the eighteenth century, under the Enlightenment of Carles III, the swamps were completely drained under the direction of the Royal Society of Friends of the Country. The dragon obviously didn't exist. What did exist were people who, due to heavy fogs or whatever, got lost in the bogs, fell into the marshy waters and drowned. And all that was later transformed into your typical myth of the dragon and the fair princess, which appears in many cultures."

Bernat the Wise scratched his neck as he answered, "What you have just explained with facts, Fèlix, is more or less the story I told, in the form it is usually told around here. But I never said I believed it!"

"The thing is, most people—including you—don't know whether you believe or don't believe in what you say!" continued the irritated engineer.

The long night and its intimate moments, after years and years of separation, had recreated the endless chambers that opened onto a common ground and a cozy family atmosphere; it had at that idle hour broadened Bernat Taltavull's principles of harmony in a direction they seldom took: toward the unspecific and subtle gradations that enriched and deepened his sense of reality. And even if he didn't believe in mystery, at that moment he was at least enjoying a heightened sense of ambiguity. He smiled broadly and said, "You see, Fèlix? Now you've finally said something that's true. But do you know why it's true?"

"Pardon me for saying so, father-in-law, but you people aren't capable of any more than what you've got up here," answered Albornoz as he pointed to his forehead.

"Not exactly. Because if we don't get to the bottom of things, if we don't get any more specific, then we are not obligated to anything; we can observe the world from a distance, withdrawn into ourselves where we can better defend ourselves. We the Taltavulls have had to defend ourselves alone here for many centuries against pirate attacks and invasions, centuries in which we have had to survive any way we could atop these barren rocks."

"The modern world is a secure place!" declared the engineer. "And therefore it's headed in a different direction from that of the Dark Ages! Furthermore, what the hell, now there's curiosity and clarity, the bedrocks of modern civilization."

"Curiosity can set you up in a trap, and clarity can be the means through which the enemy can better expose you." Bernat smiled, then backed off in doubt. "On the other hand, I can assure you that if you move through the subtle shadows at dawn or dusk, you will discover the world has lost the sharp edges and outlines that separate things, allowing them to smoothly meld together—as if there were a mystery that didn't exist before, as if you felt a warm pulsing nearby, an energy similar to that which, even though you cannot explain it, you know exists within yourself."

Adelina got up, embraced her grandfather and gave him a noisy kiss on the cheek.

"You're charming, Grandfather, a real delight!" and added, impatiently pointing to her father, "Don't pay any attention to him. He's absolutely convinced that a cat is an irrational quadruped."

Fèlix Albornoz was dumbfounded: "And what else is a cat, if not that, my girl?"

"A cat is a cat!" the girl snapped back defiantly.

34

Joana Maria, Niní, and Pere were still playing records, even though everyone had stopped dancing some time ago.

"When I hear Tina Turner's hoarse, vibrant voice, I feel like someone's running a red-hot poker down my throat and through my breast! Ay. . . ." said Joana Maria.

"I want to learn to dance the tango!" laughed Pere.

"Well, I'll take rock to rattle my bones! But for good listening, I prefer things like "La Paloma." It feels like it's a part of me, you know?" said Niní dreamily, humming the tune:

> If a pigeon lands
> on your windowsill,
> treat it with goodwill,
> because a part of me
> is in your hands. . . .

Alexandre stood alone outside on the porch, immersed in the serenity of the early morning. Strains of Niní's tune reached him without the thumping echoes and reverberations inside the hall; outside, it became a subtle melody like the stylized silhouette of an adolescent agilely skipping across the vast horizon.

Alexandre was already seventeen. He thought that was awfully old, which created within him a sense of ambivalence: on the one hand, he felt he barely had time enough to accomplish anything; on the other hand, it seemed as if his life would never end. When he heard Dioclecià of Pula declare that everything had a solution except death, he thought: "Is there really no remedy for death? Shouldn't there be some kind of access to, let's say, eternity?" At the very moment the thought occurred to him he knew it wasn't so, and that made him feel a dark fear of death, as if his body already contained the nucleus of future rot and decay.

But at the same time he was driven by an energy, a desire so irrational and full of pure joy that it seemed to soar above all the limits on the horizon of life, just as the sun did every day at dawn when it exploded into brilliant daylight.

Adelina had just left with her parents. Their car lights disappeared around the curve at the waterwheel.

"Why do I love her so much?" Alexandre asked himself in surprise. His cousin was sixteen; her figure just filling out. Her smile made her face radiant with joy; her skin was like a new discovery, like a wildflower amid the perfumes of spring.

Alexandre had known her all his life, but last summer when the Albornoz Taltavull family had come from Burgos for their vacation, he found Adelina drawing near to him like a magnet, as if she were floating inside a rosy pink cloud, as if she could come only to him. It had happened at the beach. The sun was tepid that day, the sea becalmed, when that young girl burst through the surface of the water, shaking out her hair, coming from love for love.

He saw her again that evening sitting on the sidewalk in front of Uncle Sam, the bar his friends frequented, under the deep arches in Carrer Vell, in front of the little lighthouse nervously whipping out slashes of light at the end of the wharf. Alexandre sat down beside Adelina. She was wearing jeans and a low-cut white blouse revealing her sweetly erect nipples. She chatted with him, and then he said, "You have become a real beauty over the winter."

Adelina stared at him for a moment: "Do you really think so?"

And she started to smile, and they both fell into a silence conveying such intense emotion that it seemed to enchant the very air they breathed. She placed her arm next to his and pressed against him. The warmth of their bodies became one and joined them.

He had been so happy the whole month of July, going everywhere with Adelina. And he had missed her so much during the five months that she was back in Castile, until her return at Christmas. Adelina had become a part of him, a powerful, visceral element insistently, ravenously imposing its demands on him.

As a boy Alexandre used to read war stories, fairy tales, and comic books. And whenever he had problems in school or at home, when unwelcome walls rose before him, he would fantasize about a magician who handed him a magical sword that he could use to overcome any difficulty and obtain all the wishes and money he wanted. But as he grew older, he was embarrassed to play those ingenuous but delirious mental games any more. But they surfaced again, more luxuriant and tender than ever, with Adelina. When he was with her, all obstacles seemed to melt away. And he didn't even have to overcome anything, just fly, fly away.

He took a few steps to the side, and the triangle of the sea appeared beside the blackness of the mountain; a furtive shimmer crossed it, as if something mysterious were going on out there. In the silence of early morning the world seemed to have lost as many difficulties as made it up, offering itself to all who imagined they could possess it.

A brilliant, evanescent swirl of sparks suddenly burst forth from the chimney. Someone in the hall must have stirred the embers. Alexandre mused that whenever he thought about Taltavull Hall, he always envisioned the great hall, the crackling fireplace, and the Taltavulls gathered around it, chattering away. He always pictured himself among them. And he felt he had really touched on a truth: an instinctive force formed a part of who he was and the earth he walked, and in spite of not knowing what it was, he knew it would make him happy.

35

Carloteta woke up. It was still the middle of the night, but a slight halo of light from under the door allowed her to figure out where she was: in the big bedroom at Taltavull Hall. They had laid her down to sleep together with the Moro twins in the big double bed, and they had put Nofringo on the moth-eaten ottoman, along with his stuffed tiger.

Carloteta propped herself up on her elbow to see if she could make out the tiger's stripes and its ancient, evil face. Carloteta was afraid of tigers; she decided they were what scared her most in the whole world, and if she were able to see the tiger there in front of her she would feel atrociously afraid. But it was tucked under Nofringo's blanket. Carloteta snuggled back under the comforter, satisfied.

Warm and tightly tucked in, she started to dream of being on a swing. She decided she liked to swing best of all in the whole world. She thought of telling herself a story, but she suddenly realized that all the ones she knew were terribly boring. Happy at the thought of having got rid of that bothersome problem, she fished around in one of the twin's hair until she surfaced with a barrette decorated with the head of a gnome Carloteta was deliriously in love with—even more than swinging, she mused. Or, she could swing with the barrette in her hair. Perfect! She placed it close to her ear, which started to ring at that very moment. And since that meant somebody was thinking about her, she felt a wave of satisfaction and hopped out of bed.

But the tiger was there, and she caught a glimpse of the two pictures on the wall: one was the god with the crown of thorns, and the other a group of sad women wearing long dresses. Both of them scared her so much that she stepped outside onto the small flat roof at the left corner of the house where the chimney rose up from the great hall below, right beside the immense pine that marked the beginning of the woods.

The first thing she saw was the vast curve of the sky. Dawn was breaking. The pale stars, where perhaps the angels lived ... she wasn't sure of that, but she promised herself to ask somebody about it. And as she was trying to make out the angels in heaven, a brilliant, evanescent swirl of sparks burst forth from the chimney. Carloteta exclaimed, "Oh! Oh! ... Oh!" and the crackling sparks disappeared.

The brief explosion of light had awakened some birds sleeping in the pine. The voluminous black outline of the tree stood there back-lit against the sky as if it were a huge star that had stopped to sleep overnight at Taltavull Hall, awaiting the first rays of dawn. The birds were fluttering about in the dense boughs, half-awake, chirping nervously. One of them started to warble. Carloteta stood and marveled: it had never occurred to her that birds woke up. She was convinced it would be nice to give the barrette with the little gnome to the bird who had first started to sing. That way the twin wouldn't know who had filched it.

Carloteta felt a chill and hurried back to the warmth of her bed. She decided if she covered her head with the comforter she wouldn't see the tiger or the sad pictures on the wall. And then she fell asleep in a wink, dreaming that she was still awake, waiting for the birds to get up and fill the sky around Taltavull Hall with song.